Pistols at Dawn

Pistols at Dawn

Michèle Ann Young

Five Star • Waterville, Maine

First Edition
First Printing: June 2006

Published in 2006 in conjunction with Tekno Books.

Set in 11 pt. Plantin.

Printed in the United States on permanent paper.

Library of Congress Cataloging-in-Publication Data

Young, Michele (Michele Ann)
    Pistols at dawn / by Michele Young.—1st ed.
      p. cm.
    ISBN 1-59414-460-5 (hc : alk. paper)
    I. Title.
PR9199.4.Y69P57 2006
    823'.92—dc22   2005036761

To my husband, Keith,
and my daughters Angela and Fiona,
thank you for believing in my dream.

Acknowledgements

To my Agent, Scott Egan, for your persistence and encouragement; to my critique group Mary, Maureen, Molly, Sinead, Susan, Theresa, and teacher Linda, you guys are the greatest, without your help I never would have dared reach so high; to the rest of my large family in England and Canada, thank you all for your continued support.

Chapter One

"Are you ready, gentlemen?"

Simon (Satan) St John, seventh Earl of Travis, nodded and sensed a similar movement from Yelverton at his back. The dueling pistol felt comfortably familiar through the thin kid leather of his glove. Simon eased his grip.

A damned duel over what amounted to little more than a handful of guineas and a property in Kent already mortgaged to the hilt. Vowels left strewn on a battered gaming table in one of London's grimy hells and none of it worth a man's life at twenty paces.

Distant trees loomed from the fog like harbingers of death, gallows-arms spread wide. The early morning mist, laced with the smell of London's thousands of coal fires, felt damp on his hair and cheeks and burned his tongue with its acrid taste. Each intake of breath rasped loudly in his ears.

"One," counted the second. Simon's heart picked up speed. He took the first of ten paces, which would somehow satisfy honor. His shining black boots scattered and crushed the fog's crystalline residue on the emerald grass.

Curse Yelverton for a hotheaded fool. He had allowed Ogden's taunts to aggravate the quarrel until the only option left had death lurking over their shoulders in a remote corner of Hyde Park.

Damn it. If he killed Yelverton, he'd have to leave the country. A second, fatal duel in a year would not escape the magistrate's attention. He didn't particularly wish harm to Yelverton and he didn't want to leave. He had other plans.

"Ten." He turned and faced his opponent, small across the open space. Mist eddied like seafoam around Yelverton's feet. A light breeze ruffled his hair and tugged at the great-coats of those watching with morbid curiosity: the seconds, the doctor and the coachmen with their carriages some distance off. Steaming breath from the horses and men drifted up to mingle with the dawn fog.

How odd that men should want to kill each other in the face of such peace.

Simon breathed in a steady, even rhythm and lifted his arm. He obliterated all but the feel of the pistol in his hand and saw only the man who wanted him dead. His eye drew a line, a gossamer thread, from his outstretched pistol to the center of his opponent's forehead. The path the bullet would follow.

A flutter of white. The handkerchief hung suspended, then dropped to the ground.

Yelverton lifted his arm. He swayed and the thread wavered.

Hell and damnation. The fool was drunk. What a bloody mess.

Yelverton fired.

Simon saw the spark, then the puff of smoke. The explosion ripped the quiet asunder. Rooks took wing from nearby trees with harsh cries. The bullet buzzed, hot and angry, past his ear.

His gaze traveled down his line. An easy mark, the madman didn't even have the sense to turn sideways.

Simon carefully adjusted his aim. He fired.

Yelverton crumpled to his knees with a strangled cry. Honor was satisfied. Perhaps other eager bucks anxious to try their luck against Satan would learn a lesson from this, but St John doubted it.

From behind, he heard the sound of feet scuffling through the grass and breathless sobs. Simon turned. Long, black hair flying, a young woman ran toward him. Tied with ribbons at her throat, her straw bonnet bounced against her shoulders, while her blue skirts, held high, revealed shapely ankles. A Dresden shepherdess in full flight, lacking only her crook and her sheep. Except no artist, no matter how good, could capture the anguish on this beauty's face. What in hell's name was she doing here?

Ogden's voice rang out. Simon whirled around. Both seconds ran toward Yelverton and Simon frowned. He knew he'd fired wide. He would never make a mistake like that. His gaze riveted on his opponent, he watched him toss the dueling pistol aside and pull a smaller gun from his pocket.

The girl passed Simon in a headlong rush toward the kneeling man, crying out in fear.

Simon froze as Yelverton aimed his weapon at him. There was to be no honor on this field today, then. He turned his body slowly and faced the armed man, square on. What would be, would be. Besides, if Yelverton hadn't hit him the first time, why would he succeed now?

Everyone converged on Yelverton. Simon watched with fascinated horror. Yelverton's attention shifted to the running woman and despair twisted his features. Simon stepped forward, a warning shout on his lips. Too late. Yelverton turned the gun and placed it against his temple. A chorus of shocked cries rose up from all sides. The shot cracked and Yelverton pitched forward onto the grass.

The woman's scream carried back to Simon, flat, deadened by the mist, but piercingly heart wrenching.

Bloody hell. Simon strode to join the group around the slumped figure lying on the grass.

Ian Fortain, the Marquess of Lethbridge and Simon's second, arrived at his side like a Norse god, huge, blond and simmering with suppressed anger. He took Simon's dueling pistol, pressed it into its place in the white satin and closed the black, silver-bound case with a snap. "What the deuce is going on?"

Simon shook his head. The woman lay where she had flung herself on the fallen man.

Viscount Ogden, his blond hair tousled, bent over her, trying to lift her away. Why Ogden had befriended Yelverton, Simon couldn't begin to guess. Some fifteen years Yelverton's senior, Ogden was renowned for his elegance of style and manner. He also had a reputation for luring green youths into London's gaming hells, but Ogden usually plucked far more wealthy pigeons than this young man had been.

"Your man was drunk," Simon accused Ogden.

Ogden glared angrily at him over the woman's head. "Then you should have refused to continue, my lord."

Heartless cur. With a friend like him, no wonder Yelverton lay ruined and lifeless. "You were his second. You should have made sure he got here in good order, or withdrew."

"No! He can't be dead, he just can't be," the girl cried out.

Simon glanced down at the body beneath her sobbing form and grimaced. A deadly wound right through the temple. Blood and brains scattered in the grass, Yelverton didn't have a chance. Holding a limp wrist in his fingers, the doctor shook his head.

"It's no good, Victoria," Ogden said softly, pulling at her

shoulders. "It's too late. Come away."

The sight of Ogden fawning over the weeping girl sickened Simon. He took in the shabby pelisse, the black curls tumbling around her shoulders and the beautiful, distraught face pressed against Yelverton's chest. Her small hands clutched at his coat. Anguish emanated from her in waves and touched him in a place he thought he'd frozen out of existence a long time ago.

He drew in a sharp breath. "Gad," he said in a low voice to Lethbridge. "She almost intervened. Who is she, his doxy?"

At the sound of his voice, the girl looked up, her expression wild with grief and her white face wet with tears. Large purple eyes stared at him, eyes so deep a man could lose his soul in them. If he had a soul left to lose.

"You!" she said, her voice a choked whisper. "You killed him!" Without warning, she leapt to her feet and rushed at him, reaching for his face.

Simon caught her. Her cold hands fluttered in his like the wings of a sparrow he'd once picked up from the hearth, frantic for freedom.

"You devil," she cried out.

"At your service, madam." He pushed her at Ogden. "Get the doxy out of here."

Ogden caught her around the shoulders. "Damn you, Satan," he said over her head. "You are a black-hearted fiend. She's his sister."

She sank to the ground beside her brother, sobbing.

Sister? Here? Unbelievable. Worse yet, the poor fool had responsibilities and had risked everything on the throw of a dice and then accused Simon of cheating. Shaking his head, he moved apart from the group clustered around the dead man. This melodrama was over for him.

Lethbridge handed him his greatcoat and he shrugged his shoulders into it.

Ogden strode to Simon's side, a sneer on his face. "What will you do with the girl?"

"Do with her?" Simon stared at the slender, fashionably attired viscount. Ogden's gray eyes in his pale face held an unspoken challenge. "What the deuce should I do with her?"

Viscount Ogden glanced at the girl still prostrate beside her brother's remains. He moved closer, his voice hard. "You took it all, Satan, you and your devil's luck: his money, his house and his sister."

Aghast, Simon retreated a step. Yelverton had been headed along the path to ruin long before last night; Simon merely hastened the process by winning the last of his fortune in a single sitting. "Not a chance, Ogden. The girl is nothing to do with me. He killed himself."

Triumph flickered in Ogden's eyes. "She's out on the street, then. He was all the family she had, and you ruined him."

Simon stared at him. "You take her in, if you're so anxious about her welfare."

"You might just as well have killed him when you won everything he had left. She's your responsibility. Have you no honor, man?"

"I think I proved my honor today, unless you're disputing it."

Ogden licked his lips. "Nay, I'm not doubting your honor."

Men rarely dared impugn his reputation, unless they cared to risk death. Simon chuckled softly. "Very well then."

Something clearly on his mind, Ogden hesitated. Simon waited for him to speak.

14

"It would be better for the sister if this was reported as an accident." Ogden paused.

Simon offered him no encouragement.

"The scandal will completely ruin her. We can say his weapon went off while he was cleaning it. What harm would it do?"

It wouldn't matter whether it was reported as an accident or a suicide, Simon would be blamed and the news of this morning's work would be all over town by noon. He didn't care one way or the other and Lethbridge would go along with whatever he asked. "As you wish."

"You'll pay for the burial?"

Simon nodded. He knew Ogden to be hard-pressed financially and had prepared for the worst.

Ogden pulled out his watch. "We best leave before the constables get word of this. I'll take his horse and leave the hackney for Miss Yelverton."

A slight bow was all the reply Simon deigned to give.

A pity about the sister. His gaze flicked back to the girl, who watched and wept while the coachmen loaded her brother's lifeless form into the doctor's waiting carriage. Even grief-ravaged, her beauty shone like a rare jewel. No doubt some young buck would snatch her up and take care of her. Ogden? The bastard wanted her, despite his taunts. It showed in his eyes. He'd forced the duel, and he never did anything unless he had something to gain.

With her brother gone, along with his fortune, she likely had no dowry. No woman, even if she was a lady, ought to fall into hands of a man like Ogden. A vague sense of unease twisted in his gut, a strange troubling emotion, something he rarely felt anymore. No one deserved the horrors of abandonment.

Damn it. She was not his responsibility.

After a word to the girl, Ogden mounted a fine-looking bay mare and rode away.

Lethbridge strode back to Simon's side, grim about the mouth. "That's it, then." He had obviously finished the details with the doctor and provided the necessary funds to see Yelverton properly interred. Simon had given him enough bills the previous evening to cover that eventuality, no matter which man fell.

"Put the woman in my carriage and have her taken to Travis Place." The words issued from his mouth almost before he formed them in his mind.

Lethbridge's hazel eyes filled with concern. "Don't do this, Satan. She's an innocent. I swear she's not your type at all."

Simon stared at him. Lethbridge snapped his mouth shut. Simon nodded; he was in no mood for an argument.

The Travis coachman brought up Simon's black stallion and he mounted. Ahead of him, the doctor's black carriage rolled out of Hyde Park, disappearing into the teeming London metropolis where men died every day with little remark. If Ogden spoke the truth, Yelverton was the last of his line, except for his sister.

Simon glanced at the girl—Victoria, if he recalled correctly. Unresisting, she allowed his footman to help her into his carriage. A roll of the dice had put her in his power.

Victoria slumped back against the red squabs and closed her eyes, allowing the carriage's rocking motion to soothe her. Somehow, she had been too late. Ogden had told her the appointed hour was seven when he delivered Michael's note in the small hours of last night. Arriving at half-past-six, she should have been in plenty of time.

An image of Michael's limp body on the blood-soaked

grass, so still and so strangely empty, tore at her mind. She covered her face with her hands, trying to blot it out.

If only he had listened to her. Time out of mind, she had begged him to stay away from the gambling tables. He'd just laughed at her, certain his luck would change.

Mother would have known how to convince him to stop. Victoria had failed miserably. Sobs filled her heart and her throat and drowned her breath. She clutched at the plush seat cushions, the soft fabric a comforting lifeline to the real world.

The carriage drew up and a footman opened the door and let down the steps. She blinked to clear her sight. This wasn't her home on Golden Square.

Her stomach plummeted. She had no home. In his note, Michael had said she must leave or find herself in debtor's prison. Ogden explained how Michael had lost everything. The sickening realization struck her like a blow. Michael killed himself to avoid the fruits of his folly and had left her to face them alone.

"Whose house is this?"

"The Earl of Travis, my lady," the footman replied without expression, as if the arrival of an unchaperoned female at his master's house was a routine occurrence.

"Whose?" Unable to make sense of his words, she looked around. The Travis coat of arms and the name, carved in a stone above the front door, confirmed his declaration.

The man who had dueled with Michael this morning was the Earl of Travis. Viscount Ogden had referred to him as Satan. Now she remembered. Satan St John, a well-known rake and gambler. One of the richest men in London, Michael had admired this man from a distance like some hero. Now Michael lay dead.

"There has been a mistake. Take me to Golden Square immediately."

The coachman climbed down from his perch. "No mistake, miss. His lordship directed us to bring you here."

She knew better than to be intimidated by anyone's minion. She fixed him with an angry stare. "Well, I do not wish to be brought here. You will take me to Golden Square."

The sound of a horse trotting up the drive halted the argument. The coachman retreated. No doubt the cause of all her troubles had arrived. Pushing her hair back from her face, she readied herself for battle and turned to face him.

Formidable astride an ebony stallion, only his white cravat relieved the austerity of his dark clothes. If they named him Satan for his appearance, the sobriquet suited him. Black hair curled above a broad forehead. Bronzed by the sun, his saturnine, hard-planed face showed no emotion. Sternness surrounded him like a mantle. His eyes, piercing blue beneath straight black brows, seemed to see right through her with a frightening lack of curiosity.

She drew in a steadying breath to still a sudden shiver. "How dare you bring me here."

Relaxed on his glossy black mount, he stared down at her. He raised one eyebrow and his lips curved in a faintly mocking smile. He said nothing.

"I demand to be taken home at once."

"Home?" He dismounted in an agile, fluid movement, far more graceful than she would have expected from so tall a man. He handed the reins off to a groom who seemed to appear from nowhere.

"Yes. Home," she said.

He sauntered closer.

"Number twenty-six Golden Square." She looked around for the portly coachman, her legs trembling with the effort of standing her ground.

Travis took another step. "You have no home, Miss

Yelverton, except that which I am prepared to offer you."

The indifference in his voice and his arctic cold stare chilled her to the marrow. She stepped back toward the carriage.

"Your home is here," he said. "I won you at dice last night, or did your brother neglect to tell you that?"

The servants, their eyes averted, drew away. Dear God. Wild and reckless as he was, Michael could not have made her part of his bet. She retreated another step and her back jarred against the carriage wheel. "You lie."

A wry smile twisted his lips as if he could read her doubts. "We will discuss this inside."

She had never met the Earl of Travis, but everyone knew of his licentious reputation. If she went inside his house, she would be ruined. "No."

He grasped her by the wrist, a manacle covered in soft leather. A startling impression of a menacing power checked only by the force of his will swept through her. She gasped and tried to tug away.

A strong arm encircled her shoulders, pulling her tight against his hard body, and he propelled her forward, up the steps to the massive front door. It opened the instant they reached it and they passed inside.

Breathless, her heart pounding in her ears, she dragged her feet, resisted his insistent forward motion, to no avail. He marched her along a sumptuously decorated, marble corridor and thrust her inside a room.

He kicked the door closed.

Red, blood red, filled her vision, seeming to run down the walls and puddle on the floor. Victoria swayed and closed her eyes against the surge of dizziness.

His strong hands gently maneuvered her across the room and, aware of the chair behind her, she sank into it. Nauseated, she kept her eyes closed. She propped her head on her hand and heard glass clink against glass and the sound of liquid being poured. His hand fell on her shoulder, a gentle, comforting touch.

"Drink this."

She opened her eyes. The room steadied and she looked around her at the floor-to-ceiling shelves crammed with books, many with red covers. The armchairs were covered in dark red upholstery, thick red velvet curtains looped back from the windows and fell to the floor. It was a magnificent library, an all-male domain. Unreasoning fear caused her limbs to tremble. She did not want to be here.

Alcohol fumes from the brandy snifter he held to her lips caught in her throat. She shook her head, knowing only too well the effects of strong drink on a person.

He sauntered to the large mahogany desk and leaned against it, watching her. "I don't believe we've been introduced." His deep, beautifully modulated voice expressed utter boredom. "I am Simon St John, Earl of Travis, Miss Yelverton." He bowed with elegant formality.

"Why have you brought me here? This is kidnapping."

A dark brow winged up. "I told you. I won you at dice. You are now my responsibility."

"And just what does that mean?"

The remote expression on his darkly handsome face communicated nothing of his thoughts. "That all depends on you."

She narrowed her eyes. This cold devil, standing before her as if he now owned her, would have to say exactly what he had in mind. If he thought she would willingly become the mistress of one of the most well-known libertines in London, a surprise awaited him. He had as good as murdered her brother and he deserved a knife in his back or poison in his food, not his victim's sister in his bed.

She met his icy glance with a haughty look. "I don't under-stand."

"I know you would like to murder me right now."

Her mouth dropped open in horror at his perception. "Your brother's unfortunate demise has left you in an awkward predicament," he continued.

She stared at him. He'd forced Michael into an impossible position by financially ruining him, and now he stood there looking down his nose at her with sapphire-hard eyes, as if she was to blame for her presence here.

Goaded beyond endurance by his cynical expression, she rose and planted herself in front of him. "Unfortunate demise? You practically murdered him."

His lip curled in a sardonic sneer. "Don't be ridiculous."

Anger, hot and wild, like nothing she'd ever experienced, bubbled in her veins. In blind fury, she lashed out at his cold face.

Catching her hand with ease, he forced it behind her back and pulled her close. His breath warmed her cheek; his lean body pressed against her. The ice in his gaze froze her blood.

"Let us be quite clear about this, Miss Yelverton. I did not murder your brother. He issued a public challenge and I had to accept it. After he failed to kill me, he killed himself. And now we are all going to pretend it was an accident."

Guilt squeezed at her heart. She should have realized long ago how bad things were with Michael instead of burying herself in her own affairs.

Pressed against the earl's hard form, she became aware of his powerful frame, taut, magnificent and so close the scent of sandalwood filled her nostrils. To strike out at a man like this was pure madness.

She stiffened her spine, and tipping her head back, raked a

scornful gaze over the granite planes of his jaw and cheek-bones. She absorbed the impression of the firm, straight line of his mouth, before her glance traveled back to his cold, un-feeling, blue eyes.

Anger flared in their icy depths. It was the first emotion she had seen from him and, for some strange reason, it eased the pain around her heart.

Even as she watched, the glacier melted and blazing blue heat licked at her, scorching her face, traveling down her neck to rest deep in the pit of her stomach. Her heart tumbled over in a way she'd never felt before.

Stiff and precise, he pressed her firmly back into the chair and stepped away.

She took a deep breath to cool the unwelcome glow of her skin. "You can't make me stay here." How weak and pitiful she sounded.

He strode to the window and, hands behind his back, stared out. Massive against the light, his shoulders spanned the frame and cast a huge shadow across the patterned carpet.

The silence dragged out. Victoria slanted a glance at the carved oak door and freedom. He could not force her to remain under his roof. She rose from her chair.

"The servants won't let you leave without my permission," he warned.

A flutter of disquiet and something akin to excitement raced through her. He could not keep her here against her will, she reasoned. She hastened to the door. It resisted her pull.

His boots silent on the rug, Travis had crossed the room behind her. One hand on the oak panel above her head, he held the door against her efforts to open it enough to let her pass through. The handle slipped from her grasp as he closed it with a determined click. "Don't put my servants to the embarrassment of having to stop you."

She backed against the door, away from his towering presence. "What do you want with me?" She hated the fear in her voice and tossed her hair out of her face, resisting the quiver of weakness low in her stomach.

His laid his hand flat against the door beside her head, his eyes splintered shards of blue glass. "Now you ask a sensible question, Miss Yelverton. We have been brought together by circumstances beyond our control."

Dark brows drew together at her derisive snort. "I am not prepared to defend my actions to you. I recognize I have some responsibility for your current situation, and since your only other alternatives appear to be the street or debtor's prison, I will take on the role of your guardian."

"Is that what you dissolute libertines are calling it now?"

"Miss Yelverton, my first impression of you was that you were a doxy and, from the tenor of your conversation and the direction of your mind, I can only assume I was correct."

She gasped and stared at him, speechless.

An expression of arrogant satisfaction crossed his face. "You will live here as my ward, under my protection, until you find a husband, and that is all I have to say on the matter." He spoke as if he had just announced the purchase of tickets for a play.

"But I don't want a husband." All the years of misery, first with her father and then her brother, burst like a swollen spring river from its banks. "I hate men and their arrogant, stiff-necked, stupid, idiotic, ridiculous code of honor, drinking, gambling, lying . . ." She ceased her litany of low-voiced invective at his appalled look and slightly upraised hand.

As she had learned to do these past few years, she swallowed her frustration.

"Are you quite finished?" he asked.

Needled by his biting tone, her tongue refused to be silent. "No," she bit out. But she had nothing left to say.

"I will not have you speaking like that, do you understand? It's time someone taught you how to behave like a lady."

Reining in her temper, she raised a brow. "Oh, and you think you are the sort of person to do it?"

He threw her a considering look, leaned one shoulder against the door and folded his arms across his chest.

Simon saw pride in the tilt of her chin and anger edged with sorrow in her depthless eyes. Sweet Christ, what a hellion.

In daylight, up close, her beauty struck him like summer lightning: large expressive eyes, her petite, slender body poised to flee, and her black hair falling around her in magnificent abundance.

The features, which had looked weak on her brother, curving lips, slender nose and pointed chin, were rare beauty, full of strength and will, on this small woman. Astonishingly, his body had responded instantly to the feel of her slender figure pressed against him. He, who prided himself on his iron control where women were concerned, wanted her fire and passion in his bed. *Badly.*

The realization twisted his gut. Bloody hell. Women fell into two categories in his world. His usual fare, the demimonde, sold their favors for jewels and money without scruple or deceit. And then there were the kind who spoke of love and devotion and welcomed wicked rakes like him into their beds behind closed doors and their husbands' backs. The lying, cheating ladies of the *ton*. He preferred the first kind, and this young lady definitely belonged to the second group—or she would, some time in the not too distant future. He cursed himself for a fool for even giving her a passing thought.

He'd made a mistake bringing her here knowing the attraction he'd felt the moment he saw her. If she were different from the rest of her kind, then she truly would despise him.

He cast a glance heavenwards at his own folly. But having made a decision, he was committed to it. His honor required it. She had seen her brother die, and lost her home . . .

He gentled his tone. "Why don't you go and freshen up? I will have Mrs. Pearce, my housekeeper, show you to your room and send someone to Golden Square to fetch your belongings. I must make the arrangements for your brother's funeral tomorrow."

Tears glistened in her pansy-colored eyes.

He had not wanted to remind her, but she could not hide from the truth behind her anger at him. Her brother was dead and she was Simon's to do with as he wished.

Chapter Two

Alone in a third-floor bedchamber decorated in varying shades of rose, Victoria's mind began to function with something like its usual precision. She picked up the silver-backed hairbrush from the gleaming surface of the rosewood dressing table and attacked her wild mane with rhythmic strokes.

She needed to think instead of reacting to Travis's autocratic edicts. The Earl of Travis would naturally assume marriage offered her the only option under the present circumstance, but there had to be some alternative. She'd managed the house for her father and brother since her mother died, and before that had taught Sunday school at their local church in Kent. In those days, they talked of opening a Parish school, and Victoria had volunteered to teach English as well as participate in the running of it. A housekeeper or schoolteacher at a seminary for young ladies were surely positions worthy of consideration.

She set the brush down and pinned her hair into a neat knot at her nape. This hairstyle made her look older and more self-assured. She nodded at her reflection. The earl would have to listen if she presented a sensible plan.

Whatever the future held, she needed to leave his house as soon as possible.

She strode to the bellpull beside the bed and gave it a swift jerk. Rose silk hangings suspended from the canopy brushed her cheek. She fingered the exquisitely delicate fabric.

This must be where his women slept.

A shimmer of awareness blossomed deep in the pit of her stomach and her heartbeat quickened. She closed her eyes against the unaccustomed sensation, only to find his dark enigmatic features and blazing blue eyes a vivid picture in her mind.

No man had ever invaded her thoughts like this. Today's events had unhinged her reason. She must not allow his disturbing presence to divert her.

She paced around the bed. Walking always helped her think. If only her friend, Lady Julia Garforth, were in Town, she might know of a suitable position for Victoria. Newspapers listed jobs, or the Servants' Registry. A pang of dismay pierced her chest. Always she'd felt secure in her life, but now the future seemed shrouded in impenetrable mist.

A quiet knock at the door halted her steps. A blond dab of a chambermaid entered carrying a jug of hot water. She introduced herself as Elsie.

Moments later, the efficient-looking Mrs. Pearce marched in, followed by two footmen with Victoria's shabby trunk hefted between them. The liveried men deposited the trunk next to the dressing table and departed.

"His lordship asked that, when you have refreshed yourself, you attend him in the library," Mrs. Pearce said, whisking back the curtains and flooding the room with light. With brisk steps, she crossed to Victoria's trunk and opened the lid. "Now, what do you have in here to wear?" She pulled out the three or four dresses Victoria had packed. "Is this all you brought with you?"

Too numb to protest, Victoria nodded and gazed at the sum total of her unfashionable and frequently mended wardrobe. New clothes had taken second place to paying off Father's debts over the past four years and, more recently,

Michael in his turn had spent every penny on gambling and horses.

"This one is rather nice." The housekeeper lifted a pale lilac gown from the pile. One of Victoria's favorites, it complemented her eyes.

"I'll wear the brown one," Victoria said. The closest thing she had to black, it seemed the most suitable for mourning.

Michael. The recollection of his dreadful wound battered her senses. She shuddered and wrapped her arms around her waist, fighting the hollow ache in her chest.

The housekeeper placed the lilac silk on the bed. "Elsie will help you change. She has been assigned to you until we can hire a proper ladies' maid." She left the room in a rustle of stiff skirts.

A ladies' maid? Victoria stared after her. She wasn't staying long enough to need a maid. Clearly, she still had to convince the autocratic earl to let her go.

She smiled at the nervous-looking Elsie. "Perhaps you can help me with these buttons."

Less than an hour later, dressed and ready to face the earl, Victoria left Elsie hanging the rest of her gowns in the wardrobe and made her way to the library. This interview with Travis would be quite different from their earlier discussion.

A footman sprang to attention as she traversed the entrance hall. He led her to the library and knocked on the oak door.

"Come."

Victoria stepped over the threshold of the comfortable room with a firmness she did not feel.

With what seemed to be his perpetually bored expression, the earl rose from a chair behind the desk and came around to meet her. "Miss Yelverton, I would like you to meet my cousin, Miss Maria Allenby."

He gestured toward a plump woman of middle years in a ruffled turquoise morning gown. Seated on the small sofa at the hearth, she beamed and nodded from behind an oval table set with a silver tea service. "She is going to be your companion and chaperon while you are here."

A chaperon? Lost for words, Victoria gazed at the moon-round face observing her with marked curiosity.

Miss Allenby stretched out a pudgy, mittened hand. "My poor dear Miss Yelverton, let me offer you my condolences."

Grappling with the unexpected turn of events, Victoria found herself crossing the room and taking the hand.

"There, there, you poor dear," Miss Allenby said, holding fast to her. "How you must be suffering. Such sad news. Your poor brother. Do sit beside me." She patted the sofa and Victoria sank down next to her. Miss Allenby gazed at her with sympathy, her fingers stroking the back of Victoria's hand.

"Thank you," Victoria managed. This was not the interview she'd envisaged on her way downstairs.

Perplexed, she raised her glance to the earl.

Expressionless, he leaned one slim black-clad hip against the edge of the desk and crossed his arms over his chest.

"Travis tells me you must find a husband before the Season is over," Miss Allenby said.

Victoria gasped and snatched her hand back. "I do not want a husband."

Maria looked from her to the earl in puzzlement. "But Travis, I thought you said—"

"His lordship is mistaken," Victoria rushed to say. Was this woman some fiendish trap by a licentious libertine designed to set her mind at rest?

The earl frowned. "Do you have any relatives who will care for you, Miss Yelverton?"

Victoria's tension eased with the memory of a gaunt, disapproving face. "I have an aunt, my mother's sister, Gertrude Warburton."

Keen interest flickered in Travis's gaze.

"You mean the Gertrude Warburton who used to be Miss Gertrude Crowhurst?" Miss Allenby asked.

Miss Allenby poured two cups of tea and offered one to Victoria.

She declined with a shake of her head. "Why yes, ma'am. Crowhurst was my mother's maiden name. Do you know of her?"

Miss Allenby addressed the earl across the room. "It won't do, Travis. Won't do at all."

Victoria frowned. "I beg your pardon, Miss Allenby, but I really do not see—"

"Oh, you poor dear, no need to beg my pardon. How well do you know your aunt?"

"Not well." Victoria answered with care, unsure where the question led. "She lives in Harrowgate, but our families have never been close." Her father had despised his wife's sister as a prosy bore.

Her chubby face full of sympathy, Miss Allenby nodded. "I suspected as much. I knew Gertrude Crowhurst at school, you know. She married a parson. I met her again last year when I visited Harrowgate. The waters there are said to be very good for all manner of ailments." Nodding her head, she lifted her cup to her lips.

Travis glowered. "What has that to do with the matter at issue?"

"Why just that 'tis a very small world, I suppose. Your aunt spoke very ill of your father, Miss Yelverton. His losses at cards, his . . . Well, we shan't dwell on that."

She tapped Victoria's hand with her finger. "You'll pardon my frankness, I know. Gertrude has become a veritable antidote and is not at all the sort of woman with whom a young lady would wish to end her days. Why, I don't suppose she would consent to see you at all."

"Come now, Cousin," Travis said. Despite his casual stance, Victoria sensed his tension, coiled and tight. "Are you sure it is the same person? Surely a parson's wife would come to the aid of a destitute family member?"

The callous words stung like a slap on the cheek. "Miss Allenby cannot speak for my aunt."

"No, indeed," Travis agreed.

Miss Allenby pressed her lips together. "While I am sure I am right, I will not argue. But, Travis, you cannot put Miss Yelverton in a coach and send her to Harrowgate unannounced and unexpected. She must write to her aunt for permission to visit."

The earl straightened, strolled to the window and stared out.

What did he find to attract his attention out there, Victoria wondered. The midday light cast his countenance into taut planes and shadowed hollows, like the statue of a fallen angel carved from granite.

"You are right," he said. "It should take no more than a fortnight to receive a reply. I hope, Cousin, you will consent to stay until then?"

"Nothing would please me more." Miss Allenby smiled, her brown eyes merry. "Living at someone else's expense is always an enticing proposition."

Swept up in the current of their decisions, Victoria cast about for rescue. *Julia.* "I will visit a friend until I hear from my aunt."

The earl turned his head in a sharp movement, his eyes narrowed. "What friend?"

Victoria met his piercing gaze with a cool stare. "My

friends are not your concern, my lord."

"Tell me the name and address of your friend and I will have my coachman take you there."

"There is no reason for you to trouble yourself, my lord. I can take a hackney."

He reached the sofa in three lithe strides and towered over her. "There is no friend."

Quelling an urge to shrink beneath his menacing presence, she tilted her head to meet the suspicion in his sapphire-hard eyes. "Do you call me a liar, sir?"

He recoiled, clearly taken aback by her accusation.

"If you must know, my friend is Lady Julia Garforth and I can assure you—"

"So, you know Lady Julia Garforth?"

She nodded, wary of the cynical curve to his lips.

"Really, Miss Yelverton," he said, lifting a brow. "You will have to do better than that if you wish me to believe you. Lady Julia is presently on an extended visit to the Lake District with her brother. As a *friend* of hers, you should know this."

Victoria's heart sank. She had not expected the Earl of Travis to know of Lady Julia's movements. She struggled to retain her calm. If she lost her temper with this infuriatingly arrogant man, she risked losing the battle, and she had no intention of allowing that to happen again. "Lady Julia is expected to return any day now."

Travis fisted his hands on his hips. "Then I suggest you write yet another letter. We shall see whether your aunt or your friend will take you in."

His harsh words stormed her defenses. With Michael gone, she really was alone. Tears prickled behind her eyes and she blinked them back.

The sharp-eyed Miss Allenby handed her a handkerchief.

"Travis, do bite your tongue. See, now you have upset the poor dear."

"I'm not upset." Her voice came out husky and thick. She blew her nose. She never cried, but this man seemed bent on bringing the evils of her situation home to her. As if she needed any help.

The earl stifled an impatient sigh, returned to his seat behind the desk and leaned back. He cast a long-suffering glance at the ceiling. "I beg your pardon, Miss Yelverton. What I should have said is, we will await the results of your missives, and in the meantime my cousin is at your disposal."

A niggling fear stirred in her stomach. Neither the earl nor Miss Allenby had any reason to take control of her life and they had no reason to care about her preferences. Left to their own devices, they would pack her off, willy-nilly, to her aunt in Harrowgate before she had a chance to decide her best course of action. She rose to her feet. "I have decided to become a governess. If you will assist me in this by recommending me to some suitable family, I should be grateful. If not, then I shall endeavor to find a situation myself."

She stared, affronted, as the earl started to laugh. Just a small chuckle to begin with, it became a rather loud and deep laugh. Warmth curled in her stomach at the pleasant sound. She frowned at him.

"Forgive me, Miss Yelverton," he said, his mirth finally subsiding. "Can you imagine the face of any worthy mother, were I to recommend a lovely young female as a governess for her children?"

Lovely. The word echoed strangely in her ears. With her outmoded gown and unfashionable hair, it seemed unlikely a hardened rake would describe her thus.

Her eyes twinkling, Miss Allenby nodded. "He's right, you know."

At least *she* had the grace not to laugh out loud. Victoria pressed her hands together. "Surely, Miss Allenby, you could be of assistance?"

Miss Allenby's plump face turned serious. "I suppose I could."

"It's quite out of the question," Travis said. "I will not turn you out onto the street to fend for yourself. Either you go to your aunt in Harrowgate or you get married. I don't care which. This is what your brother would have wanted."

Michael never gave a thought to her future or her wishes.

Travis stood up. "Write to your aunt, Miss Yelverton, I will frank the letter."

Trust a man to think everything was so simple.

Before she could frame another objection, the earl bowed. "If you ladies will excuse me, I have an important engagement." Like a well-fed tomcat, all sleek and self-satisfied, he strode from the room.

Miss Allenby held out a cup to Victoria. "After you have finished this nice cup of tea, we will visit the *modiste*. Travis tells me Madame Claire has instructions to have a gown ready for your brother's funeral tomorrow."

Weighed down by the recollection of Michael and the thought of his funeral, Victoria silently sank onto the sofa and accepted the cup and saucer.

Simon smiled as he shrugged into his driving coat. The interview with Miss Yelverton had turned out better than he'd hoped. The spirited young lady might not hesitate to heap invective on his head when they were alone, but apparently her upbringing did not permit her to do so in company.

All he had to do now was wait for her aunt's reply and make sure never to be alone with the young woman who unaccountably stirred his blood.

Not too great a challenge. His interests did not lie with virtuous females and dear cousin Maria, completely up to the knocker in society's eyes, bored him to death.

He took his hat and whip from the lackey at the door and stepped outside.

As for Miss Yelverton's faradiddle about being Lady Julia Garforth's friend, he mused, he wasn't green enough to be taken in by it. Philip Garforth, the Earl of Rutherford would have mentioned a friend of his sister's as beautiful as Victoria, and Simon surely would have met her at one of the Rutherford's many parties. In choosing a family well known to him, she'd picked the wrong name from the society columns.

Out on the drive, Diablo pawed at the gravel and tossed his head, while a frazzled groom clung to his bridle. A swift pat on the beast's neck calmed him enough for Simon to mount. He turned out of the gate and headed for Hyde Park.

Even at this early hour, there were a few members of the *ton* walking and driving in the park. Acknowledging the odd acquaintance as he went, he observed the fashionable set's barely concealed whispers over his latest *affaire*. Not that he would ever commit the sin of bad *ton* and own up to dueling, but they would all know of it and be titillated by the latest *on dit*. None of them would believe the story of an accident.

Hell. Just for once, it would be nice not to be the villain of the piece.

A dark blue barouche, its wheels picked out in red, had pulled over at the side of the path. Buxom Miss Cassandra Eckford waited, exactly as he had instructed in his note. He crushed a vague sense of disappointment. In a brief moment of weakness, he thought she might be different from all the others. Lucky for him she wasn't or he'd be looking again, and he had invested much time in her these past few weeks.

He brought Diablo alongside her carriage and cast a glance over the blond-haired, blue-eyed chit and her pouty lips.

"My lord, I thought you were not coming. You are late."

Her maid looked scandalized, as well she might. No respectable young lady would *arrange* to meet him, though no one would balk at a chance meeting in the park. But Miss Eckford was out to bag an earl if she could, or his wealth if she couldn't. Wry satisfaction filled him. Without a doubt, the beautiful and money-hungry Miss Eckford would take a slip on the shoulder as swiftly as she would take a wedding band. And that suited him perfectly.

"My apologies," he whispered leaning close. He smiled at her rewarding little shiver and dropped his gaze to where her blond curls brushed the nape of her lovely neck. She was a delicious morsel indeed.

He gestured toward the lake with his riding crop. "Would you care to take a stroll, Miss Eckford?"

"Oh, what a simply lovely idea," she replied in a breathy whisper. "Smith will mind your horse."

He smiled. "Nay, I'll not trouble your groom with this beast." Diablo was far too valuable and unpredictable to entrust to anyone. Simon dismounted and assisted Miss Eckford to alight.

With Diablo following behind, they strolled side-by-side across the spring-green lawn, beneath the spreading ancient oaks, skirting the fronds of blowing willows. He selected a stone seat with a fine view of the ornamental lake and strategically placed Diablo between them and the chaperon. He assisted Cassandra to sit and lounged beside her, admiring her perfect profile.

The determined set of Miss Yelverton's features flashed into his mind. She made no bones about telling him what a dissolute wretch she thought him. An ache of loss settled like a cold, hard lump in his gut. She was right, and there wasn't a damned thing he could do about it.

Miss Eckford peeped at him from beneath fair lashes. A tremulous smile curved her perfect rosebud lips—a diamond of the first water and readily available to the likes of him.

He captured her fingers in his, rubbing her gloved palm with his thumb. She blushed delightfully. He lifted her hand and brushed his lips against the inside of her wrist. Her fingers trembled and her breath quickened. He recognized the signs. She was his.

Boredom crashed over him. This shallow barter of flesh for money was all he would ever have, all he deserved.

Damn it, he'd been wooing the simpering Miss Eckford for weeks. Was he so jaded that, now he had her in his grasp, he didn't want her? The events of this morning must have addled his brain or destroyed his appetite.

"I'm leaving Town soon," he said.

"When?" She sounded nervous. They all were, at first. His reputation ensured it. But she'd be better off with him than some of the other men sniffing around her like bloodhounds, tempted by the bait laid out by her mother. As least when he parted from her, he'd leave her financially secure for the rest of her life, free to choose her partners. It was more than most men offered their cast-off paramours.

"I'm not sure when. I will send for you. Will you be ready to come with me?"

Anxiety filled her expression. "I think so."

Her hesitation gave him pause. He wouldn't force her; not when there were so many others who were willing. He gentled his tone. "You are free to say no, if you do not wish to come."

A tremor shook her hand and she raised her gaze to his. "Of course I wish it." She dazzled him with her smile.

Heaving an inward sigh of relief, he brought her hand to his lips. "I'll send you word." As soon as he could safely leave Miss Yelverton in the capable hands of his cousin, he'd seek his own amusement.

Miss Eckford nodded, her ringlets caressing her lovely face.

"Paris, Rome, wherever your heart desires, you just have to tell me," he offered in a rush of generosity.

Her china-blue eyes sparkled with anticipation. "I'll let you choose."

Ennui enveloped him. He shook it off. All that mattered was her willing agreement, and to hell with the disappointment eating at his soul.

He held out his hand. "Come, we must go back. No one must suspect." He played to her pretence of innocence, all part of the game he'd won more times than he cared to count.

Assisting her to rise, he gazed intently into her eyes. He needed the warmth of a woman after this morning's debacle, even if it was only fleeting, shallow and false. Her youth and freshness satisfied his need for something other than a tired courtesan.

She would entertain him as he taught her how to please him. He would bask in the warmth of her adoration, even if she only adored his wealth.

For a while, he would forget how much he despised himself.

Chapter Three

Simon wanted his old life back.

He repressed the desire to close his eyes against the sight of dozens of garish plaster statues depicting leering Poseidons and bare-breasted mermaids, strategically draped with seaweed, in every niche and corner of Lady Corby's ballroom.

On the opposite side of the dance floor with Maria, Victoria gazed around her with an expression of wonder.

"If you keep staring at her like that, they will think you have designs on her yourself."

The voice at his elbow held amusement. Simon dragged his gaze away from the debutantes at the edge of the ballroom floor and turned to meet Lethbridge's smiling face.

Simon kept his tone light. "Nothing of the sort. I'm just keeping an eye on things."

"Ah, the dutiful guardian."

Ian's smile widened, and for a moment, Simon felt like punching him. With a short laugh, he gained control. "I'll be glad when she finds a husband."

Almost a month had passed since Michael Yelverton's death and, at Simon's urging, Maria had convinced the denizen's of the *ton*, the patronesses of Almack's, to signal their approval of Victoria's come-out.

Lethbridge gazed past him. "Looking like that, she should be off your hands in no time at all. She does you justice."

Simon resisted the temptation to turn around. His thoughts had followed the same path before Lethbridge arrived, except he wanted to have strong words with Maria about the smoke-gray wisp of silk Victoria wore. The bodice revealed an indecent amount of skin and clung to every curve. She had been wearing a velvet cloak when they left the house or he would have marched her straight back up the stairs to find something modest, more suited to an innocent young lady.

He forced his mind away from the picture of creamy flesh rising in curving swells above the beaded neckline. It delighted and infuriated him at one and the same time. He tugged at his neck cloth. "I need a drink."

They strolled to the refreshment table covered in swaths of blue muslin and decorated with balloon glasses containing, of all things, goldfish. Enough to put a man off brandy for life.

"It's surprising the sister of an idiot like Michael Yelverton could turn out so well," he said to Lethbridge, careful to select two glasses of champagne, not fish. "She's positively . . ." He hesitated. "Honorable." Applied to a woman, the word tasted foreign on his tongue, and Lethbridge's jeering hoot of laughter jangled his nerves.

Lethbridge shook his head. "Kind of an odd thing to say, Travis. Attractive definitely, beautiful perhaps, but honorable?"

Women didn't know the meaning of honor. "You're right. It's just that she's determined to pay me back for everything when she marries." He frowned as he recalled the rest of her words: or out of her wages if she didn't.

Lethbridge glanced around the crowded ballroom. "Well, my friend, there are plenty of likely prospects here tonight. The whole of London must be in attendance."

"I had the same thought myself."

A strange sinking feeling invaded the pit of his stomach. He'd successfully avoided Miss Yelverton these past several weeks, only running into her occasionally. Each time he crossed her path, the surprise of finding her in his house lifted his spirits. He savored the scent of her jasmine perfume when he traveled down a hallway or entered a room after she had been there. He liked hearing her soft voice conversing with Maria as he passed the drawing room. The unaccustomed feeling of pleasurable warmth troubled him. He had a duty to fulfill, nothing more. He ignored the stab of regret as he envisaged his house after she left.

Lethbridge lifted his glass in the direction of a young man in a burgundy coat crossing the room in front of them. "How about young Greely? Good family, plenty of the ready, not too high in the instep and looking for a wife."

"Greely?" Simon could not keep the scorn out of his voice. "He's too short."

"That shouldn't be a problem. Miss Yelverton is not particularly tall."

True. She barely reached to Simon's shoulder. She was dainty in an elfin sort of way. As delicate as fine porcelain, but not as fragile as one might think. If he tried, he could encircle her tiny waist with his hands. He forced the vision of her slim body beneath his touch back where it belonged, in his dreams.

"What about old Monteith, there?" Lethbridge continued, clearly enjoying his role as matchmaker.

Simon inspected the grizzled Colonel Charles Monteith stepping out a lively cotillion and already perspiring. "He drinks too much and he's far too old. Besides he's married."

"Widowed. Got a couple of children. He's looking for someone to take care of them."

Simon's stomach churned at the thought. Victoria

41

Yelverton deserved better than to play nursemaid to a couple of spoiled brats for a man who spent most of his time away from home on military service. He shook his head. "I don't think so."

"Surely you're not expecting a title?"

"Why not?"

"It's unlikely you'd get someone like a Marquis Deveroux or an Earl of Pelham," Ian said, indicating the two youthful rakes in question. "With their encumbrances, they must marry money and land. No, what you need is some eligible, youngish bachelor with an easy competence and a pleasant disposition. And if he has a title, all the better."

Simon couldn't see a single male who fitted the description. "Precisely."

"I think I might have a go at her myself," Lethbridge said, a hint of laughter coloring his voice.

Simon swore silently. He'd been caught, and nicely, for Lethbridge had indeed just described himself. If Simon hadn't known his friend had no interest in looking for a bride, he would have planted him a facer.

"Please do," he answered in cool tones.

A restless look crossed Lethbridge's face. "How long are you going to stay? Will you join me at White's later?"

Simon groaned. "I'm down for two waltzes with Miss Yelverton. According to Maria, I am required to be the first to lead her out. After all, it is her introduction to the *ton*. Maria made me swear to dance with at least three other females, just to allay the gossip."

Lethbridge grinned. "Parenthood is hell, isn't it?"

Simon had just about had enough of his jests. He was seriously thinking about inviting his friend to a couple of rounds at Jackson's Saloon when an intense expression replaced Lethbridge's mocking smile.

"There's one man you won't want to encourage."

Lethbridge would not catch him out again. Simon kept his voice cool. "Who?"

"Ogden."

Swinging around, Simon saw a smug Ogden with Victoria's gloved fingers pressed to his lips. Simon scowled. "Damn him. I told her to have nothing to do with him."

Lethbridge placed a restraining hand on his sleeve.

"If you'll take my advice, you'll tread warily. He's a vile cur. You know it and so do half the men in this room. But it's all conjecture. He's never caused a scandal and he was her brother's friend. The more you press it with her, the more she'll cling to him. She trusts him."

To hell with that. Simon started in their direction. Maria arrived at Victoria's side. Simon halted in mid-stride, released his breath and remained where he was. Maria would look after things; he'd given her his instructions.

"I'll meet you later at White's," he promised Lethbridge. He needed another drink. After that, he would do his duty and dance with every unattached female in the room, if it meant he could indulge himself and hold the delicate Miss Yelverton close for a few minutes. Besides, it was one sure way to keep her out of Ogden's clutches.

At Maria's side, Victoria watched Ogden's trim, black-coated back as he sauntered through the crowded ballroom and into one of the adjoining salons.

She sighed. Gambling held all these men in its thrall. Still, his kindness in requesting a dance warmed her and she looked forward to a further conversation with him, especially since Maria had almost chased him away.

The last three weeks had been a whirl of appointments at the dressmaker's and a decorous round of morning calls. Under Maria's careful guidance, Victoria had been introduced to the *ton* as the Season got slowly underway. With the approval of Maria's friend, Lady Sally Jersey, her position on the marriage mart was known and accepted. Putting off black gloves only a month after Michael's death had raised few eyebrows. Everyone seemed to agree with Travis and Maria, a long period of mourning was a luxury she could not afford.

"Are you enjoying yourself, Victoria?" Maria asked.

Not for the first time that evening, Victoria gazed in awe at Maria's startling combination of an emerald *robe de chine* and a crimson turban perched on her gray curls. "Of course. How could I not?"

"What do you think of Lady Corby's decorations? She's known for them."

Victoria glanced around at the statues, walls and pillars festooned with blue and green silk, among which the cream of London's *ton* talked and laughed in a noisy babble. In the glare of thousands of candles, their sparkling jewelry danced in the gilt wall mirrors. "It is quite extraordinary."

Maria beamed. "I'm so glad you approve." Moving closer to Victoria, she lowered her voice. "You know, Travis would prefer you not to spend time in the company of Viscount Ogden."

Victoria stiffened. She had not missed the earl's glowering countenance across the room while Ogden paid his respects.

Seemingly oblivious to Victoria's reaction, Maria fluttered her ostrich feather fan. "If Ogden has any idea at all about marrying, and I've not heard he is on the marriage mart, he needs to marry money. The Du Plessys never have a feather to fly with. Gamblers, all of them, and his father the worst of the lot. He'd gamble his last farthing on the turn of the dice."

"Like Travis," Victoria said, once more catching sight of the earl across the dance floor talking to the Marquess of Lethbridge, whom she'd met at Michael's funeral. A fraction taller than the earl beside him, he was a cheerful Viking god next to a dark, implacable angel.

While she did her best to ignore Travis's presence, his athletic grace, commanding height and dark, enigmatic looks made it impossible. Particularly elegant tonight in black evening dress, his coat hugged his broad shoulders as if it were sewn in place. His dark hair, swept back off his broad brow, emphasized the hard planes of his face. On rare occasions, he could be warm and charming, like now, when a grin lit his face as he parted company from Lethbridge.

"Nonsense," Maria said. "Travis never gambles recklessly. Why, he's known for his luck at the tables and the race track."

The devil's own luck. The words summed up Simon St John very nicely. A dark fiend who profited from other men's foibles.

The earl's threat to provide a husband constantly nagged at the edges of her mind. She shrugged it off. No matter how ruthless or how powerful his connections, the Earl of Travis could not force her to marry against her will. As soon as Julia returned to Town, Victoria would enlist her aid to find a suitable situation and to the devil with him.

The crowd around the dance floor ebbed and flowed. Travis strolled toward them, carrying two glasses of something pink. He bowed and handed one to her and the other to Maria. Victoria looked at it askance.

"Fruit punch," he explained.

"Thank you, my lord." She had promised herself she would be cool and polite to her self-appointed sponsor. She preferred the word sponsor; it sounded less personal than guardian.

"It's almost time for our dance, Miss Yelverton. Maria, I assume you were successful in seeking permission for Miss Yelverton to waltz?"

Maria's cheeks swelled into rosy apples as she smiled. "Naturally. And I obtained tickets for Almack's."

"Every maiden's dream." His dispassionate gaze ran over Victoria as if she were a prize heifer on market day.

Heat rushed to her cheeks. If he intended to put her out of countenance, he had succeeded admirably. She smiled with all the sweetness she could muster. "Do I have a smut on my face?"

His gaze locked with hers and something warmer than frost flickered within the winter-sky blue of his eyes. He stepped back a little. "Certainly not. Whatever gave you that impression?"

"You were staring."

"I was simply paying attention to your words."

He had been staring, and his reaction said he knew it, too. She repressed a childish urge to poke out her tongue.

The corner of his mouth kicked up in a funny little half smile as if he guessed her thoughts.

The orchestra struck up the first notes of the waltz and he took her glass and handed it to a nearby lackey. "Are you ready?"

"Indeed I am." She loved to dance, although she had never danced a waltz in public. This was the highlight of the evening.

Her hand disappeared inside his large one and he grasped it lightly, his warmth penetrating the double layer of their gloves. Effortlessly, he swept her into the dance. Despite the lightness of his touch on her hand and shoulder, he controlled her movements as they swirled to the music.

His leg brushed her skirt, inducing a sensation far too intimate for comfort. The spicy scent of his cologne enveloped her as they whirled around the turns. A flush of warmth drifted up her body. Sapphires caught in a beam of sunlight

46

gazed down at her. Breathtakingly handsome, a smile of pure enjoyment lit his face. For a second, her heart forgot to beat.

"You dance well, Miss Yelverton."

His low tones rippled pleasantly over her skin, sending a shivering tingle down her spine. She stiffened. This must be how he charmed his conquests.

She raised her brows. "Surprisingly, so do you."

A wary look came into his eyes. "Why would you be surprised?"

"I didn't think you would bother with such boring, social activities. After all, dancing with unattached females on the marriage mart is a rather dull obligation for a . . ."

A muscle tightened in his jaw and his face grew dark.

She had gone too far, again. His eyes, so warm and friendly moments ago, held cold remoteness. His expression hardened. The strangest sense of having hurt his feelings squeezed her chest.

"A what, Miss Yelverton?" he asked, his tone insistent.

The heat of embarrassment traveled up her neck and face. "It was nothing. I have forgotten."

He swung her around the end of the dance floor, avoiding an elderly couple who turned in the wrong direction. "Now, I wonder exactly what you planned to say?"

She dared not look up, he sounded so derisive.

"Let me see," he said. "Perhaps you had in mind a dissolute libertine?" He threw her words back at her, words spoken in rage and anguish.

She had let her unruly tongue run away with her and spoil their dance. "I beg your pardon. I should not have spoken as I did. I would be obliged if you would escort me back to Maria."

"Courage, Miss Yelverton. You only have a few more minutes of my dissipated company and it will be over.

Surely you can manage that?"

She had no choice. To leave the floor in the middle of the dance would occasion remark. She concentrated her gaze on the diamond pin in his cravat and her mind on the movement of her feet; anything not to look at his hard expression. His steps remained smooth, his grasp on her hand hadn't changed, but tension sparked across the space between them. His dark mood hammered at her senses, sharpening every nerve to taut awareness.

"And now, Miss Yelverton, you will oblige me by addressing some unexceptionably commonplace remark to my face."

Her breath hitched at the suppressed violence in his tone and she glanced up.

His lips curved in an ironic smile: the smile he hid behind.

She smiled back, determined to make amends for her rudeness. "The weather is quite warm for this time of year. Perhaps that is why it seems so hot in here this evening."

He nodded. "Indeed. Perhaps you would like some air at the conclusion of this dance. We can step out onto the balcony, if you wish."

She did wish. It would be dark out there, a chance to catch her breath, regain some composure and cool her blushes. "I believe I should like that, my lord."

"It will be my pleasure." Remoteness once more colored his voice.

They circled the floor again, spinning and gliding between other couples. He moved easily through the crowd and, as the music filled her mind, she relaxed in his arms.

The last notes died away and he drew their dance to a close beside one of the open French doors. Retaining his hold on her hand, he led her outside.

The balcony ran the length of the back of the house and

overlooked a high-walled garden. Flaming sconces cast pools of light along the stone gallery. A couple conversed in low voices at one end. Travis drew her in the other direction and they stood silently in the shadows, looking out.

Shame pierced her. It was unlike her to be so mean-spirited, but the arrogant Earl of Travis seemed to bring out the worst in her. "I'm sorry I was rude."

His features cast in shadow and one arm leaning on the balustrade, he turned to face her. "Don't believe everything you hear. A lot of it is gossip."

"But not all. 'Tis said there's no smoke without a fire." Oh, her traitorous tongue. She'd spent too long ruling the roost over her father and brother and seemed to have lost the art of common courtesy. Overcome by remorse, she squeezed her eyelids shut for a moment.

He smiled, a white flash in the dim light. "You're right. Not all, I'm afraid."

The timbre of his deep voice resonated deep in the pit of her stomach. Gooseflesh raced across her shoulders and down her back, hot and cold and confusing.

She made an attempt to lesson the sting of her condemning words. "I'm not completely surprised. Michael always disparaged stuffed shirts who moralized about gambling and . . . and the like. He said it was his duty to sample all life had to offer before he settled down to a family."

He laughed, a sound so natural and cheerful, she breathed a sigh of relief.

"I think your brother was a little too free with his information. It's not unlike things I've heard many young bucks say, though. A man is expected to sow his wild oats. The sowing just requires a cool head, or there are consequences."

Victoria reached out and gripped the rail in front of her. The rough stone snagged the delicate fabric of her gloves.

"Consequences, yes. But did it have to be ruin and death?"

"Victoria, I'm sorry. I wasn't speaking of Michael in particular. Your brother needed guidance and he didn't get it."

"I know." If only Michael had listened to her. She had failed utterly in her attempts to make him see the error of his ways. A hard lump blocked her throat.

He reached out, his warm hand cupping her jaw. He swore softly. The pad of his thumb grazed her cheek. "Don't cry."

Her laugh sounded shaky. "I'm not crying."

He tipped her face toward the light and dabbed at it with the handkerchief he pulled from his pocket. "I know it's hard. You have been so brave."

His soft words surprised her as much as his gentle touch. How would he know? She'd scarcely seen him since arriving at his house. She stared into eyes reflecting the flickering torchlight. If she had any sense, she would leave here at once. Drawn by his virile masculinity, she inhaled his spicy cologne mingled with smoke from the flambeaux. Her heart fluttered and skipped at his intoxicating nearness.

She wanted to reach out, to touch his face, to feel his hair where it waved silkily over his stiff, white collar. A sudden urge to trust him rocked her foundation. The man exuded danger. She didn't care.

His head bent toward her, so close she could feel his breath on her cheek. His hands fell on her shoulders, warming her skin. Inches from her mouth, his full sensuous lips held her gaze. She leaned into him.

Simon gazed at her beautiful heart-shaped face, golden in the glow of the torches. His heart clenched. He drew in a sharp breath. He shouldn't be here. He was supposed to be finding her a husband, not trying to seduce her.

With her lovely elfin face tipped to his, her magnetism drew him in to her aura of light. He wanted to pull her hair down around her shoulders, the way he had first seen it. He wanted to run his hands through its heavy waves, see it spread ebony across white linen, across her naked skin, and his.

Her lips parted, the whisper of her breath caressed his chin. He had only to lower his head a fraction to plumb the warm depths of her mouth, to feel her soft, slender shape against him. The scent of jasmine drifted around him, tempting him to press his mouth against her throat, inhale her perfume and her womanly scent.

His heart drummed in his chest drowning out the music from the ballroom. If he did this, there was no going back.

"A fine guardian you make, Travis." Ogden's words rent the quiet air.

Victoria jerked back, one hand to her mouth.

Simon bit back a curse.

"Ogden," he said, and turned to face the interloper. "What are you doing, sneaking around in the dark?"

"I might ask you the same thing," Ogden sneered

To Simon's disappointment mortification filled her expression. She was embarrassed to be found alone with him, ashamed no doubt to be caught with a notorious rake. And of all people, it had to be Ogden.

"If you gentlemen will excuse me," she said, edging around Simon. She lifted her skirts aside to avoid contact with either of them.

Simon reached out to catch her arm. He wanted her to stay. "Victoria?"

Hell. It sounded like a plea. He let his hand drop.

She hurried into the ballroom in a whisper of silk, the scent of jasmine lingering on the night air.

Simon eyed Ogden grimly. Damn it all. What kind of idiot had he become? She was just too damn alluring. He'd forgotten she was a lady and not for him.

"Wait till this bit of gossip is heard around the clubs," Ogden jeered.

"Damn you to hell. We were talking and getting some fresh air." Simon wouldn't be believed, not with his reputation. "You are supposed to be a friend of hers. Why would you want to ruin her?"

"This is not about her."

Bloody hell. Simon sighed wearily. "What do you want?"

"You know what I want. Miranda, back where she belongs."

"Not in my lifetime. You'll have to think of something else."

"Bastard! Then keep your filthy hands off Victoria Yelverton. I'll see you pay dearly if you come anywhere near her. For now, you can send your man around to my lodgings with a hundred guineas. My luck at the tables has been quite out this month."

Simon's hands balled at his side, but he kept his expression blank. The sound of the departing Ogden's mocking laughter stayed with him as he stared out into the darkness.

One day he was going to have to settle his score with Ogden, permanently.

Bloody, bloody hell and damnation.

Chapter Four

Several men, approved by Maria, asked Victoria to dance. Men with perfect manners and pleasing, open countenances, including two of Michael's friends and one rather elderly baron. None of them set her heart fluttering in the manner of a frightened bird the way Travis had.

She had not seen Travis since she practically threw herself into his arms on the balcony. Ogden had also disappeared. He probably thought the very worst of her. A dismal notion.

"Who is she?" asked a debutante to Victoria's right. Victoria glanced across the room in the direction of the discreetly pointing fan. She shook her head. She knew few people present and certainly did not recognize the blond beauty lingering beneath Poseidon's trident.

On the other side of Victoria, a tall brunette in lemon silk turned to look. "It's Satan's latest flirt. Cassandra Eckford. How he ever got Lady Corby to invite her, Mama said she'll never understand." She smiled wryly. "Except he can charm the birds out of the trees, and Lady Corby is some sort of distant relative of his."

Satan's latest flirt. The words scraped at Victoria's nerves. Beneath the stars, she had played into his hands like some silly schoolroom chit.

With a dispassionate eye, she observed the ravishing girl across the room. The gossamer-thin shawl draped over Miss

53

Eckford's bare, white shoulders did nothing to hide the feminine roundness of her figure. With her alabaster complexion, perfect features and golden curls, it was easy to see why the males of the company eyed her with frank appreciation, although she seemed oblivious to the warm glances cast her way. Restless fingers twisted the fringed edges of her wrap as she scanned the room.

The girl in yellow chuckled. "Sickening, isn't it? Her family is barely acceptable, and there she is with the richest, most eligible bachelor dangling after her." Hiding her face with her fan, she edged closer. "The rest of us can only look on in wonder and despair. My brother says they are taking wagers at White's as to whether she'll snare him or he'll get her first."

Victoria frowned. "What do you mean?"

"No lady has ever come close to bringing him up to scratch. They are betting he'll offer her a *carte blanche,* and the odds are she'll take it rather than lose him. Look, there he is now."

Dark and sinister in the glittering surroundings, Travis sauntered through the crowded room. Women turned to watch him pass; men stepped out of his way.

"He's seen his quarry," commented the girl.

Quarry indeed. He stalked across the room with all the lithe grace of a panther, and he looked just as dangerous. Victoria could not tear her gaze away from the fascinating sight of Miss Eckford freezing in his hunter's stare. Reaching her side, the earl took her small hand and pressed it, palm up, to his lips. Those same lips had almost kissed Victoria a few moments ago. Kisses meant nothing to him. The idle flirtation of a careless rake bent on entertaining himself. Her stomach fell in a sickening plunge.

Miss Eckford blushed and fluttered the fringes in her

other hand in protest, but the curve of her full lips welcomed him all the same.

"She looks scared," Victoria murmured.

"So she might. She's no match for him. My brother says she's a silly widgeon without a thought in her head, except fashion and frivolity. She must know Travis's intentions are dishonorable."

As if she were a fragile flower, he led Miss Eckford onto the dance floor.

A cold hand clutched at Victoria's heart at the sight of him smiling down at the ethereal beauty. She turned away. It was beneath her to gawk at them as if they were freaks at the fair. They made a handsome pair and she wished them well.

"My quadrille I believe, Victoria," Ogden's voice came from behind her.

She whirled around. "My lord."

Following hard on her feelings of dismay, the sight of an old friend lifted her spirits. "I thought you might cry off after—"

"What, and leave Michael's beloved sister in the lurch? Never."

The sting of embarrassment at their encounter on the balcony faded and she smiled at him.

With her hand on his sleeve, he led her into the nearest set.

The music began and she curtseyed to his bow.

"I'm sorry, I suppose I really should call you Miss Yelverton now." He sounded regretful, as if he had lost something important.

They crossed to opposite corners of the set. Ogden's slender figure showed to advantage in evening clothes, despite his age.

The steps brought them back together and their hands met in the middle of the square. She shook her head. "You may continue to call me Victoria. Michael would have wished it."

His face lightened as if she had bestowed a precious gift.

The changing formation separated them, and Victoria nodded and smiled at her new partner, a pleasant-faced, short young man in a burgundy coat and pink waistcoat.

A few bars of music later, Ogden partnered her again. She revolved slowly beneath his outstretched arm.

"I'd really like the chance to talk to you alone," he said. "Somewhere we won't be interrupted. Do you think you can escape the dragon lady for an hour or so?"

In another set across the dance floor, Travis sent Victoria a glacial stare over the heads of other dancers. She pretended not to notice. She had no intention of turning her back on a man who had befriended her brother to satisfy the whim of a reprobate who flaunted his courtesan in the face of the *ton*.

With her hand resting on his, Ogden guided her around the square, his questioning gaze fixed on her face.

"I quite often go to Hookham's first thing in the morning," she murmured. "Maria is never up and Travis usually rides out first thing."

A warm smile lit his pale face and deepened the grooves beside his mouth. "I might have guessed. You were always bookish."

He had teased her gently when he found her reading in Golden Square and she'd often put down her book to converse with him while he waited for Michael. She smiled at the recollection.

A serious expression crossed his face. "I'll try to see you there tomorrow. If not, perhaps later in the week. I have something important to tell you."

Once more, the short man claimed her with a bow. What could Ogden want to say that was so important it could not be said here?

When he finally took her hand, his pale gaze raked her from head to toe, lingering on her bosom. "I never saw you look more lovely, Victoria."

A twinge of embarrassment flicked her conscience. She'd never thought of Ogden as anything more than friend and had given him no reason to think otherwise. After witnessing her disgraceful embrace with Travis, he must think her no better than Miss Eckford. Her heart sank. Was that why he wanted to meet her alone?

When he fleetingly squeezed her hand at the conclusion of the dance, she flinched, and a wry, self-mocking smile twisted his lips.

She had no wish to lose a friend. She would meet with him alone, but only to clear her name.

Ogden escorted her through the animated groups around the dance floor and delivered her to Maria, who was sitting on a sofa against the wall with several other older ladies.

"Thank you, Miss Yelverton," he said. "I shall look forward to our next meeting with great anticipation." He bowed and strolled away.

Moments later, Colonel Monteith, a robust man with a full set of graying whiskers and splendid in his hussar uniform, whisked Victoria into a minuet with military efficiency. A hero of Waterloo, according to Maria, the medal on his chest attested to his bravery.

Beyond the dancers, Victoria caught a glimpse of Travis steering Miss Eckford out onto the balcony. Another female was about to fall under his spell beneath the night sky. A vision of him with the incomparable Miss Eckford in his arms left a hollow ache in the region of her heart. Mortified by the direction of her thoughts, she focused her attention on Monteith.

"Excuse me, Miss Yelverton, I hope I didn't step on your foot."

Victoria blinked, surprised. Heavens above, she must have glared at him. What was the matter with her tonight? "No, indeed, Colonel." She cast him a brilliant smile and his florid cheeks turned a darker shade of red.

It was none of her business what Travis did. She'd allowed him to charm her, in spite of what she knew of him, and she was annoyed by her own stupidity. The rarified atmosphere created by his rakish smile and piercing blue eyes would not make her lose her senses again. She fixed her gaze on Monteith's face and the soldier beamed at her.

At the end of the set, he bowed smartly to Maria promising to call on them the next day. He also pressed Victoria's hand before he departed with brisk steps. Perhaps Ogden had not been so very forward after all?

Satisfaction oozed from Maria's broad smile. "I think he's hooked."

Victoria stared at her. "Hooked?"

"Monteith. I think he's interested in you. He's definitely looking for a wife."

Victoria stared after the portly gentleman in his scarlet coat and tried to imagine herself married to him. A black pit opened in front of her feet. She must plan her escape from Travis and his organizing cousin soon, or find herself walking to the altar with the first man who made her an offer. If only her aunt would reply to her letter. It had been almost four weeks now, and not a word had she heard.

The last waltz belonged to Travis. The arrangement had made sense when Maria proposed it, since they would go all home together. After watching him with Miss Eckford, Victoria had no desire to dance with him again. She dallied beside the refreshment table, hoping he would forget.

Her heart skipped at a tap on her shoulder, and she turned to find him standing behind her. Her breath caught at the intensity of his sapphire gaze. The way her pulse quickened at the sight of his manly figure and devilish handsome face left her feeling foolish.

"My dance, I think?" A question lurked in his eyes, as if he sensed her tension.

"I'd really rather prefer to sit it out, if you don't mind."

"But I do mind," he drawled. "I would have left hours ago if not for this."

The blasted man always had an answer for everything.

Keeping her expression pleasantly indifferent, she gave him her hand. "Since you put it in those terms, how could I possibly refuse?"

"*Touché*, Miss Yelverton."

With a manner as distant as if they were strangers, he swept her into the waltz already in progress.

Victoria relaxed. She found his cold demeanor far easier to ignore than his bone-melting smile. "I must thank you once again, my lord. I have enjoyed this evening immensely."

"You are very welcome, Miss Yelverton."

She raised a brow. "And you? You seem to have enjoyed yourself. I gather congratulations are soon to be in order?"

Almost imperceptibly, he stiffened. His expression remained bland. "I know of no reason for congratulations."

She smiled blithely at him. "I must have misunderstood. Surely you and Miss . . ." The grasp on her hand tightened like a vice, then eased.

"Once more, it seems I must remind you not to listen to gossip."

An icy mist of danger blanketed the air between them. She shivered. Whereas her father and brother only grumbled and growled when she sharpened her wit on them, baiting Travis proved to be a risky pastime. This untamed creature might actually bite.

59

She forced herself to speak in even tones. "I understand Lady Corby is a close friend of yours? She certainly has a flair for unusual decorations."

His gaze held hers for a long moment. "Did you find a bridegroom, Miss Yelverton?"

She couldn't hold back her gasp. So, he thought to pay her back in kind. She lifted her chin. "There are three or four quite likely prospects."

A muscle tensed in his jaw. "No doubt I can expect some or all of these worthies to present themselves to me in the next day or so? Please be good enough to give me a list and an indication of your order of preference. I will take it into consideration in making my response."

She narrowed her eyes. "Do my suitors have to address themselves to you for permission, then?"

He swung her around the turn, their movements in perfect harmony. He really was a wonderful dancer, adapting his long legs to her steps, perfectly in tune with her.

"Naturally."

The one word spoken, with all the calm assurance of an arrogant male, sparked her anger. "I think not, my lord. You will send the gentlemen to me for my decision."

His eyes widened and darkened to midsummer blue. "Don't think to choose Ogden."

"Your dispute with Viscount Ogden has nothing to do with me. Unless, of course, you care to tell me the facts of the matter and let me be the judge as to which side has the right of it."

He surprised her by hesitating.

Anxious to understand him, she held her breath, sensing that she hovered on the brink of discovery.

Puzzlement lurked in the crystal depths of his eyes. His black lashes lowered and swept his thoughts away. "It's private, not something I can discuss. It involves another."

Probably a woman. "I can well imagine."

"Dammit." He sighed, short and sharp. "Why can't you trust me in this?"

She smiled. "I wonder."

A fleeting shadow crossed his expression. For the second time tonight, she felt as if she had the power to wound him and the sensation left her uncomfortable.

Absurd. A man like him had no deep feelings. She kept her face as expressionless as his. He would not tell her whom to marry. In fact, she would not submit his will in anything.

Simon had no trouble spotting Ian's large form slumped in the deep wing chair in his normal corner of White's card room far from the hearth, his fair head sunk on his chest.

Simon cursed silently at Lethbridge's obviously inebriated condition. He'd have to get him home to bed again.

"I half expected you to be gone by now," Simon said. He sank into the soft leather chair opposite Lethbridge. A two-thirds-empty brandy bottle and two full tumblers sat on the round table between them.

Lethbridge peered at Simon. He looked like hell, eyes red-rimmed and bleary, hair and clothing rumpled. His deceptively warm, lazy smile did nothing to hide his agony of spirit.

" 'S'all right. I've been keeping you company." He must have seen Simon's confusion, for his shoulders shook in ghostly laughter.

"First," Lethbridge said, picking up one tumbler and waving it vaguely in Simon's direction, "I drink to you." He downed the golden liquid in one swallow, blinking as the fiery alcohol hit the back of his throat. "Then you drink to me." He picked up the other glass, chinked it against the first and disposed of its contents in one smooth motion. He leaned forward and, holding the bottle in both hands to steady it, began to refill the glasses.

Simon kept his frustration out of his voice. "You've had enough."

Lethbridge shook his head and looked at him owlishly. "Can't have." He paused, considering, then shook his head again. "Nope, not yet. It still hurts. It still damn well hurts, Simon. It won't stop hurting till I'm dead drunk, or dead, whichever comes first."

Damn all women to hell, and especially Genevieve Longbourne, the woman Lethbridge loved and stubbornly refused to accept he couldn't have. Simon didn't understand why Lethbridge had let himself become so besotted with a woman who had proved beyond a doubt she didn't give a tuppenny damn for him.

Simon never allowed anyone to get that close. Not since Miranda. And even then, not like this. Lethbridge had simply lain down and died instead of fighting back. A strong, good man, he was no coward, but if he didn't pull out of this soon, he would be a dead one.

Simon ran a hand through his hair and stood up. He grasped Lethbridge by the arm. "Come on, old fellow, let's get you home."

He'd been acting as nursemaid to the man for weeks. He didn't know what else to do. Most nights he managed to stop Lethbridge from getting this sotted. Every now and again, Lethbridge escaped him and then he had to force the blond giant out of some hell or other; no easy task when he didn't want to be rescued. But for Victoria Yelverton, Simon would have seen Lethbridge home hours ago. Damn his charitable urges.

Lethbridge struggled up. He swayed and braced his legs apart.

"Not going to cast up your accounts, old chap?" Simon asked, a trifle anxiously.

"No." The blond head swung from side to side in exaggerated slowness.

Simon trusted him to know. "Come on then. We'll pick up a hackney outside."

When they descended the front steps onto St James Street, there wasn't a hackney or a chair to be seen. He swore freely. Any other night, even at this early hour of the morning, there was the odd jarvey hanging about outside White's looking for business. But not tonight, when he desperately needed one. A couple of jeering link boys offered to light them home and Simon sent them scuttling off with a formidable glare. "No help for it, old chap. We'll have to walk."

He grabbed Lethbridge's arm and drew it over his shoulders. He staggered as Lethbridge leaned on him. "Get a grip, man, for Christ's sake."

"Sorry," he mumbled.

To Simon's relief, Lethbridge pulled himself upright and began a slow plod. One foot placed ahead of its previous location, it was more a disjointed stagger than a walk, but it took them in the right direction. Thank God Lethbridge lodged close by on Jermyn Street.

Fifteen minutes later, breathing hard and with sweat trickling down his forehead, Simon glanced around in dismay. Still no sign of a hackney. Hell. Ian weighed what felt like a hundredweight. If he wasn't carrying the marquess, it was as close as he ever wanted to get to it. Simon forged on, one step at a time. The slow progress irritated him, but footpads and Mohawks plied their nefarious trade in the twisting back alleys, and he didn't dare leave Lethbridge and go for help. They wouldn't hesitate to take advantage of a drunken toff temptingly laid out like Sunday dinner.

He turned the corner and glanced up the carriageway, which led to the mews behind Lethbridge's townhouse. The back entrance seemed a lot closer than the front door. Simon hoisted his burden higher on his aching shoulder and turned into the gloom of the narrow, stinking alley running between the walled gardens of the imposing Mayfair townhouses.

They had traversed only half the distance to Lethbridge's gate when footsteps echoed behind him. He swung around. Three shadowy figures closed in on them. Damn. No chance to run with Lethbridge weighing him down like a shackle.

The scum would likely leg it at the first sign of a fight. "Who's there," he called out. "Show yourselves."

A burly shape moved closer. "That's 'im," a coarse voice muttered.

They carried weapons, wooden clubs from the look of it. They swung them menacingly in the shadowy moonlight.

This night had definitely gone downhill, and it had been bad from the moment it started. At a low point when his heart lurched at the sight of the dark-haired Miss Yelverton, her rosy lips parted and her cheeks delicately flushed with anticipation, as she stood under the chandelier in his hall waiting to go to Corby's ball, it was now at rock bottom.

Lethbridge stumbled and almost brought him down. Simon had no choice but to let Lethbridge slide to the slimy, cobbled ground. He propped him against the rough, stone wall, then straightened to face his assailants.

Three to one. Not bad odds, given the nature of these cowardly footpads. Two to three would be better, but Lethbridge remained unconscious, totally oblivious and already snoring loudly. Simon almost laughed at the sound. Instead, the lessons of his youth fresh in his mind, he poised himself on the balls of his feet and took a deep and calming breath. He cleared his mind of all thought except awareness of the men who meant them harm.

They had weapons, but fists and feet were as effective as any club. Mr. MacIver had taught him well. He relaxed and waited to see what they would try. The narrow alley favored him. They had to come one at a time.

A solid shape loomed out of the shadows. Simon tensed, listening. A scuffle, a foot slipping on cobbles, heavy breathing, all revealed his opponents' movements. Simon dodged a swooshing rush of air, thick with the smell of manure. A cudgel swept past his head.

He reached out, grabbed the man's arm and wrenched it up behind his back. He swung a left hook. It failed to connect with the man's head. Simon lurched forward. He kicked high and his boot jarred with a satisfying crunch against the flesh and bone of unprotected ribs.

The man swung his club in a wide arc and Simon twisted away. Another shadow surged in and a wild jab made vicious contact with Simon's shoulder. He staggered back, his breath rasping loud in his ears.

"We've got 'im now," one of them said.

This was no robbery, Simon realized vaguely. These men were out for blood. A red haze of anger gripped him. He tamped it down. Rage dulled the senses. He concentrated on the sounds made by shifting shadows in the gloom.

"Simon." Lethbridge struggled to rise at Simon's side. His hands clawed up the wall.

"Stay back," Simon warned.

Momentarily distracted by fear for his friend, Simon almost didn't sense the next blow aimed at his skull. He fended it off with his forearm. Hell. The shattering pain brought him to his knees. His eyes watered. He forced himself to close his mind to his body's protest. He buried it deep inside, the way he had learned to do as a child.

Beleaguered lungs fighting for air, Simon staggered to his feet. He grabbed at the cudgel raised to finish him. Caught off guard by Simon's upward momentum, his opponent slipped on the greasy filth underfoot. Simon roared in feral triumph and pulled the weapon free.

The odds had changed. He was armed. He tested the weight of the rough, wooden club and prepared for battle.

"Simon. Here," Lethbridge called out.

A glitter of steel. Simon deftly caught the wicked-looking blade. Swinging the cudgel, he landed a blow to the downed ruffian's head. The man grunted and sagged, a dark lump on the ground before him. The other two crouched and came in low. Simon slashed at the one on his right and missed.

Lethbridge launched himself at the feet of other. A crack of wood on bone and Lethbridge's grunt bounced off the stone walls. It was the help Simon needed. He thrust at the closest shape and felt the knife sink deep into soft flesh. A gurgling cry of pain rewarded his effort. He pulled back, ready to strike again.

With muttered oaths, the cowards broke and grabbed their fallen comrade between them. Their boots clattering and scraping on the slippery stones, they stumbled to the end of the alley.

Doubled over and desperately sucking in air, Simon saw them silhouetted against the street lamp, and then they were gone, melting into the city's underbelly.

At his feet, Lethbridge groaned and Simon sank to his knees, beginning to know the damage to his battered body and fists.

"Lethbridge? Ian?" Simon nudged him. "Are you all right?"

At the sound of his friend's faint chuckle, relief overwhelmed him.

"Can't hurt a drunk, you know that."

"The devil you say. Can you stand? It's only steps to your door. I don't think I can lift you." One arm numb, but seemingly not broken, Simon watched Lethbridge get to his feet and pull himself along the wall with halting steps. When they reached the welcome refuge of the gate, Simon yanked on the bell. Its urgent clang broke the silence like a call to arms.

"Who goes there?" cried a quavering young voice after long minutes.

"Dammit! It's me, young Ben. Your goddamned master," Lethbridge shouted back.

"My lord?" The boy held a lantern high over the wall and gasped with horror as the flickering light spilled over them.

"For God's sake, boy. Let us in and lock the bloody gate behind us," Lethbridge urged.

The moment the sturdy gate was closed and barred, Simon slumped to the ground next to the collapsed Lethbridge. "Fetch a couple of footmen," he gasped to the wide-eyed boy.

"Yes, my lord." Ben fled toward the house.

Chapter Five

The morning after Corby's ball, gray skies required candles to be lighted in the cozy breakfast room. Even the sunny yellow curtains and upholstery seemed unable to brighten Victoria's mood. She sipped her tea and watched the rain run down the tall window. She could not blame Travis for her disturbed sleep last night. He'd not come home.

She always knew when he came in, no matter the time. Her months of listening for Michael's stumbling, cursing progress after a night on the town had left her a light sleeper.

She sighed. She would never hear Michael again. Better not to think of about it, or about Travis's nighttime adventures. Rain or no rain, she longed to stretch her legs.

She rang the bell and the butler appeared in moments. "I am going to Hookham's this morning, Benton."

Stony-faced, the butler bowed. "I will order the carriage brought around, Miss Yelverton."

"I prefer to walk. There is no sense asking people to get wet."

"I don't think his lordship would allow it, miss."

The earl had stricter notions of propriety than her father or brother ever had.

The butler's serious face offered the faintest of smiles. "Young Wilson would be more than happy to oblige you with an umbrella. He'd sooner do anything than polish the silver."

Victoria smiled back. Benton, beneath his austere exterior, was a rather nice man. "Wilson it is then. I'll just be a moment getting my coat and hat."

"Very good, miss."

Followed by the liveried Wilson, who somehow managed to keep the large black umbrella above her head, Victoria wove between the other pedestrians on Bond Street, keeping a wary eye out for dirty waterfalls splashed up by passing carriages.

At Hookham's, she left Wilson seated on the bench beneath the dripping eves and ducked inside. The lack of customers amongst the rows of shelves attested to the miserable weather. There was no sign of Ogden at the stacks or in the area set aside for reading.

The smell of new leather and old dust pervaded the room. She browsed the shelves and exclaimed in triumph when she located Miss Austen's *Emma*. A work dedicated by the author to the Prince Regent, Victoria had wanted to read it ever since it came out. Not ready to return to Travis Place, she lost herself in the array of books and titles, some old favorites and others she had yet to read. She pulled out a copy of Lord Byron's *Bride of Abydos* and dipped into the first few pages.

Jostled from behind, her nose barely missed making contact with her book's pages. *Emma* slid out from under her arm and landed on the floor with a soft thud.

She whirled around. "What . . ." Her gaze fell upon the perfectly formed features of Miss Cassandra Eckford.

What bad timing.

"Forgive me," Miss Eckford said. "I do beg your pardon. I wasn't looking. At least, I *was* looking, but the other way. I hope I didn't hurt you."

Every instinct warned Victoria to leave immediately. "Not at all." Victoria replaced Byron in its place.

"Please don't leave on my account." The soft tone held a note of pleading.

Victoria gazed into a pair of concerned, sky-blue eyes fringed by long golden lashes exactly on a level with her own. She waived a deprecating hand. "I had finished."

She reached down to recover her book just as Miss Eckford stooped and retrieved it from the floor beside her feet. Crouched on the floor, Victoria stared into the beautiful Miss Eckford's apologetic face and watched as she blushed; a glorious pale-rose suffused her dazzling, white skin. No wonder she entranced the earl.

The thought left Victoria feeling strangely hollow and she stood up. She accepted the book from Miss Eckford's outstretched hand. "Thank you." She turned away.

An odd shuffling noise drew her back. Miss Eckford had removed several books from an eye-level shelf and now peered through the gap towards the front door.

"What are you doing, Miss Eckford?"

With a wide-eyed, startled expression, Miss Eckford put a finger to her lips. "Hiding from Mama," she whispered.

Victoria doubted her sanity. "She must know you are here."

Miss Eckford shook her head. Her golden curls bounced beneath the brim of her ruched blue bonnet. "I told her I was going to Hatchard's, then slipped in here instead. I always get them mixed up." Her fair eyebrows drew together. "This is Hookham's, isn't it?"

"Yes."

"But it's no use. She'll find me, and then I'll miss him, and I'll have to go with her to see the Elgin Marbles, and I did so want to go on a picnic with Albert. I promised."

Victoria raised a brow. "If you promised, then you should go."

"I can't." The distraught tone held impending tears. "Mama has it on good authority that *he* is planning to be at the British Museum, and therefore I must go."

A strange stillness invaded Victoria. She predicted the answer before she asked. "He?"

"Travis, the earl of," Miss Eckford replied with a pout.

"Oh," Victoria said, her guess confirmed. "Quite. It has been exceedingly pleasant speaking with you, Miss Eckford, but I really must dash along now, my footman is waiting outside."

"Do I know you?"

Victoria hesitated, surprised.

Miss Eckford went on, "I mean, you know my name, but I don't believe we've met, have we?" The wide, blue eyes demanded an answer.

"Yelverton, Victoria. I mean Victoria Yelverton." She wanted to leave. Now.

"Yelverton? Didn't you move into Travis's house after he killed your brother?"

Shock froze Victoria to the spot. She had no idea Travis was accused of killing Michael. "It was an accident," she blurted out. "If you will excuse me, I really must be on my way."

The foolish girl just didn't seem to listen; she clutched at Victoria's sleeve. "Oh, I am so sorry, Miss Yelverton. So very sorry. If I lost my brother like that, so young, it would be so very dreadful. Not that I have a brother, I have a younger sister. But I can imagine how you must feel."

Astonishment held Victoria transfixed. How could Travis spend more than five minutes with this pea-brained goose without giving her one of his scathing set-downs? A cold hand fisted in her chest. He wouldn't. Engrossed in Miss Eckford's other attributes, he probably never listened to a word she said.

In the same nervous manner Victoria had noticed at Lady Corby's ball, Miss Eckford twisted the ribbons of her bonnet and glanced over her shoulder.

Victoria frowned. "You don't want to meet the Earl of Travis today?"

"I want to go on a picnic with Mr. Runcorn."

"Mr. Runcorn?"

"He's a friend. I've known him all my life." Miss Eckford sounded defensive. "Mama doesn't like him because he doesn't have a title or a fortune. But Grandmamma approves of him. He lives close by her home near Worthing. He's only in Town for a week, and he asked me to go on a picnic today, and Mama promised I could, but now I have to bump into Travis at the museum and waste the afternoon looking at old stones." Her lower lip trembled. Sweet heavens, she was going to cry.

"Don't you like the earl?"

"Oh, yes. One must of course. He's the richest man in London and very good *ton.*"

The matter-of-fact tone chilled Victoria. Travis had met his match in this beautiful woman with veins of ice. Victoria couldn't stem her curiosity. "Rumor is that you plan to marry him."

Miss Eckford blushed again and peeped at Victoria from beneath her lashes. "Mama is hoping he will make an offer. If not, he's sure to make me a very handsome arrangement. Don't look so shocked, Miss Yelverton."

Victoria closed her mouth.

Miss Eckford shook her head sorrowfully. "You see, we only have enough funds for my come-out. Grandmamma doesn't like my half-sister Lucy and won't help her at all. Mother says, sometimes we have to sacrifice ourselves to help our loved ones. So, if Lord Travis is prepared to . . ."

Victoria raised her hand. This was more information than she ever wanted to know. Pity for the worldly wise but somehow vulnerable, Miss Eckford, swept away Victoria's disgust. Between her mother and Lord Travis, she had been netted and caged like a wild linnet. A travesty whichever way she looked at it. "You mean you would prefer to go to the picnic with Mr. Runcorn than meet the earl?"

"Yes. You see, Albert wants to marry me, but Mama won't agree. Not when there's a possibility the earl might make me an offer. Think how much better off we all will be." She sighed, and a big fat tear rolled delicately down her china-doll cheek. "Grandmamma condoned the match with Albert, but Mama says—"

"Miss Eckford, I am presently staying with the earl." Victoria almost choked at having to make an admission she had been denying to herself for weeks. "He is my guardian. If you tell your mother I am going on this picnic with you and I am expecting the earl to accompany me, do you think she might change her mind?"

A small crease marred the perfection of Miss Eckford's fair brow. "It wouldn't be of any use at all. Albert doesn't like the earl and Travis is sure to say something unpleasant."

Victoria clung to her patience. "I didn't mean he would really come with us."

"Lie to Mama, you mean." The rosy lips formed a shocked O and her eyes opened wider.

Fruitless. Victoria edged away and tears welled up in the confused china-blue eyes. Out of pity, Victoria made a final effort. "It's not much different from hiding and more likely to be successful. The earl might be expected to accompany me, but expectations do not always materialize."

Miss Eckford smiled. Sunshine after rain. "I see. It's in the realm of possibility, but unlikely. That's something Grand-mamma often says."

At least someone in the family had a brain. Victoria nodded.

"I'll do it," breathed Miss Eckford.

Wonders would never cease. "Then so shall I." Victoria held up her book. "Are you going to borrow anything, Miss Eckford?"

"No. I hoped to meet someone, but he doesn't appear to be here."

"Mr. Runcorn?"

Miss Eckford blushed yet again. She did it on purpose, a carefully orchestrated color wash, which she executed at will. "No, someone else. Please, Miss Yelverton, it's not what you think."

Victoria realized her face had once more revealed shock and schooled her features into something akin to sympathy.

"He's a friend, an older gentleman, who is kind to me, but he doesn't have money, not like Travis."

Victoria could well believe Miss Eckford collected men who wanted to be kind to her, like a lamp collected moths on a warm summer night. "Who is he?"

"Viscount Ogden."

Ice filled Victoria's veins. This was the reason Travis hated Ogden. Two dogs fighting over the same bone. Quite laughable, if it weren't so awful for Miss Eckford and so typical of arrogant men.

Miss Eckford wanted neither of them. The inertia gripping Victoria since Michael's death fell away. She resolved to teach Ogden and Travis a well-deserved lesson. They could not simply help themselves to what they wanted without any thought of the consequences for others.

She headed towards the desk where a clerk waited to

record her loan. Miss Eckford trotted beside her.

"Now, let's find your mother," Victoria said.

It did not take them long to locate Miss Eckford's mother. She stood on the pavement just outside Hookham's, accompanied by a sulky-faced girl of about fifteen.

Gimlet-eyed, with thin lips, she reminded Victoria of a ferret their old gamekeeper used to keep for hunting. Her toilette, a puce walking dress topped off by a crest of peacock feathers on a yellow bonnet, created an awesome picture.

"There you are, my girl," Mrs. Eckford said crossly, apparently not noticing Victoria.

"Mama," protested Miss Eckford.

"You had me traipsing from one end of Bond Street to the other and here you are all the time." She raised her carefully plucked brows at Victoria.

"Miss Yelverton, my mother, Mrs. Eckford, and my sister Lucy. Mama, this is Miss Victoria Yelverton, she is Lord Travis's ward."

"Indeed," Mrs. Eckford said, her magnificent bosom swelling. "I heard something about Travis acquiring a ward."

Victoria blinked. Did this woman assume Victoria was her daughter's rival? A sinking feeling invaded her stomach, but she kept her tone friendly. "How do you do, Mrs. Eckford?"

"Good day, Miss Yelverton, I'm sure." Mrs. Eckford sniffed and turned to her daughter. "Come along, Cassandra. We must finish our errands or we will be late."

"Mama, Miss Yelverton expects Lord Travis to accompany her to Albert's picnic this afternoon."

The words came out in a rush and Mrs. Eckford halted in her tracks. Victoria could not help sending Cassandra an admiring glance.

"It was so kind of Miss Eckford to invite me," Victoria said with a sweet smile. "I know so few people, having only just come to Town, and we were quite at a loose end this afternoon."

Mrs. Eckford's pouter-pigeon look subsided, but she cast a sharp, discerning glance at Victoria.

Lucy thrust out her bottom lip. "Why can't I go?"

"Because you weren't invited, Lucy," Miss Eckford said.

"How is it she can go?" Lucy pointed at Victoria. "She wasn't invited, either."

Victoria spotted Wilson shifting from foot to foot nearby. She had kept him waiting far too long, and Mrs. Eckford seemed wholly unconvinced. "Perhaps you know my companion and cousin to Lord Travis, Miss Maria Allenby, Mrs. Eckford. She will be more than delighted to accompany us if a chaperon is required."

At the sight of Mrs. Eckford's defeated expression, Victoria gave thanks for Travis's provision of a chaperon known for her exemplary morals.

The routed Mrs. Eckford tossed her head. "Miss Allenby will not be needed. I am quite sure of that. The party is all arranged. I certainly would not permit Cassandra to attend if it were not properly chaperoned."

Victoria hid her relief. She doubted Maria would be persuaded to accompany Miss Eckford and her friends even if she were not touted to be Satan's next mistress.

Mrs. Eckford glanced up at the leaden sky. "It's sure to rain again. Mr. Runcorn will be forced to cancel the outing." The prediction seemed to give her a modicum of satisfaction.

"No, Mama. Albert has it all arranged. Primrose Hill has a pavilion where we can picnic under the roof. The band will play at tea time, rain or shine. Do say yes, Mama, please."

"It sounds very enjoyable," Victoria added, unable to resist a mischievous smile. "Just the sort of thing Travis likes."

"Very well," said Mrs. Eckford. "But you remind Mr. Runcorn not to go arranging any more outings without consulting me first. Come along girls." After a piercing stare at Victoria, she turned and set off down the street with Lucy trailing obediently behind her.

"I'll send the carriage for you at two," Miss Eckford said with an anxious smile.

In the wake of her family members, the incomparable Miss Eckford picked her way daintily around the puddles on the pavement. Men turned their heads to watch her pass. How could a mother force her daughter into such a disgraceful liaison when she loved another man? And how could Travis take advantage of the situation? It was not to be borne.

"Girls, less noise please," the severely thin Miss Prudhomme remonstrated, not for the first time.

Giggles echoed beneath the pavilion's high roof. From her nearby bench, Victoria glanced over at the blanket on the ground where Cassandra and Mr. Runcorn's school-aged cousins, a pair of dark-haired and merry-eyed imps, sat. Louise, the youngest, had plump cheeks and eyes like raisins, and Jean looked skinny enough to blow away in a high wind. They were as happy as larks on a summer day. Their high spirits and the gangly Mr. Johnson's teasing had turned the game of consequences organized by the spinsterishly neat governess into a romp.

Happy and unaffected, they enchanted Victoria.

And what a stolid country gentleman of serious demeanor Mr. Albert Runcorn of Gosford near Worthing had proved to be. He stood protectively behind Miss Eckford. Ruddy-faced, of average height and build, his attire was neat and well-tailored. Fair-skinned with tawny hair and rather sad brown eyes, only when his gaze fell upon Miss Eckford did his heavy features brighten.

He was not alone. Several of the other gentlemen strolling around the pavilion adopted a particularly besotted look upon encountering the lovely Miss Eckford. Much to her credit, Cassandra seemed unaware of their admiring glances and laughed with blithe enjoyment at the antics of the young Runcorn girls.

Victoria repressed a twinge of guilt. When she had declined Maria's invitation to go with her to visit an old acquaintance, Victoria had indicated her intention to spend the afternoon reading and had deliberately not said where.

"Miss Yelverton," Miss Prudhomme called. "Mr. Runcorn. It's time for tea."

Tucking her book in her reticule, Victoria smiled and joined the party on the blanket around the governess.

"Mr. Runcorn, sit next to me," Miss Eckford cried, beaming up at him.

"Now, Cassie, Miss Yelverton is your guest," said Mr. Runcorn in a gentle chiding tone.

"Oh, I'm so sorry, Miss Yelverton, I forgot." She patted the blanket next to her. "You will sit next to me, won't you?"

"I should be delighted," Victoria responded with a smile.

Mr. Runcorn seated himself between his cousins and opposite Mr. Johnson. Miss Prudhomme unpacked the picnic baskets and passed out plates and napkins.

"How long are you staying in Town, Mr. Runcorn?" Victoria asked as the plate of ham sandwiches made the rounds.

"Not long enough," Miss Eckford said.

Mr. Runcorn shook his head. "Just until tomorrow. It's longer than I should stay, as it is. The farm won't run itself."

"I do miss your farm, Mr. Runcorn," Miss Eckford said, a sandwich delicately hovering in front of her cupid's bow mouth. She turned to Victoria. "He has the prettiest chickens, a really gentle horse I'm not afraid to ride, and a herd of the sweetest black-and-white cows, Miss Yelverton."

"And they miss you," Mr. Runcorn said with a sad, faintly bovine expression.

Victoria turned away lest he see her pity at his misery. The Runcorn girls whispered and giggled behind his back.

"Girls," Miss Prudhomme rapped out. "If you can't share your conversation with the rest of us, then keep silent."

"Jeannie thinks Miss Yelverton is just as pretty as Cassie," blurted out the younger sister, Louise.

Heat scorched Victoria's face, but she managed a smile. "Thank you, Jean."

"Do you have a suitor?" Louise asked. "Cassie has ever so many."

"Louise, mind your tongue," Miss Prudhomme said in shocked accents.

"Do you?" The slender Jean stared at Victoria curiously. "Just because Cassie is *à la mode* doesn't mean girls who have dark hair and eyes can't get a beau. I think you are as pretty as Cassie."

Victoria choked on a bite of her sandwich.

Silence hung over the group. Mr. Runcorn stared across the circle, a frown on his face. "A pale English rose and an orchid, two beautiful but different flowers," he managed in a strangled voice, his face brick red.

His wit might not be of a high order, but his generosity of spirit only improved Victoria's good opinion of him. She quelled an urge to lean across the blanket and pat his arm.

"An exotic bouquet," Mr. Johnson mumbled, clearly not wishing to be outdone.

"Louise, pass the lemonade," Miss Prudhomme said. "Girls, hurry up and finish eating. We will have time for one more game before the band begins."

"This time, may I sit next to you, Albert?" Miss Eckford asked.

"You let Miss Prudhomme arrange the seating, Cassie," replied her strict swain. "She'll know what's right."

The picnic over, and anxious to discover how Emma fared, Victoria went back to her seat on the bench and opened her book. The squeals from the girls made concentration impossible. After reading the same paragraph three times without taking in a single word, Victoria closed her volume with a sigh.

"You do not enjoy games, Miss Yelverton?" Runcorn's pleasant, low voice pulled Victoria's attention to him standing beside her.

She kept her voice light. "Of course. I am just not in the mood this afternoon."

His expression held sympathy. "Miss Eckford told me of your loss."

His sympathy was misplaced. Michael's death did not hold her back from the amusements. Memories of her own schoolroom days, happier times when their country home had been full of laughter had suddenly returned to haunt her.

She shot him a rueful smile. "I must apologize if I am casting a damper on the day." Victoria stuffed *Emma* into her reticule. "I am happy to join in whatever game Miss Prudhomme arranges to entertain us."

A frown furrowed his forehead. "Actually, Miss Yelverton, I'm right glad to have the chance to talk to you. It pleases me to see Cassie—I mean Miss Eckford—so happy, but I'm that worried." In his anxiety, a trace of Sussex accent infected his normally precise speech. "It's this Travis fellow. He's got her head so turned, I don't know what to do."

Victoria glanced over at Cassandra, one of nature's rarest creations. This poor young man did not stand a chance of winning her with Travis in the running.

"Do you love her?" The question popped out before she thought about it.

"Aye. I always have. For years. Her grandmother encouraged me to hope. She said I was good for her, steady like." He shook his head, a lock of brown hair falling over his forehead. "Then that mother of hers comes to visit, looking for money, takes one look at Cassie and fills her head with titles and nobility and the like. And if that weren't enough, she tells her Lucy's happiness hangs on her success. Cassie is too soft by half. She can't bear to think of making anyone suffer and especially not her own family." His hands clenched suddenly. "I'd like to kill that Travis."

Victoria recoiled.

Runcorn's face flushed a mottled red. "Please, excuse me, Miss Yelverton. I forgot myself. I have no wish to insult you."

Insult was the wrong word. While shocked by the extremity of his threat, Victoria empathized with his sentiments.

Impatient strides took him away and then he paced back, fists clenched at his sides. "If I thought he'd make her happy, I'd stay out of it. 'Tis my guess he don't mean to do right by her."

Uncertainty tortured his expression. Instinctively, Victoria knew Miss Eckford would throw away something far more valuable than a title or jewelry if she walked away from this man's genuine adoration. If Victoria were ever blessed with this kind of honest devotion, she would count herself fortunate indeed.

"You wish to marry her, then?"

"Aye, what else?"

His belligerent tone only enhanced his worth in Victoria's eyes. "Can you not persuade her grandmother to interfere?"

"Nay. The old lady's out-of-reason stubborn. I tried talking to her before I came to Town. She was that miffed when Cassie went off with her mother, she threatened never to see her again. The old lady is too proud to go back on her word. A stickler she is, from a long line of sticklers. They cut the son off when he married Cassie's mother and regretted it ever after, especially since he died, leaving Cassie the last of the line. A crime it is. She don't even bear the name. She took the stepfather's."

Something in the way he described the family gave Victoria a glimmer of unease. "Just who is her grandmother?"

"Lady Elizabeth Halsted of Sussex."

Cold chills ran down Victoria's spine. Did the earl have any idea of Cassandra Eckford's connections? No doubt Mrs. Eckford would delight in telling him when it was too late to draw back. Foreboding filled her. What sort of life would Cassandra have with a rake forced to make an offer? Cassandra Eckford might well end up wedded to an earl, but the price would be her happiness.

Victoria kept her voice low. "I cannot promise much, but if I am able to divine the earl's intentions toward Miss Eckford, I will send you word." She rose to her feet.

Taking her hand, Mr. Runcorn pressed it briefly with his capably square, warm one. "I don't know how to thank you," he murmured. "I was none too pleased when Cassie said you were to come today. But as soon as I saw you, I knew you were true blue, Miss Yelverton."

Nervousness fluttered in her stomach. She had absolutely no way of knowing whether she could keep her promise. "Time enough for thanks, Mr. Runcorn, if they are deserved."

The balance of the afternoon passed pleasantly enough. Victoria enjoyed a game of consequences with the merry group, the band made up in enthusiasm what it lacked in skill and, at the end of the afternoon, the party made its way home in Mr. Runcorn's carriage, well satisfied with the day's entertainment.

Victoria, the last one to be delivered home, could not remember when she had passed such a delightfully carefree afternoon. She gazed out the carriage window, seeing only the rain streaking against the glass. Papa's problems had overshadowed everything for years. No, it had been a very long time indeed.

Against her wishes, Mr. Runcorn insisted on seeing her home and very properly handed her out of the carriage and delivered her to the earl's front door.

"Whatever you can do, Miss Yelverton," he said with a stiff bow as he bade her farewell. He lumbered back into the rain and the waiting carriage.

Victoria smiled at Wilson holding the door and stepped inside.

"Who was that?" Travis loomed out of the shadows. "Where have you been? Cousin Maria has been in a dither for the past hour."

Jolted by his sudden appearance and accusing tone, her heart raced. To recover her composure, she focused on removing her coat. "Thank you, Wilson."

"Well?" Travis said, his voice louder.

Her pulse skittered in the most annoying way. She did not fear him. She arched a brow. "What has made you so out of reason cross?"

He stepped into the light of the chandelier.

She gasped.

Livid bruises discolored his jaw and a cut split his lip, no doubt from some drunken fracas. Remembering Michael's testiness when worsted in a brawl, she resisted the desire to sympathize. "Now I see. You must have lost your fight. There's no need to take your spleen out on me."

"I did not lose the fight. I want an answer."

She glared at him.

He narrowed his eyes. "I'll see you in the library. Now."

She stiffened, refusal on the tip of her tongue. If only she didn't feel so guilty about sneaking out without telling Maria—and she certainly didn't want to continue their argument with the servants looking on.

She nodded in acquiescence and passed through the door he held open for her. Prepared to be reasonable, she turned to face him. "While it is none of your business, I received a last-minute invitation from a friend to go to Primrose Hill for a picnic."

"It is my business, Miss Yelverton. You told Maria you planned to stay at home this afternoon. I want the truth. Where did you go and with whom?"

He spoke as if a naughty child stood before him, and her anger at his arrogant assumption of control bubbled to the surface. "Are you calling me a liar?"

"If the cap fits—"

"How dare you." She headed for the door.

His hand shot out. Warm on her upper arm, his strong fingers held her fast. He swung her around to face him. Energy charged the air, prickling the back of her neck. She drew in a sharp breath.

He swore and dropped his hand as if he also felt it. Cool air replaced the heat of his hand. "You will not leave, Miss Yelverton, until I have an answer."

Her heart thundered. She resented the need to dissemble, and if he were not such a despicable rake, she would not be forced to prevaricate. "I have said all I intend to say. Now if you will excuse me . . ." She sidestepped him.

In a swift, unexpected motion, he caught her chin, forcing her to look up at him. His fingertips fired her blood and flames raced to the center of her being. Her breathing quickened. Just like on the balcony, she stood transfixed, caught in the aura of his dark presence.

His mouth, cut and swollen, hovered a mere inch away from hers, sensuous, compelling. She could feel his warm breath on her cheek. He smelled of . . . witch hazel?

Blue flames flickered in sapphire depths as he gazed into her eyes, his expression intense, watchful. Deep longing unfurled in the pit of her stomach. Not again. She jerked her chin away.

Rising and falling in a controlled rhythm, his broad chest filled her vision as his anger erupted in savage tones. "You went to Ogden, didn't you? You arranged to meet him."

He thought her morals as bad as his own. He'd learn the truth when she spoiled his sport with Cassandra Eckford.

She met his hard gaze boldly. "Let me pass, please."

He caught her by the shoulders, his fingers digging into her flesh. "Not until you tell me the truth."

His dark expression and the bright fury in his eyes gave her pause. He looked ready for murder. She took a deep breath and spoke calmly. "I told you. I went on a picnic with friends. We played consequences. We listened to a band and I read." She rummaged in her reticule, yanked out her book and waived it under his nose.

He stared at her for a long moment, his gaze fixed on her mouth.

Breathless, she let her hand fall and licked her lips.

A sigh hissed between his clenched teeth and his hands grasped her shoulders and pulled her close. He pressed his lips against hers.

Soft and warm, their pressure stifled her gasp of shock.

85

Pleasurable shivers slid down her back to the pit of her stomach and emptied her mind. The heat of his body warmed her, his hands softened on her shoulders, moved over her back with gentle caresses. Steel-hard against hers, his body thrummed with a tension she felt in her heart and soul. Irresistible. It felt as if she'd always known him, her body molded to his familiar shape, his thigh between hers, his hip against the curve of her stomach, her breasts flattened against the wall of his chest. She arched against him.

His sharp in-drawn breath broke the silence.

Utter madness. Folly. This man destroyed everyone in his path.

She pulled away, desperately seeking to still her shaking limbs and catch her breath. She had lost her senses. "I think we better agree this never happened."

Puzzlement and yearning lingered in his expression. Fire flickered in his eyes then banked to white heat.

His lip curled in a sneer. "Do you say the same thing to Ogden?" He ran his gaze over her face and down to her heaving chest. "And does he make you feel like that, Victoria?"

"Enough. I will not tolerate your insinuations. The viscount is a gentleman, unlike . . ."

Pain shattered his brilliant gaze. He grimaced. "Unlike me."

Her stomach squeezed at his hurt. Wishing her words unsaid, she gentled her tone. "My lord, I am telling you the truth. I am sorry if I worried Miss Allenby, but I truly expected to return before her. I will beg her pardon immediately. Please excuse me."

He didn't reply, just stared, his expression remote, unbelieving.

"I assure you, I never lie. I wonder if you can say the same thing?"

"My apologies," he said, his face like granite.

The urge to say more, to convince him of her innocence pressed on her chest. The sardonic curve to his lips stalled her words. What was the point? He would never believe her.

She swept past him and out of the door.

Simon watched the sway of her curvaceous hips, the swirl of her violet gown. He controlled the urge to recapture her in his arms, to force her to yield her passion only to him.

He cursed softly. Much more of this, and he would carry her up to his room and make sure he had the right to question her every waking moment, to kiss her when he would.

He stilled. Marriage. The word choked in his mind, even as longing clawed at his heart.

Bloody hell, he had lost his reason. Honeyed lies dripped from her tongue, just like the rest of her kind. Hadn't he learned his lesson? This was lust, pure and simple, and any woman would fill the need. Love was an emotion promulgated by self-serving women and madmen like Byron. It was designed to trap a man and break his spirit. He would not be caught again.

He strode across the hall to his study. He had no intention of becoming cup-shot like Lethbridge, but a fortifying brandy would not come amiss.

He heard the echo of her voice down the corridor as she spoke to his cousin in the drawing room. He paused in the doorway, listening . . . soft tones, beautiful face, intelligent, full of passion . . .

He slammed the door behind him.

Chapter Six

Lethbridge pushed away the plate of White's famous roast beef. He'd barely eaten anything.

"You're going to fade away to skin and bone," Simon said.

It sounded a ridiculous charge when applied to the huge Lethbridge, but he'd already changed. Bleariness dulled his eyes, hollow cheeks emphasized the planes of his face, and his once-healthy skin had a sallow cast.

"No appetite," Lethbridge said, picking up his glass and swirling the golden liquid. The square fingers clenched for a moment, then he tossed it off. "How's your arm?"

"It's fine. Don't change the subject. The brandy might ruin your appetite, but before long it will take what's left of your brain." Lethbridge needed something other than Genevieve Longbourne to think about.

Lethbridge answered by refilling his glass, lifting it in a silent toast to Simon and swallowing it in one gulp.

Simon thought to distract him. "I think the attack last night was deliberate."

"You said as much this morning. Any idea who'd want to kill you?"

Simon grimaced. "Why me? Could just as easily be someone after you. They weren't explicit."

With a flash of his former self, Lethbridge grinned cheekily. "A husband?"

"God. No married women for me." He grinned back.

"The last thing I need is a jealous husband."

"They can be inconvenient, certainly."

Simon poured himself a brandy. "No. No wives, no widows, only ladybirds from now on. Much less complicated." And no virtuous young ladies with violet eyes and hair as black as night.

"There's going to be a gnashing of teeth and beating of breasts among the noble matrons of the *ton*."

Simon shrugged.

"So who then?" Lethbridge asked.

"How about one of your old enemies. Europe is rife with intrigue now Napoleon's been put away. Everyone's jockeying for position."

Lethbridge looked glum. "Jesus. What I'd give to be back in the service. Anything to alleviate this bloody boredom and . . ." He shook his head. "I shot my bolt there. Castlereagh'll never have me back. Not after Longbourne complained."

"What about Longbourne? He hates you enough after what happened with Genevieve."

"Aye. And he's sneaky enough. But what reason would he have? Genevieve gave me the right about last time I saw her and now she's engaged to the duke of her dreams. Damn his eyes. I'm finished and Longbourne knows it."

Simon nodded. Washed up as a spy, though he'd served England nobly over the last years of war with France, Lethbridge's cover had been stripped away along with his political aspirations. Once thought to be one of Castlereagh's up-and-coming young men, his aborted attempt to elope with Longbourne's sister had ended his career hopes. Simon stared into his glass.

"Ogden?" Lethbridge suggested.

Simon considered the issue dispassionately. Ogden hated

him with good reason. "It doesn't make sense. If I die, so does the golden goose. He's nothing to gain except revenge, and a great deal to lose."

"I thought you weren't going to pay him any more?"

He didn't want to, but his father's will required it. "Oh, I'll pay. Till the day I die, I'll pay. Actually, it would make more sense if I killed him."

Lethbridge poured another brandy.

A long night stretched ahead. Courageous and honorable, Lethbridge had made a stupid mistake over a spoiled little bitch. Genevieve had been a fool to pass him up. He would make a good husband, kind, generous to a fault and with no skeletons in the family cupboard. The perfect man for Victoria Yelverton. The thought of Lethbridge and Victoria together slid, like sharp steel, into his ribs.

"I need you to do something for me," Simon said.

Lethbridge flicked an eyebrow. "What?"

"Maria has me escorting Victoria to the theater and an endless list of balls. Join us tomorrow night at Covent Garden."

"Ye gods, no. Not my style at all."

"Dammit, Ian. What else have you got to do? I'm dying of boredom. I need some moral support around these damned society wenches, some decent male conversation."

Lethbridge raised his hand. "I can't do it. I might run into Genevieve."

Simon leaned back into the leather wing chair and took a deep swallow from his snifter. "You can't go running like a rabbit into a burrow every time Genevieve is in London. You're going to have to face her sooner or later. Talk will die down all the quicker if you get it over with."

Lethbridge looked unconvinced.

"Besides," Simon continued, "if there really is someone

out to get me, or you, we should stick together and see if we can't catch the bastards." There was no one he'd rather be in a fight with than Lethbridge. When he was sober.

Lethbridge's expression brightened. "It makes sense." He leaned forward. "If they do try again, we'll know for sure it wasn't a random robbery. If we catch them at it, we might be able to figure out who is after whom. I'll do it." He groaned. "How many balls did you say?"

Simon grinned at him. "Good man. Never mind the balls, I think we have Almack's on Wednesday."

"Curse you. You failed to mention that."

Simon laughed. "Listen, no drinking on this mission, at least not until the end of the evening. You have to stay sober around the ladies."

"I can do that."

Simon certainly hoped so. He got up and stretched his shoulders. "How about a hand of piquet? I need to relieve you of some of your fortune."

Lethbridge heaved himself to his feet. "Not here though, Satan. Let's go somewhere we can get as pickled as herrings and no one will care. Somewhere they have warm and welcoming ladies."

The prospect of Lethbridge as drunk as a wheelbarrow was no more enticing than the thought of a *fille de joie*. The last thing Simon needed right now was a woman. At least, not the kind he could have. He sighed. "You're going to kill us both."

Lethbridge merely grinned.

After tonight, the marquess would be too busy escorting Victoria to drink himself to death in some hell. Lethbridge liked Victoria; he'd indicated as much at Corby's ball. She would divert him from his troubles.

Simon tasted the bitter ashes of disappointment. He

clenched his jaw and slapped Lethbridge on the shoulder. "I know just the place."

Green Park offered a delightful vista, and clear blue skies lightened Victoria's mood as the breeze blew away her worries about the impending interview with Travis. Perhaps he'd heard from her aunt at last.

Its emerald grass bedewed with yesterday's rain, the park provided a haven of pastoral quiet in the heart of bustling, dirty London. Even the air smelled fresh for a change. A distant herd of cows sheltered in the shade of an oak so ancient it counted its age by hundreds, and a goose-girl chivvied her flock toward the pond. Victoria breathed in the sense of peace.

Here, she remembered being young, happy and carefree in her old home in Kent.

Trailed by Elsie, her maid, Victoria tramped across the open grass uncaring of the wet and mire creeping up the hem of her gown. She avoided the pathways, where officious nurse-maids walked their charges and dodged steel-bright puddles.

This morning, Travis had left the house to go riding long before Victoria reached the breakfast room, and Maria never rose before mid-day. At Golden Square, Victoria ran the household and before they were forced to come to London, her work raising funds for a Parish school had occupied much of her time. The trivial social round and enforced idleness of her current situation left her enervated. A brisk walk would set her to rights. Inhaling a lung full of fresh air, she picked up her pace.

"Victoria." The figure of a man crossed the grass to meet her.

She squinted into the sun. Ogden. She greeted him with a smile.

"I hoped I might find you here this morning," he said, taking her hand and raising it to his lips.

She continued walking and he strolled at her side. "My lord, however did you guess I would be here this morning?"

"I believe I know your habits well enough by now. It's a fine day and, unless you have your nose glued to a book, you are walking out. Green Park is close to where you currently reside and quiet and so voila . . ." He bowed with a flourish. "Here I am."

Irritated by his faintly condescending tone, Victoria frowned. "Am I so predictable?"

He laughed. "I would not dare say such a thing, but even Michael remarked on your penchant for early-morning walks."

Those last few months, Michael hadn't expressed an interest in anything except his horses and the precision of his cravat. "I didn't think he'd noticed."

Ogden stopped and grasped her hand for a moment, squeezing her fingers. "You are wrong, my dear. Your brother worried about you. Your lack of dowry grieved him. He always hoped to win enough at the tables to restore your fortunes."

Cold enveloped her. Michael had lost everything because of her? It couldn't be true. "He knew I didn't care about money or position. I just wanted us to be happy, the way we were before Mama died."

Before her father, racked by guilt, drank himself into a stupor and let everything slide away from him. If only she had tried to find out what troubled Michael, instead of tearing into him about his drinking and gambling each time he set foot in her drawing room.

Ogden shook his head sorrowfully. "Incorrigible young rogue. I tried to talk to him. But you know how he was. He laughed at danger, always sure the next turn of the die would be in his favor. I had no idea he had joined Travis's bank. He'd lost everything by the time I got there."

Victoria closed her eyes against the shattering memory of Michael's last moments. Ogden had often talked to her of her brother's folly. To discover she had caused his recklessness pained her beyond belief.

"Come, you need to sit for a while." He indicated a bench set beneath a spreading oak and she sank onto it.

Dawdling behind them, Elsie chatted with a nursemaid from a neighboring house. A little boy of about three years took advantage of his keeper's distraction. Feet stomping in a puddle at the far reaches of his leading strings, he giggled as muddy water soaked his petticoats.

The little scoundrel. Victoria chuckled.

"I admire so much about you, Victoria," Ogden said, one arm stretched behind her along the back of the seat. "So full of good sense." He stared at the ground, his expression solemn. "I just can't help wondering . . . Well, it really is none of my business, I suppose."

Her heart sank. "What?"

He took her hand. "I'd like to think we are more than friends."

An uneasy prickle skittered down Victoria's back. She'd dreaded this, and knowing he also pursued Miss Eckford gave her a slightly sick feeling. She eased her hand from his.

His jaw tightened. "Victoria, I care about what happens to you. As your brother's closest friend, I can't help wondering why you agreed to accept the hospitality of a man like Travis."

As Michael's friend, she owed him some explanation, some assurance that nothing was untoward. "It all happened rather suddenly. Somehow Travis learned I had nowhere to go after Michael's death and he insisted he had some responsibility for my welfare." She no longer believed Michael had lost her to Travis in a wager, and she certainly wasn't going to mention it to Ogden.

"You must be careful, Victoria. You know his reputation, and that's not the half of it."

His barely veiled insinuations made Travis sound evil, and a strange desire to defend him hovered on her lips. "I've barely seen him, and Maria Allenby is a formidable chaperon. Travis wants me gone just as much as I want to leave."

Ogden's gaze searched her face, his expression full of concern. "Don't be fooled by his charm."

Charm? He either issued autocratic commands or avoided her. Except when he kissed her. A wicked quiver taunted her with the memory and warmth infused her. She bit her lip.

"Do you know how many beautiful young innocents he's ruined?" Ogden asked. "His nickname is well deserved." He must have sensed her disbelief. He sighed. "I know it's hard for you to imagine, but even now he has another in his toils."

He meant Miss Eckford. "Please, say no more."

Deep furrows creased his high, pale forehead. "Don't trust him, Victoria. Let me take care of you. I can't offer you marriage, or great wealth, but I can protect you."

She gasped. Her face flamed at his offer of a *carte blanche*. She felt soiled. "How dare you." She rose to her feet.

He leaped up and caught her elbow. "You mistake my meaning; it was not well said. You are like my own dear sister. I just want to help you leave Travis. I know to my cost what he's like. A member of my own family . . ." He pressed his lips together, strain showing in the grooves around his mouth and in his forehead.

Cold fingers clutched at Victoria's heart. She no longer

knew what to believe. "Who? If you have firsthand knowledge, you must tell me."

Ogden rubbed his chin, a disconsolate expression in his pale eyes. "To speak of it would harm an innocent. You must trust me. Michael didn't listen to me and see what happened."

Victoria didn't know what to think. Ogden had been a true friend to Michael, whereas the Earl of Travis had taken everything he had left. Not true. Michael took his own life.

Despite his autocratic commands and his icy exterior, she had never feared harm from Travis. And yet Ogden had been a true friend to Michael. Nothing made sense anymore.

The drumming of approaching hoofbeats disturbed her whirling thoughts. Man and beast in perfect harmony, dark and powerful and awesome, thundered across the turf towards them. Rainbows splashed up around the beast's great hooves. Travis.

In spite of herself, relief washed over her. With Travis here, Ogden would leave.

"The devil," Ogden said. "I was sure he always exercised that beast of his in Hyde Park."

One reason she came to this place.

Travis drew up and dismounted in a fluid motion. Victoria snatched up her parasol from beside the seat.

"The earl can't tell me with whom I may or may not speak," she said as Ogden brought her hand to his lips.

"I can and I will," Travis said, his expression tight.

Ogden curled his lip. "Don't be a boor, Travis."

Travis drew off a gauntlet and ran it through his palm. He flicked a black brow. "Challenging me, Ogden?"

"I'll not brawl with you in front of a lady." Ogden bowed to Victoria. "Don't forget what I said, Miss Yelverton." He nodded stiffly at Travis and headed towards his curricle waiting on the street.

Travis, his face thunderous, watched his departure. "Another tryst, madam?"

"Certainly not, my lord." She nodded. "If you will excuse me, I should like to continue my walk."

He reached out and grasped her arm. "I specifically told you not to go abroad without Maria, and I find you meeting the cur alone, after I instructed you to have nothing to do with him."

This was second time this morning a man had questioned her morals. She lifted her chin. "Don't lay your lack of attention to society's rules on my head, my lord. I met Viscount Ogden quite by chance. And, if you will turn your eyes in that direction," she waived her parasol at Elsie, "you will see my maid. Now, if you wouldn't mind releasing my arm, I will go . . ."

The word home stuck in her throat. She had none. "I will be on my way."

She set off at a brisk pace, leaving Elsie to follow.

"Victoria, wait."

She heard the plea in his voice, like that night on the balcony, and his boots scrunching on the gravel path behind her.

"Miss Yelverton. Please wait."

He gained swiftly on her. Others strolling on the pathway stared at them. She whirled around to face him. "Well?"

He smiled. Warm, friendly and unutterably charming. Her heart skipped a beat.

"I'm sorry," he said. "I spoke in haste. I should have given you a chance to explain."

"I don't have to explain anything to you."

He grinned, charmingly rueful, a boy with his hand found

97

in the biscuit barrel, and not the least bit put out. "You're right. I'm sorry."

She shook her head. What could she say faced with such sweetness? It was as if he wanted to make up for his unacceptable behavior yesterday. The thought pleased her more than she expected. "Apology accepted."

"Thank you." He sounded equally pleased. Perhaps they could begin anew.

The horse nudged him in the back. Victoria put out a hand as Simon lurched into her.

"Sorry," he muttered. "Diablo, behave."

She glanced sideways at him. "Imagine. You named your horse after yourself."

His cheeky grin reappeared. "Ironic, no?"

Far too charming when he wanted to be. She ignored the flutters of her pulse and fixed her attention on the horse. "He's a beautiful animal." She reached out to stroke Diablo's nose.

"I wouldn't if I were you," he warned.

She smiled at his astonishment as Diablo snuffled into her hand. "He and I are friends. I visit him some afternoons when Maria is napping. He has a sweet tooth."

"You like horses?"

She evaded the question along with the empty feeling in her stomach. "My father used to breed some beauties."

He looked at her curiously. "Do you like to ride?"

Attractive and perceptive, he asked the inevitable question. Might as well get it over with. "No, I don't."

"Afraid?"

If only her brave-hearted mother hadn't followed Papa over the wall. The little mare broke her leg on the steep drop on the other side, and Victoria never rode again. "Yes."

He frowned. "You surprise me. I thought of you as fearless. Were you in an accident?"

She nodded, blinking back blurring tears, refusing to embarrass herself. She pointed at Diablo. "He's magnificent. You should breed him."

"I did," he said. "This past year. He sired a fine colt which will do well on the racetrack." Joy, sunrays bursting through thunderous clouds, gave him a youthful and impossibly attractive expression. Her chest tightened against her swelling heart. She must not let him charm her again.

She kept her voice light. "I didn't know you bred horses."

He quirked an eyebrow. "There's a lot you don't know about me, Miss Yelverton."

A smile tugged at her lips. She liked this gentler, teasing side of him. "I'm sure there is, Lord Travis. Do you breed your horses for riding or racing?"

"Racing mostly. I have a likely filly running at Newmarket next race day." Pride flashed in his eyes, then he became serious. "But you know, you really should ride again. The best thing after a fall is to get right back up and try again."

Get him talking about himself. It always worked with Michael and Papa. She continued strolling and sent him a questioning glance. "That sounds like the voice of experience speaking."

"I've had the odd tumble," he admitted. For a moment, he fought with Diablo's bridle as the horse snorted and tossed his head. "I'm sure I must have something gentle enough for you in my stables. If nothing there suits you, I'll see what Tattersall's has next week. I'd be delighted to tutor you."

"No, thank you. I used to ride with my parents as a child. I haven't ridden for years and have no intention of doing so now."

His smile cajoled her and sent her heart leaping wildly beneath her ribs. "I would never let you fall. There's nothing like riding at speed for freeing the spirit."

She couldn't think about it, let alone do it. She tried to speak around throat-choking tears at the vivid recollection of the day her life had changed forever. Burdened with guilt, Papa had sold every horse they owned for a pittance within a week of Mama's funeral and disappeared inside a bottle. Michael had run wild, and Victoria had failed to take her mother's place.

She scrabbled for her handkerchief and blew her nose. She tried to smile at him. "My mother fell from her horse in a riding accident when I was twelve. I watched her die. I see it and I hear it every time I think about getting on a horse. The sound of her falling, the horse screaming, my father crying. I have never been able to get up the nerve to ride again."

Cold reserve turned his sunlit eyes to glacier blue. His expression stony, he stared off into the distance.

Seconds felt like minutes.

He cleared his throat. "You've certainly had more than your fair share of tragedy."

Delivered like an accusation, his biting words lashed at her. She drew in a sharp breath.

A muscle flickered in his jaw. "Excuse me, Miss Yelverton. I must return home. I will see you in my study at eleven, as arranged."

He leaped into the saddle, his riding coat swirling around him. The black brute stood quietly under his hand. He nodded stiffly, wheeled Diablo around and galloped away.

Victoria stared after him, wishing she had not revealed her fear. A man with melted snow in his veins, he had been disgusted by her lack of courage.

On arrival at the park entrance, numb after her dismal admission to Travis, she absently checked for Elsie. Once more, Travis had brought home to her everything she'd lost. She really had to find a way to leave his house.

Chapter Seven

Usually, Diablo's speed gave Simon a sense of deep satisfaction, but not today. All his thoughts were focused on leaving the source of his increasing frustration behind.

He'd been so unforgivably stupid.

A shout broke his thoughts and he jerked Diablo tight to the curb to avoid a carriage by inches.

He glanced around. God. He'd never live it down if he ploughed into some dull matron driving sedately around Mayfair.

He forced himself to calmness, relaxing his clenched hands, easing the urge to rake his heels into Diablo's sides and send him flying to hell and gone. He maneuvered through the traffic, determined his inner turmoil would not gain the upper hand.

At his stables, he tossed the reins at the waiting groom and glared as the man looked hesitant. If the fool couldn't stable his damned cattle, he'd no business in his employ.

He cursed when a footman impeded his progress through the side door into the house. "Get out of the way, idiot."

"May I take your hat and coat, sir?" the brawny young man asked.

Simon peeled off his coat and shoved it into the footman's hands. "Wilson, isn't it? Tell Benton to bring brandy to my study. Now." He shouldered his way past the servant.

He thrust the study door open and pushed it shut with his

heel, the force enough to rattle the porcelain ornaments on the shelves and in a glass-fronted cabinet.

Damn. Damn. Damn.

He kicked a spindly Sheraton chair out of his way and paced the width of the room in front of his desk. What the bloody hell was the matter with him? She said she didn't like riding. She changed the goddamn subject twice. He'd been too busy fantasizing about riding beside her, her black hair blowing long and free in the wind, her face flushed with fresh air and her lips parted in enjoyment. He'd missed every sign.

Hell and Hell. He hadn't been such an idiot with a woman since his misbegotten youth. He'd sworn never to let any woman get her claws in him again and here he was, almost thirty, for Christ's sake, so wrapped up in his own pleasant dream, he'd been oblivious to her mood.

He flung himself in the brown leather armchair, staring blindly at the polished mahogany of his desk. He'd lost his grip.

A knock sounded on the door.

"What?"

Benton eased through door. "Your brandy, my lord."

Simon jerked his head toward the desk.

"Will there be anything else, my lord?" Benton asked, setting down a square crystal decanter and one balloon glass on a silver tray.

Simon grimaced at the admonition in Benton's tone. Having served Simon's father and known Simon in short coats, Benton's opinion carried weight. Embarrassment washed over him. He'd stormed into the house as if he truly was a devil. He abhorred rudeness to servants in others, and was now guilty of it himself.

He shook his head. "No, thank you, Benton. Apologize to Wilson for me, would you? I was a bit short with him on the way in. No fault of his."

"Yes, my lord." Benton bowed himself out.

Simon took a deep breath. At least Benton seemed mollified. What the hell could he say to Miss Victoria Yelverton?

He poured a brandy and stared into the depths of the glass. What must she have thought?

Last night, he'd decided to convince her to marry Lethbridge, but in her presence, his purpose slipped from his grasp.

It wouldn't have been so bad if he hadn't found her with Ogden. She'd lied; he'd seen it in the way her eyes refused to meet his. They were all the same, the ladies of the *ton,* liars and cheats. Disgust for his sense of disappointment gnawed at his gut.

Dammit. Lethbridge was right, the more he said against the viscount, the tighter she hung on to him. *Because she doesn't trust you.* While he hardly blamed her for that, the thought galled him.

He'd done his best to win her over, burying his anger at her treachery, engaged her in pleasant conversation, watched the smile dawn on her face and lighten her eyes from mysterious dusk to the color of sky just before dawn. With success in his grasp, he'd badgered her to let him teach her to ride for no good reason at all. The hurt in her eyes and the tremble of her tragic mouth when he'd forced her to admit the reason for her fear twisted his gut and left him speechless.

He hadn't sensed such anguish in another person since the day his father banished him. Since then, he hadn't allowed himself to care enough to feel.

Somehow, her pain had pierced his carefully guarded defenses and his throat had burned until he thought he would choke, a feeling so foreign it frightened him to the depths of his being. He couldn't remember what he had said after that.

Something idiotic from the expression on her face.

And he still had to do something about Ogden.

None of Simon's inquiries had provided more than vague hints of how Victoria's brother had gone from carefree to desperate in the months after his father's death, the months when the notoriously cash-strapped Ogden had become his closest friend. Without proof of any wrongful intent on Ogden's part, Victoria would always blame Simon for her brother's death. Winning her trust remained elusive.

Ogden also played some deep game of his own. He had thrust the girl at Simon, then proceeded to meet the chit alone. The Marquis of Northdown would insist on his son wedding a girl who could bring a significant marriage portion into the family coffers, therefore whatever Ogden intended with regard to Victoria Yelverton, Simon doubted it was honorable.

Damn. He never should have brought her here. Why on earth had he let Ogden prick his ego? Icy fingers fisted in his gut. Ogden had nothing to do with it; Victoria did.

He got up and prowled the room, touching the Meissen china figures that adorned every available surface, calming himself with their intricate, cold beauty. Like a piece of fine china, Victoria's exquisite beauty tempted him. Unlike china, hot blood ran beneath her translucent skin; her expression changed with each new mood, her luminous eyes revealed her feelings. He'd been drawn to her the moment he saw her, before he knew she was a lady. The sooner he left London and took his mind off Victoria Yelverton, the better.

He glanced at his reflection in the gilt pier mirror between the windows. His hair showed signs of his raking fingers. He'd wrecked his cravat. He put the glass to his lips with a wry grin; if he didn't watch his step, he'd be keeping Lethbridge company in the worst possible way.

He rang the bell for Benton, who arrived in moments.

"Ask Miss Yelverton to wait for me in the library. I need to change."

"Yes, my lord."

He hurried upstairs and changed swiftly. On his return, he was gratified to find Victoria reading by the window in the library.

Enchantingly, her lips moved slightly as her eyes skimmed the page. Piled high on her head, her black hair drifted in a cluster of luxuriant curls to her shoulder and rested on the gray silk of her morning dress. He paused, savoring the sight of her.

She must have sensed his presence for she glanced up. Her cheeks flushed at the sight of him, no doubt from embarrassment at his earlier rudeness. He clenched his jaw. He would not allow her to affect him again. Cold reserve had protected him in the past and it would continue to do so.

"Miss Yelverton," he said with a cool smile. "If you wouldn't mind stepping into my study."

She rose gracefully and brushed softly by him in the doorway, her skirts caressing his legs, her jasmine perfume drifting around him. He gestured to the open door. "This way, if you please."

She perched in the delicate Sheraton chair in front of the desk. He'd never liked that chair before today. Her glance wandered around the room, her violet eyes widening at the sight of the porcelain ornaments filling every available surface: the console beneath the mirror, the shelves behind him, the mantel. Only his desk remained unadorned, apart from his inkwell, quills, and the tray of brandy.

"I collect porcelain," he said.

"It's beautiful." She frowned. "The pieces are so delicate. I'm surprised." She colored and looked away.

His short laugh sounded strained to his own ears. He forced himself to relax, to be in control. He knew what she meant. "So unlike anything you would expect me to appreciate?"

"Pardon me. I didn't mean to be rude."

"It is you who must forgive me for rushing off just now. I had forgotten Diablo's visit to the blacksmith today. All our talk of horses reminded me." A small lie, but it salved his conscience. He waived a dismissive hand. "Enough of my foibles. I have something more important to discuss." He paused. How to say this?

Hope filled her expression. "You have heard from my aunt?"

"Aunt?"

"Yes, Aunt Gertrude. Has she replied to the letters?"

He frowned. Too bad the aunt hadn't replied. Perhaps she'd agree to take Victoria off his hands. He shook his head. "No. Not as yet."

Distress filled her eyes and he stilled the desire to comfort her in his arms. "You are correct. We should have heard from her long before now. I will write to her again. But my desire to speak with you is about another matter entirely."

Her gaze rested on his face, her fine, black brows arched in question.

"I had a visit from Colonel Monteith yesterday afternoon, when you disappeared on your picnic." He frowned. Her disappearance still rankled. "To cut to the chase, he made an offer. He asked for your hand."

Thoughts traveled rapidly across her lovely face: confusion, comprehension, fear. Fear of what? That he had said yes? That he had said no? Wariness followed fear.

Her hands clenched in her lap. "What did you say?"

"What did you want me to tell him?"

"You agreed not to make any decisions without consulting me."

"I am consulting you now. What are your thoughts on the matter?"

She got up and strolled to the cluttered console by the window. Her delicate, white fingers traced the outline of an elfin piper perched on a fallen log. Delicate, green ivy trailed around cracked and pealing bark. He held his breath.

She glanced briefly in Simon's direction, then her fingertips continued their gentle stroking. "I don't know him well. We met at Lady Corby's ball, for a few moments only. I am astonished he would make an offer on such a short acquaintance."

Simon compelled himself to stop watching her hand. "He informed me he's been ordered back to India next month. He does not have the time for a lengthy courtship."

"India?"

She sounded breathless. He could not see her face. Did the promise of exotic travel entice her? He kept his voice matter-of-fact. "Yes. I gather he wants the issue of a wife settled before he leaves. His children need a mother."

"He has children, then?"

"Two. Both under five. A boy and a girl. His wife died in childbirth last year."

She turned with an expression full of sorrow. "How sad."

It was a long time since anyone had looked on him with such pity. He shrugged. "Unfortunate. I agree."

She hesitated. "He seemed pleasant, a man I could respect, but in truth, I do not feel I could agree to marry without knowing more of him, his character and nature." She shook her head. "I must say no. I hope you will convey my regrets to the colonel."

Simon breathed a heartfelt sigh of relief. He had not expected her to say yes, but her desperate circumstances and her desire to get out of his house, might lead her into doing something she would regret.

No. Lethbridge provided the best the answer to the dilemma. Simon could live with that. He froze at the vision of his friend caressing her creamy skin, cradling her slender, shapely form. Simon could bear it, if he didn't think about it. He spoke calmly. "That is what I told him."

She frowned. "You had no business responding before speaking with me."

"I reached the same conclusion you did, only earlier."

She glared at him. "Still, you had no right."

There he was, doing it again, saying things better left unsaid. He never usually explained anything at all to females, but with Victoria, he couldn't seem to help himself. He raised his eyebrow. "I can tell him I was wrong if you like. Then you can give him the good news yourself."

Anger flashed in her eyes and her hand clenched on the ornament. For one horrible moment, Simon thought she would throw it at him. Mentally, he flinched. She wouldn't be the first woman to throw something at him for his arrogance and no doubt she wouldn't be the last. But he'd like her to be. The thought rocked his carefully ordered life, leaving him off balance. Yet again.

She slowly relaxed her grip and assumed a calm, superior expression. No destructive tantrums for this young lady, then. He released his breath.

She tilted her chin at him. "Since you have done no harm, I will say no more. However, I would remind you, we have an agreement. You will not speak on my behalf without consulting me first."

He nodded, relieved to be let off so lightly. "Agreed. Come, Miss Yelverton, a truce. We both know you prefer not to reside here. However, rest assured, I have nothing but your best interests in mind."

She opened her mouth to speak, but he raised a silencing hand. "Let me finish."

He moved to stand in front of her, determined to hold her attention. Her gaze did not waver under his intense scrutiny. She had more courage than many men of his acquaintance, but she would not be pleased at what he had to say.

He softened his tone. "On several different occasions, I have found you conversing alone with Viscount Ogden." He saw a protest on her lips and continued swiftly. "Almost alone then. My attempts to dissuade you from associating with him cannot have escaped your attention."

"Dissuade is far too weak a word," she cut in.

"No matter the description, the results have been the same. You have ignored my request. I know he was your brother's friend and was welcome in your home. While I cannot prevent you from speaking with him at social occasions, it is my duty to remind you of your search for a bridegroom, not a protector. Ogden must marry money if he wants to keep his family estate intact. Continue to welcome his advances in private and you will ruin your chances of a good marriage. This has nothing to do with my personal opinions of the viscount. It is simply good sense."

She stepped closer to him, her expression determined. He imagined her slender body pressed against him, his hands exploring her curves. Need throbbed in his veins. He moved to the door and opened it.

She tipped her head on one side, clearly puzzled by his retreat. "Thank you for your warning, Lord Travis. The viscount also insists he has my welfare at heart. Finding me a bridegroom is your idea, not mine. I would prefer to go and live with my aunt, or find a position as a governess. Therefore, I don't think there is any cause for concern about the *ton*'s opinions of my friendship with Viscount Ogden."

She awarded him a sweet smile and it hit him like a rock in the center of his chest. She arched a brow. "If there is nothing else you wished to see me about . . ."

The stubborn wench refused to listen to logic, so he wouldn't try to reason with her. He'd arranged things the way he wanted them. "Not quite all. I will now take it upon myself to ensure you receive a *suitable* offer. To begin with, you will drive with me each afternoon in Hyde Park."

"Every day?"

He smiled ruefully at the horror in her voice. "Not so distasteful, surely? You have been hiding your light under a bushel for far too long. From today, you can expect to be occupied, day and evening. Prepare yourself accordingly. Maria is well aware of my wishes, and she will provide you with a list of the entertainments she has organized. You won't have time to slip away on picnics or assignations with Viscount Ogden."

Let her make of it what she would. She was going to spend as much time with Lethbridge as Simon could manage.

She opened her mouth to retort and anticipation coursed through his veins. Once more, she surprised him. She curtseyed stiffly, a bare inflection of her knees, an imperceptible movement of her proud little head. "If there is nothing else, my lord?"

Unaccountably disappointed by her refusal to continue crossing swords with him, he shook his head. "Nothing at the moment." He bowed politely as she passed him.

The scent of jasmine lingered long after she vacated the room. He inhaled deeply. He would miss it when she left.

A pervading sense of loss filled his soul.

A high-perch phaeton waited at the front door. Its black

body, trimmed in silver, hung on the longest, most precarious, swan-neck springs Victoria could imagine. Four beautifully matched ebony horses sidled impatiently in the traces.

It reeked of danger. She hesitated.

Travis raised an eyebrow. "Does it frighten you? Shall I request Maria's landau be put to instead?"

She clenched her jaw. She might be afraid to ride, but she wasn't going to let him think she was a complete coward. "Certainly not."

His mouth flicked up at the corners in a brief smile. Sensing he mocked her, tested her courage, she took a deep breath, tamped down her anxiety and strode to the open carriage door. Heavens. The step was at her waist. She glanced up Travis. Dark lashes swiftly covered a wicked flash of blue.

"Allow me to assist you," he said.

His hands encircled her waist. Victoria's heart skipped and danced to an erratic rhythm at his touch. Dash it. After his coldness yesterday, she had sworn she would not let him affect her again.

Mere inches from her face, his broad chest in a snug black coat with gleaming silver buttons radiated warmth. His sandalwood cologne filled her in-drawn breath. A frisson of awareness shivered through her at the invading recollection of his kiss. A kiss that filled her dreams.

She must be suffering from spring madness. The only reason the wicked rake had for taking her up in his carriage, for displaying her like one of his fine china ornaments, was to auction her off to a husband.

Brilliant blue in his taut face, his eyes focused over her shoulder on the groom and his horses. She tried to ignore the large hands filling the hollow between her ribs and hips ready to lift her. She grasped his arms for balance. Beneath her fingers, hard muscles tensed and strength surrounded her. He protected his own. The thought echoed in her mind and her heart thudded in her ears.

The carriage shifted backwards an inch or two.

"Easy now," Travis said to the groom. "Hold them."

They waited, a frozen tableau, while the groom brought the horses under control. Travis's chest rose and fell inches from her cheek. She sensed his heart's rhythmic beating.

"Are you ready, Miss Yelverton?" His voice, soft and low, carried on a warm breath across her cheek. Sharp-pointed needles showered her skin, leaving her breathless. If only he would hurry up and place her in the blasted carriage.

Lifted as if she weighed no more than a child, she hung above him, gazing into his handsome face. The purple bruise on his jaw had faded. His lips, still bearing signs of battle, softened and curved seductively. The word handsome did not do justice to his dark, satanic looks; it was far too weak. Her heart beat faster. She forced herself to meet his sapphire gaze and risked a smile.

Heat flared between them. He blinked and swept the fire away. "There you go, Miss Yelverton," he said and deposited her on the high platform.

The carriage rocked unsteadily beneath her feet and she dropped thankfully onto the seat. The vehicle pitched as Travis climbed up beside her and she grabbed at the side.

"Let 'em go," he called out. The groom stepped back, then smartly leaped up behind them.

With a twist of his strong wrist, Travis flicked his whip above the leaders' heads. The horses jostled a little, then settled into a smooth walk. He deftly eased them into the heavy London traffic with sure movements of firm, strong hands. "Chin up, Miss Yelverton. Today you will experience all the joys of the afternoon ride in Hyde Park."

"You do not sound as if it is something you enjoy."

His expression remained bland. "It's well enough, I suppose, for those who like to gossip, to see and be seen. For myself, I'd sooner drive these beauties down the long stretch of road between here and Brighton, than dawdle slowly along Rotten Row."

"Maria mentioned you might be going to your Hampshire estate next week."

A muscle tensed in his jaw. He guided his team around a coal-heaver's dray. A muffin man's bell and the clatter of horses' hooves on the cobblestones drowned out his reply.

Victoria leaned closer. "I'm sorry, I did not hear what you said."

The carriage jolted. She lurched forward with a small cry. He lashed out an arm and pulled her close, safe, his lean hip pressed hard against hers. A strange, knowing feeling stirred in her stomach. Heat travelled from her throat to her hairline.

Pure wickedness gleamed in his quick sideways glance. "All right now?"

He'd done it on purpose, the odious man. She nodded, pretending not to notice his powerful grip around her shoulders. He released her.

"I said," he continued, "I have some business that requires my presence. Maria knows how to reach me if any matters arise which require my personal attention."

Like a proposal of marriage? Still, his absence might allow her to find a governess position. "You are going to see Diablo's colt?"

"Him, too," he said. "You will be well entertained while I am gone. I plan to leave directly after our trip to Vauxhall next Tuesday."

"How long will you be away?"

His expression became remote as if her prying annoyed

him. "It will depend on my level of engagement with the planned endeavor."

The wry tone sent warning bells clamoring in Victoria's mind. His oblique responses seemed out of character. He must be planning his rendezvous with Miss Eckford. An unreasonable sense of disappointment churned in her stomach. She should be glad of his departure.

"And here we are," he said, turning through the gate into Hyde Park. "London in all her myriad guises."

All of society did seem indeed to walk or ride in the park. The fine afternoon had brought out half the population, it seemed. Flower sellers, ladies in elegant walking dresses, demi-reps ogling ladies in passing carriages and strollers in silks and jewels mingled at the fashionable walking hour of five o'clock.

Travis bowed to a lady and gentleman in a carriage. "Lord and Lady Ralston," he murmured.

Victoria wrinkled her nose at the noise and the smells. "It's very crowded. I can see why you might prefer the open road. Goodness. Who on earth is that?"

Travis looked in the direction she indicated and chuckled. "The mincing, elderly popinjay, you mean? Sir Giles Willowby. And over there," he nodded at a portly fellow with two white poodles on leashes following in his wake, "is Lord George Montmarcy and Romulus and Remus."

Travis's expression of disdain, devoid of malice, made her laugh. He had a dry sense of humor.

"And over there?" she asked, indicating a handsome young buck, attired in the height of fashion, strolling with a splendidly buxom female in a purple satin gown which concealed only a fraction of her luscious curves.

"The Duke of Hawkfield and his latest inamorata, the incomparable Carmelita di Consuello of the *corps de balle*, otherwise known as Betty Dodds from Wapping."

Victoria stared, fascinated. The duke, a proud strutting peacock, displayed Betty Dodds like shimmering plumage. He'd no doubt cast her aside when her feathers faded or some new bird of paradise caught his interest.

"It's rather shallow," she mused and only realized she had spoken her thoughts out loud when he gave a short laugh in response.

"Indeed, Miss Yelverton. But to some, its very shallowness is its charm. There is no need for knowledge when the titillating whispers of hidden scandal can amuse one's acquaintances for hours, if not days. No need for skill or art, when the tongue's razor edge can shred a reputation in one sentence. No need for honor, when a man's wealth is the measure of his true worth, no matter the means by which he acquired it."

Travis puzzled her. On first acquaintance, he appeared to embrace all the aspects of the *ton* she despised: gambling, brawling and licentiousness. His words and manner told a different story. Strict with her, honorable, cynical about the *ton;* if these last were a true indication of his nature, why did he not break free of the mould and undertake some worthwhile project? Something other than herself.

More of a puzzle was the pull he exerted on her. Never a moment passed in his presence when she wasn't aware of his masculinity, his wide shoulders taking up more than his share of the carriage, his strong, muscled thigh touching her skirts and the occasional drift of his sandalwood cologne. He flustered her and she did not like the feeling.

The offside leader took exception to a strolling lady's yellow ribbons fluttering in the breeze. Travis's arms flexed as he regained control.

"Shall I go to their heads, my lord?" the groom asked from behind them.

"Thank you, no. I've got him in hand now. I didn't want him to trample her."

Travis followed the line of carriages parading along the Row. Some of the gentlemen acknowledged him and some, high-sticklers probably, did not seem to see him. Travis, apparently unaware of any slight, greeted a few friends. Several of the ladies regarded him surreptitiously, then turned their green-eyed-cat gazes on Victoria. They clawed her with their nudges and sly glances, no doubt jealous because she rode beside one of London's most handsome, eligible and disreputable bachelors. She sat taller in her seat.

"Well done, Miss Yelverton." His soft murmur shimmered down her spine and sent heat flooding to her face. He knew the curious stares had made her squirm. He seemed oblivious to all and yet missed nothing.

A rider caught them up and drew alongside. The warm, friendly smile of the Marquess of Lethbridge filled Victoria's vision. Travis eased out from behind a smart red Tilbury and pulled over to one side. A fashionable matron with two fair-haired daughters glared up at them from their landau as their coachman manoeuvred around the curricle.

Lethbridge bowed. "Good afternoon, Miss Yelverton. Travis."

Travis nodded. "Lethbridge."

The marquess looked over his shoulder. "We appear to be very much impeding progress here, Travis. Perhaps we should move?"

Travis shrugged. "If they are too cow-handed to go around us, let them wait. Miss Yelverton, I'm not sure if I told you, Lethbridge is joining us for dinner tonight and will accompany us to the theater afterwards."

Victoria smiled at Lethbridge. "How exceedingly kind of you, my lord. You must be a true friend indeed."

The marquess briefly rolled his eyes in Travis's direction and grimaced. "No indeed, Miss Yelverton. The pleasure is all mine."

He looked so out of countenance, Victoria couldn't resist teasing him. "I'm sure Miss Allenby will be delighted to have another gentleman in the party."

The marquess tugged at his cravat. "Allenby? Oh, yes, Maria Allenby. Dash it, Travis, you didn't mention your cousin."

Travis cast a sharp look at Victoria. "I did. You became so engrossed in other entertainments right afterwards you must have forgotten. Would you like me to refresh your memory?"

The marquess's fair skin flushed and he forced a smile. "Gad, no. If you say you told me, d'ye think I'm going to give you the lie?"

Victoria repressed her laugh at his obvious discomfort.

A shadow flitted across Travis's face and disappeared in an instant. "I will be Miss Allenby's escort tonight, not you. You will have the pleasure of bearing Miss Yelverton company."

Lethbridge glanced down and pulled at his gauntlet. "I'm looking forward to it."

"Begging your pardon, gentlemen," called a voice behind them, "you're holding up the traffic. Let her ladyship pass, please."

Victoria swivelled in her seat. She almost tumbled out of the carriage when she saw the redhead driving the coach behind them. Lady Julia Garforth in a mannish green coat and with a jaunty shako perched atop her auburn curls, grinned and waived. Her curricle, almost as high as Travis's and pulled by a pair of handsome grays, drew alongside. "Victoria. What are you doing here? I can't believe I'm really seeing this. Let me in, Travis."

Travis edged his horses forward. "Be careful, Lady Julia," he called out. "You'll turn that thing over."

"Fie," she retorted. "You're not the only notable whip in London."

"I don't run my horses into the backs of others," Travis muttered as he edged over a little more to give her space.

Victoria listened in amazement to their banter. The hard edges, which made Travis generally unapproachable, dissolved around Julia and Lethbridge, and the cynical expression disappeared.

Victoria leaned over the gap to touch Julia's hand holding the reins. "Julia, I have so much to tell you. May I call on you?"

Julia, her gaze stuck on the marquess, did not respond.

"Oh, excuse me," Victoria said. "Lady Julia Garforth, have you met the Marquess of Lethbridge?"

"No, I don't believe I have had the pleasure," said Lethbridge. He leaned across the curricle to take Julia's hand and her bold appraising glance ran over him, her green eyes full of appreciation.

A statuesque woman, Julia's idea of the perfect male was large and muscular. Travis, though tall and broad shouldered, looked almost slender beside this blond giant. Victoria watched as Julia's lips curved and a dimple appeared beside her mouth. Lethbridge stared, a mesmerized and confused mountain.

Victoria slid a glance at Travis. He seemed unaware of his friends' reactions.

"Will we see you at the theater tonight, Lady Ju?" Travis smiled, and Victoria's breath caught in her throat. He could be so charming when he wished. Charming and attractive, and dangerous to her peace of mind.

Julia grinned at him. "No, I don't believe so. Mama is

exhausted from our travels."

Lethbridge looked disappointed and Julia's half-smile said she'd noticed.

"Perhaps you could join us at Vauxhall on Tuesday, my lord," said Victoria.

"Oh, are you going, Victoria?" Julia's face lit up. "Philip has a box for a whole party of interesting people."

"I understand you are to join us, Lord Lethbridge," Victoria said with an encouraging smile.

Lethbridge tore his puzzled gaze from Julia's face. "Why yes. I had almost forgotten. That is," he flushed again, "now you mention it, of course, I recall." He looked back at Julia. "I'm looking forward to it."

"Pointless you wearing a domino," Travis jibed. "You can't hide a great lummox like you in anything but a tent."

" 'Tis true." Lethbridge grinned good-naturedly. Suddenly, his warm expression fled and he leaned closer to Travis, his quick, softly spoken words inaudible. The direction of his focus drew Victoria's attention to a pretty blond in a pink-and-white-striped morning gown walking toward them. Miss Eckford. Cassandra Eckford sent Victoria a swift smile and Travis a shy wave.

Travis frowned. "Excuse me, ladies. I need to speak to a friend of mine. Take their heads," he directed his groom.

After leaping nimbly from the phaeton, he moved casually through the jostling people and slow moving carriages to reach Miss Eckford's side. Victoria saw the delicate blush that greeted him as he bowed over Miss Eckford's offered hand.

Victoria forced her attention back to her companions. Lethbridge looked uncomfortable and Julia raised her eyebrows in question. Victoria pasted a bright smile on her face. "Do you also go to Almack's with us on Wednesday, my lord?"

"If you'll have me, Miss Yelverton." Lethbridge had a courtly style all his own.

"Famous," said Julia smiling at him, her green eyes sparkling with interest. "I shall also be there. Mama says I'm to get serious about making my mark this Season."

"It seems to me, Lady Julia, you would always make your mark, serious or no," Lethbridge said.

"Why, my lord," she replied, with a dimple-peeping smile, "how gallant. I shall very much look forward to our next meeting. Victoria, call on me tomorrow. Better yet. Let me take you up in my carriage. We can talk all we want with no fear of interruption. I want to hear all your news." With a flourish of her whip, she skilfully extracted her carriage and joined the throng of walkers and drivers.

Victoria frowned. Julia seemed oblivious to Michael's death. She must not have received Victoria's letter. It didn't matter. At last she had someone to talk to. Someone she trusted.

On his return to the carriage, Travis's pleasant mood seemed to have evaporated. His mouth set in hard lines, his eyes cool and remote, he bade a brief farewell to Lethbridge after confirming their arrangements for later. Since he remained deep in his own thoughts as they turned out of the park gate, Victoria mulled over how she planned to approach Julia with her request for help when next they met.

Chapter Eight

The bell clanged fifteen minutes to curtain time. A lackey hovering at the entrance to Simon's Covent Garden Theater box took Maria's cloak, while Lethbridge removed the velvet cape from around Victoria's shoulders.

Simon stifled the urge to snatch it back and wrap it around her. The damned gown had been designed by a devil incarnate. No virile male could ignore the delectable sight of her creamy skin above her dove-gray bodice, and a gentleman was not permitted to notice.

He swallowed and glanced at her face. Damn. She had seen him staring at her bosom like a lusty schoolboy faced with his first set of tits. "You must take your seats if you want to be in time for the first act," he announced.

"Unlike you to worry about missing what is on stage, Travis," Maria said with a sharp stare.

"I don't care for myself," he replied. "I thought Miss Yelverton particularly wanted to see this play."

Victoria smiled. "Oh, I do."

Her candid expression of enjoyment charmed him. He couldn't remember the last time he'd looked at a visit to the theater as anything but foreplay. A need to be met, before getting down to the business of visceral pleasure with his chosen companion for the evening. Victoria's countenance, full of eagerness for the words of the bard, not for the gift of diamonds or pearls, which would complete the evening's enter-

121

tainment, lifted his spirits.

This was not about him. The purpose of this evening was
to throw her into Lethbridge's arms. A chill settled in his gut.
He swept back the red velvet curtain to allow his guests to
pass inside. "Then let us be seated."

Steps behind the ladies, Lethbridge stopped short and
Simon sidestepped to avoid a collision.

Lethbridge cursed under his breath. "Pardon me, ladies,
I've just seen a friend I've been trying to speak to for weeks.
I'll be but a moment." He thrust Simon aside in his haste.

Simon stared after him. Now what? He glanced across the
auditorium and bit back a groan. He'd forgotten about the
Duke of Rockingham's box directly across the way. Apparently, Genevieve Longbourne had decided to put in one of
her rare appearances.

Genevieve looked as she always did, tall, blond and frigid.
No sign of Rumplestiltskin, Simon's private name for her
ducal betrothed. Like so many other young and beautiful
women, Genevieve had agreed to marry for money and left
Lethbridge eating his heart out. It wouldn't surprise Simon if
she produced the obligatory heir and invited Lethbridge into
her bed.

Simon loathed the deceit.

Sliding into the seat next to Victoria, he watched her gaze
around in wide-eyed appreciation.

"Does Covent Garden Theater meet with your expectations, Miss Yelverton?" he asked.

He sucked in a breath at the devastating smile she cast in
his direction. "Yes, my lord. I love Shakespeare, don't you?"
She returned to her observation of the crowded pit.

The urge to make her smile again raced in his veins, but he
hesitated, preferring honesty rather than the flattery of cour-
teous lies with her. "I like some of his work. I must admit

Romeo and Juliet is not among my favorites. Rather a lot of romantic nonsense, if you ask me."

Her soft gaze turned to meet his. "So, my lord, you admit to having no romance in your soul?"

The thought soured in his gut. The sickly and sentimental words of Romeo and Juliet made him cringe. The banishment, the dreadful coincidences, the betrayal; it grated on his teeth. Professions of love led to weakness and ruination. Lethbridge proved the point.

"Be realistic, Miss Yelverton. What would you say if a man you barely knew climbed through your window in the dead of night? I expect, at best you'd send him packing and at worst, he'd end up in the bushes with a broken neck."

She laughed out loud, her piquant face alive with amusement. "You might be right."

Her words lacked conviction. He imagined climbing in through her window and seeing her asleep in her bed, her black hair spread around her, her soft curves barely disguised by some flimsy nightrail.

The pleasurable thoughts pulsed blood to his loins. He shifted, widening his thighs to ease the pressure of the tight, satin fabric on his groin. His knee brushed against her skirts and his blood coursed faster. Damn. He stared down into the crowd, counting ostrich plumes, anything to avoid thinking about Victoria, her jasmine perfume, her dark curls kissing the delicate skin at the base of her lovely neck. Need spiked, hard and urgent.

What in hell was wrong with him? Women never affected him like this, not even the earthy ones he preferred. And where was Lethbridge?

Irritated beyond endurance, Simon stood up. He ought to check to make sure Lethbridge didn't make a complete ass of himself. "If you will forgive me, I will go and make arrangements for refreshments to be served at the intermission," he murmured to Maria.

"Thank you, Travis," Maria replied.

Fortunately, it wasn't necessary for Simon to run the gauntlet of the queen of glaciers. Lethbridge, red-faced and rage-filled, tacked unsteadily along the corridor as Simon arrived on the other side of the auditorium.

"What in hell's name are you doing over here?" Simon asked.

"Nothing. She wouldn't speak to me."

Simon saw what he had failed to notice at dinner. "You're foxed. For God's sake, you promised to stay sober tonight. Come back and watch the play."

"No."

A black cloud of misery hung over Lethbridge. Short of hitting him over the head and dragging him back to his seat, Simon had little hope of forcing Lethbridge to finish out the evening. "You gave your word to accompany me tonight."

"To hell with it. I told you this was a bad idea."

Hopeless. "You're an imbecile."

Lethbridge shook his head. No doubt too distraught to recall the reason he had agreed to accompany Simon in the first place, Lethbridge shoved past him.

Hell. Simon stared at Lethbridge's broad back as he lumbered down the hall. The stubborn idiot. Simon heaved a sigh. It made no difference. Lethbridge was useless in this state. Simon followed him. "Come on then, old friend, let's get you home."

In the cool night air outside, Simon watched the hackney carriage drive away with Lethbridge in its depths. He had given the driver Lethbridge's address, but whether the fool would actually go home was anyone's guess. Simon had done his best for the poor sap.

He clamped a cigar between his teeth, savoring the acrid smoke burning his lungs. Carriages lined the street waiting for their owners. Ragged street urchins held the horses in hopes of receiving a groat for their pains, whether their services were required or not.

Damn Lethbridge. Why couldn't he see past Genevieve, to a real beauty like Victoria Yelverton? Simon huffed out a breath of annoyance. Now the task of entertaining her for the rest of the evening fell to him.

Unaccountably, his mood lightened. Spending time with Victoria was certainly less of a chore than he'd expected. He'd delighted in her company on their drive through Hyde Park. Unlike Miss Eckford, Victoria's wit and understanding were needle-sharp. He could be himself, never needing to explain what he meant. He also liked her teasing laugh, her smile, her delicate, slender body. He pushed the thought away. It only led to madness and there had been enough insanity to last him all his life. Dark shadows swirled through his mind. He shrugged away a grim sense of foreboding.

He tossed his cigar onto the step and ground it beneath his heel. Well, hell. Perhaps Lethbridge had done him a favor. Just this once, he would make the most of Victoria's charming company while he still had the chance. Before someone worthy snapped her up.

In awe, Victoria gazed around the theater. Plush velvet drapes closed off the stage from view. Row upon row of white and gilt private boxes crowded with ladies and gentlemen in glittering finery lined the walls. Smoke from the oil lamps and cigars burned in her throat and filled her nostrils. The auditorium reverberated with the racket of conversation and the exchange of ribaldries from the noisy throng in the pit, where nobles and the lower classes jostled for seats. Victoria recognized some of the patrons from those she had met at Lady

Corby's ball and her outing in Hyde Park.

Not once since her arrival in London, had Victoria been to the theater. Her father had never wanted to attend and Michael claimed it to be far too dull. This was almost enough to make her change her mind about becoming a governess. Almost.

She leaned across the vacant seat to Maria. "Who is she?" She nodded to the box opposite, at the blond who held herself like a queen.

"Genevieve Longbourne," Maria said. "Soon to be the Duchess of Rockingham."

Diamonds flashed fire in her hair and at her throat with every motion of her regal head. She looked like every girl's dream of a fairy princess. "She's beautiful."

"And ambitious. Rockingham gave her a king's ransom in family diamonds on their betrothal. That's her mother behind her. The Longbournes set their sights high and they succeeded beyond their wildest dreams. The Duke is yonder, one row down, with the orders on his chest."

Following Maria's glance, her gaze encountered a large-girthed, bald man with a buxom brunette in red perched on his knee. "But surely . . ."

Maria chuckled behind her fan. "His mistress. It's a marriage of convenience. She gets the title and he gets her plump dowry and connection to one of England's most powerful financial houses."

The diamonds lost some of their glitter. Poor Miss Longbourne.

The bell rang.

"Five minutes to curtain," Maria muttered. "Where on earth is Travis?"

As if he'd heard her, Travis slid into the chair between them.

Victoria peeked across the row of seats. "Is Lord Lethbridge coming back?"

"He isn't feeling well," Travis replied. "He went home."

"Hmmp," Maria muttered.

The sleepy eyes and slight sway Victoria noticed during dinner indicated Lethbridge's illness came from a bottle. She'd seen her father on the way to drunken oblivion often enough to recognize it.

A splash of red caught her eye. She leaned forward. "Do look, Travis. Isn't that the young man we saw in Hyde Park? He has an enormous bouquet of roses."

Travis grinned. "Hawkfield," he confirmed.

"Do you think Miss Dodds, I mean *Senorita di Consuello,* is in the cast?"

"No doubt about it. Part of the chorus. I'll wager a pony, I spot her first."

Victoria stiffened, his lazy taunt sickening her. Michael had been trapped into losing everything like this. "I do not gamble, my lord."

His face went blank. "I apologize. I spoke in jest."

" 'Tis of no importance," she replied, her lighthearted mood destroyed. She sat back in her seat.

"Come, Miss Yelverton, a different kind of game," Travis murmured. "If I see Miss Dodds first, you must forfeit the rose in your hair. If you are more observant, I will take you, Lady Julia and Lethbridge to Richmond for a picnic. Does that seem fair?"

An apology from Travis? She cast him an arch look. "A rather mundane outing for a rake, certainly a forfeit for you."

He shrugged and laughed. "*Touché.* A fitting punishment, don't you think? Come, will you play the game?"

To be disagreeable to her host felt rude, and giving way to him in this had nothing to do with his attractive countenance and charming smile. She nodded. "Agreed."

He rewarded her with a grin of unabashed, boyish delight as if she had bestowed some treasure upon him. Her breath caught in her throat at the beauty of his smile and a restlessness invaded her body. Summer-day blue gleamed in his eyes as their gazes locked.

The curtain rose breaking the intensity between them. She released her breath and turned toward the stage.

The theater slowly hushed.

A pair of star-crossed lovers. Victoria knew the words by heart, but the actors gave it life and meaning as they played their parts. Around her, the theater, the crowds, even Travis disappeared from her awareness, leaving only the unfolding story of heartbreak.

The Montague ball was almost over when she recognized *Senorita di Consuello* in the *corps du ballet.* She'd almost forgotten their game. She pointed. "There she is."

"Who?" Travis asked, his voice a warm tickle against her ear.

She gasped at the pleasurable sensation and glared her disapproval. "*Di Consuello.* You forfeit," she whispered.

"So I do," he whispered back with a smile.

Her heart fluttered and skipped and she edged away from him. He seemed much too close in the confines of the box. She focused her attention on the play.

What light through yonder window breaks? Travis had it all wrong. If a man truly loved her, she would welcome him at her window.

Paris thrust, and Mercutio received his mortal wound. Victoria jerked back in her seat.

Simon chuckled. "It's not real."

"I know," she flashed back at him. "Do hush."

With a sigh, he stretched out his long legs and remained

silent. Victoria did her best to ignore the pent-up energy that seemed to surround him and her.

Intermission came as a relief. Their box filled up with callers and a footman brought ratafia and sweetmeats for the ladies. Travis preferred wine.

Several of the people she met at Corby's ball came to pay their respects, Mr. Greely and Lord Pelham among them. Travis greeted everyone with frigid politeness, especially the young bachelors who flocked into their small space.

She could not help a small smile as she caught his expression of panic when a determined, matchmaking mother and her daughter cornered him. He grimaced back at her. No doubt this was another new experience for a confirmed rake playing the worthy guardian.

The curtain bell rang and Maria urged the young gentlemen, who seemed inclined to linger, out of the box.

"Thank God," Travis breathed.

Victoria laughed at his chagrined expression as he realized he had spoken out loud.

"Damn vultures, the lot of them," he muttered and grinned back.

"Then I must thank you doubly," she said as she settled her skirts around her chair.

"Doubly? Why so?"

"Why, there can be nothing more tedious than being required to attend things one does not enjoy. To be forced into the company of people one would prefer not to meet is twice the sacrifice."

His eyes widened and his mouth kicked up in a devilish smile. "I can assure you, Miss Yelverton, I would rather be in no other company than yours."

His low, seductive voice resonated in her ear. A rare compliment, indeed. Her heart skipped, but she knew better than to be fooled by him, no matter how smooth his charm or biting his wit, which appealed so nicely to her sense of the ridiculous.

Turning her shoulder in his direction, she leaned forward and allowed the poetry to flow through her mind and heart.

The intensity of his gaze fixed on her face fought for her attention. She glanced sideways at him. With his chair slanted toward her, he couldn't possibly see the stage. His predatory expression made her feel hot and cold and strangely breathless. He took delight in teasing her.

She shot him a warning glance. "You're staring."

His dark eyebrow lifted. "Me?"

"Yes," she whispered. "Stop it."

"Be quiet, you two," Maria said.

Victoria bit her lip. She had forgotten Maria.

The corner of Travis's mouth quirked up. He leaned close, his breath warm on her cheek. "Anything you wish."

A delicious shiver hurtled down her spine. How did he do that? She frowned and he chuckled. Damn his flirting. This had to stop before she succumbed to his expert ploys.

"I wish you to watch the play," she said.

He did stop staring, but she sensed an uneasy tension in him as the performance continued. His growing irritation disturbed her and she forced herself to concentrate.

Romeo's pain pierced her heart as he drank the poison, and she clutched at Travis's arm. Through her tears, she heard his sharp in-drawn breath and seconds later he pressed a handkerchief into her palm.

She sniffed and wiped at her eyes with a shaky laugh. Her heart contracted at Juliet's discovery of Romeo's dreadful mistake and her fateful decision. Travis squeezed her hand, a comforting pressure of warm, strong fingers.

Silence echoed in the great hall for a moment, then the audience roared its approval.

The players took their bows and Victoria, numb from the depth of her involvement in the story, rose to her feet and joined the applause. She glanced at Travis. On his feet, he stared at the stage with a shuttered expression.

"Thank you so much for bringing me, my lord," she said.

As if pulled from somewhere deep within himself, he blinked, then flashed his rakish smile. "You are more than welcome. I don't know when I have enjoyed the theater more."

"You hardly watched the play at all, sir."

His eyes held sardonic amusement. "Exactly, Miss Yelverton."

Flirtatious nonsense—and yet she couldn't prevent her answering smile.

"Well, my dears," Maria said. "I for one am exhausted. I hope you don't mind if we don't stay for the farce. It's time I retired for the night. Let us go home."

Simon tried to make himself comfortable against the squabs and stared out of the window. He hated being driven. Devil take Lethbridge for leaving him in the lurch. What an idiot. Crying over what might have been never served any purpose. If anyone knew that, Simon did.

The flash of streetlights into the carriage became less frequent. Simon sat up and peered through the window. This wasn't the way to his house. Cold fingers traveled up his spine.

He rapped on the overhead trap with his cane. No response came from the coachman. He frowned and rapped harder. Across from the nodding Maria, Victoria gazed at him curiously.

"The driver has taken a wrong turn," he said.

Victoria nodded.

Simon unlatched the window and slid it down. The fetid stench of London hit the back of his throat. He stuck his head out. "Griggs. Pull over."

Hunched in his coat, the coachman did not seem to hear. Simon tried to get his bearings. Where the hell were they?

God rot it. They had passed the Seven Dials and were in one of the poorest, most unpleasant neighborhoods in London, heading away from Mayfair. The old fool had lost his bearings. "You," he shouted. "Stop the carriage, now."

The horses began to slow. Good. Now he would find out what the hell Griggs thought he was doing. He pulled his head in.

Victoria gazed out of her window. She seemed not to have any sense of the danger they were in and Simon had no wish to scare her.

The carriage halted.

"There he is, men," someone outside shouted.

A pistol cracked. The dull thud of a bullet striking the velvet squabs beside his head sent Simon diving across the carriage. He threw Victoria to the floor and pushed Maria down next to her.

The coach rocked and footsteps clattered on the street. The idiot coachman had run off. Bloody hell. Self-respecting highwaymen didn't waylay carriages in the middle of London. This was no random robbery anymore than the attack the other night had been.

"Simon St John," Maria said, outrage in every syllable.

"It's all right, Maria," he heard Victoria say as he snatched his pistols out from under the seat. "It seems as though we are being held up. You are safer on the floor."

A cool head indeed. Another shot rang out and a horse

whinnied. Simon lunged for the door, but the coach lurched as the team shot off at a gallop jolting him sideways.

Ice filled his veins. He forced himself to think, not to freeze. He stuck his head out of the window and winced. The out-of-control horses careened along the street; two men on horseback followed, and up ahead the road took a sharp turn.

Another shot cracked. Simon ducked inside.

He swore. The carriage would turn over on the bend at this speed.

He swallowed the bile in his throat at the mental picture of a wrecked carriage, water rising, a baby screaming. He shuddered.

Her face white, Victoria stared up at him from her crouched position on the floor. Trust shone from her eyes. Trust in him. He could not fail, not this time.

He had to do something. He stuffed his pistol in his coat pocket and stood on the seat. Sticking his head out of the window, he braced himself against the carriage's wild pitching. Finding a handhold on the ornamental carving above the door, he wriggled his shoulders through the window and Victoria gave his feet a boost. He sprawled across the roof, his legs hanging over the side.

He pulled himself up, threw himself into the empty driver's box and took swift stock. The reins snaked on the ground out of reach.

More gunfire.

Burning pain tore at his arm. He clutched it and his hand came away bloody. Shot, by God. He forced the pain out of his mind. If he didn't get the horses under control, they'd hit the corner at full speed. Impossible to make the turn at the rate they traveled.

Blood pounded in his ears. They were going to crash.

He eased over the front of the box, one foot on the pole,

judged the distance, and dove for the rear animal's bouncing back. Foam flew back at him. Jagged pain ripped up his arm. He clung onto the harness. The thunder of hooves drowned everything out. He gritted his teeth. They were almost out of time.

He pulled his feet up onto the rocking back.

Steady. Found his balance. *Go.*

He lunged forward at the broad arse ahead and scrabbled for a purchase. He slid sideways, cobbles rushing up and past him, ringing hooves slashing at his head.

He clung on in desperation. He would not allow Victoria or Maria to come to harm. He had to keep them safe. With steady pressure on the bridle, he talked nonsense, quieting the horse as he would a crying woman, nothing words. All tone. Assuring, gentling, sweet nothings.

The trembling creature slowed and its partner followed suit.

Their problems weren't over. Other hooves clattered toward them. The attackers were closing in.

He took a deep breath. He'd sooner face a dozen men with pistols than a runaway carriage.

The sweating horses halted, and Simon leaped down. He reached into his boot. He'd taken a leaf out of Lethbridge's book and carried a knife. He slashed the traces and cut the horses free. This carriage wasn't going anywhere.

Victoria stuck her head out of the window.

"For Christ's sake, woman. Stay on the floor," he yelled.

The blackguards were almost on them. Only two. Decent odds. Simon glanced about. Where the hell had they ended up? Wherever it was, he could expect no help from the neighbors.

Their pursuers pulled their horses up a few yards off. Cowards. He pulled out his pistols, cocked them and set one at his feet. Aiming carefully, he fired at a shadow and heard a satisfying scream. One down.

A rush of booted feet sounded in the deserted street.

Hell. Two more, arriving on foot.

"Hold your fire," one of them called out. A west-country voice. Simon narrowed his eyes, trying to pierce the gloom.

Muttered instructions and the sound of men fanning out. Shuffles indicated their positions.

Victoria stuck her head out. Bloody hell. She had a pistol in her hand. She must have found his old one in the coach holster. She fired and missed. The men hesitated. Good try.

She disappeared inside.

Thank God. Simon picked up his other gun and waited. He wanted them closer. His last shot had to count. There were at least four of them.

They rushed at the carriage. He took slow and careful aim, focusing on the target in his sights, his pistol an extension of his arm, a deadly part of him.

He fired. A man cried out. No use. The three remaining men moved in, using the body of the carriage for protection. They only had to fire inside the coach and the occupants would die. Simon put up his hands and stepped out. He couldn't let them harm the women when it was him they wanted.

A lumbering mail coach, its lantern swinging, rounded the bend. Simon stared. None of them had heard its approach. Shock twisted the driver's face as he fought to avoid the derelict carriage. The villains scattered before its terrifying passage.

Please, God, let it pass. The sickening, splintering screech of wood and metal as the stage's wheels ground against the town coach sent terror racing down Simon's spine. He could only stare, shock holding him rigid. A shout of warning died on his lips as his carriage rocked, hung balanced on its right-hand wheels for an agonizing second and finally crashed onto its side. The street echoed with the tinkle of shattering glass.

Horror churned in his gut.

He dashed to the stricken vehicle, pried the door up and pulled himself over the edge. Too dark. He couldn't see a thing inside. He heard a moan.

"Victoria. Maria. For God's sake, say something."

Shaking so hard, he could barely climb, he dragged himself onto the upturned side of the carriage.

Please, God, don't let them be dead.

He peered inside. Maria, her turban crooked and her face bloody, raised her head. Thank God.

Other people arrived, other arms pulled at the old woman. "For God's sake, hurry up. There's another one," Simon shouted.

Maria finally emerged, and the men staggered as they took her weight. The moment they got out of the way, Simon hung headfirst in the opening, his hands searching, grasping. He felt an arm. Grabbed it. "Victoria. Out you come."

Nothing. She didn't move. Dear God. No. This could not happen. Not another death at his door.

"Here," a calm voice said behind him. "Why don't I hold you and you pull her out."

With his ankles braced, Simon dropped his head and shoulders through the opening. The splintered doorframe caught on his coat as he wriggled forward. He felt around and located her shoulders. Careful not to cause her further injury, he grasped her beneath the arms. "Pull slowly," he called out.

He lifted her tiny frame with ease. She hung limp in his hand, boneless, silent. His helper pulled him from the carriage well and Simon cradled her still form in his arms. Despair washed over him.

"Sir, you're wounded. Let me take her." His helper, a serious-faced young man, held out his arms.

Fear curled in his gut. "Stand back."

She was just too damn still. Her face white, her lips bloodless, she lay like a broken doll. He placed his cheek close to her mouth and felt a faint breath on his skin. His gut clenched. Not dead. Not yet.

"Get a doctor," he yelled.

He ran his hands over her, back, arms, and legs. Nothing broken.

"Sir, let me bind your arm, you're bleeding."

He brushed him off. "I'm fine. Get a bloody doctor." The man recoiled. Simon didn't care.

She didn't move, her pallor dreadful to see. Internal injuries? He reeled at the awful thought.

"This will help," the persistent young man said and climbed up beside Simon holding a coach light. "There's a nasty bump on her head, see."

An ugly lump near her temple swelled evilly even as he stared at it. No blood. She had cuts on her arms and her gown was torn.

A cold weight pressed on his chest. She was dying.

Drops of water fell on her pale cheeks.

Rain.

His fingers shook as he gently wiped them away.

More fell.

Oh God. Not rain. He dragged his sleeve across his eyes.

He swallowed the burning lump in his throat. *Please, God. Don't let her die. I'll do anything. I'll stay away from her. I swear. Just don't let her die.*

Chapter Nine

Victoria ached all over. The musky scent of sandalwood enveloped her. Arms held her in a firm grip against a warm, hard-breathing chest. Her cheek rubbed against coarse fabric. Someone carried her.

"Benton, help Miss Allenby inside. Send for the doctor. And Benton, get the name and directions of the young man helping my cousin. Damnation, man! Don't just stand there. Make haste."

Travis's voice, harsh and demanding, echoed through her aching skull. Travis held her. His heart thrummed loud and strong in her ear. But did he have to shout? A blacksmith was using her head for an anvil. Weighted with lead, her eyelids refused to open. Victoria stifled a moan as pain stabbed into her temples.

All motion ceased.

His chest heaved and his warm breath caressed her face.

"Thank God." Travis spoke quietly this time. "Victoria, open your eyes."

She opened them a fraction, squinting against the bright light above her head.

"Good," he said. "Look at me."

A wave of dizziness rolled over her and black fog filled her vision. Her eyelids slammed shut.

"Victoria, wake up."

Why couldn't he just leave her alone? She forced herself to

look up at him. Deep lines etched the sides of his mouth and concern clouded his eyes.

"My head hurts." Her voice sounded tiny and miserable.

"I know," he said, starting up the stairs. "But you must stay awake until the doctor arrives."

She tried to frown. It hurt, too. "Did I fall asleep?"

"There's been an accident. The carriage tipped over and you hit your head."

"Oh." She wrinkled her brow. Pain rippled across the skin of her forehead. She winced. Her memory failed to reveal anything after they left the theater. "Is Maria all right?"

"She has some cuts and bruises, but she is fine. Don't talk. You must reserve your strength."

Footsteps sounded beside them.

"Open the chamber door, Mrs. Pearce."

The thought of laying her weary bones on a soft feather mattress tantalized her protesting body.

He lowered her gently. The cool sheets felt like heaven against her tortured skin. The soft pillow cradled her throbbing head. She closed her eyes.

She felt gentle hands rolling her on her side, fumbling at the fastenings of her gown. Every joint screamed in protest. She groaned at the pain that tore along her shoulder. The hands let her fall back.

"Here, let me." Travis again.

She felt his warm fingers on her skin at the neckline of her gown. His touch scorched her flesh. She forced her eyelids open to find his dark head bent over her, his expression hard. Metal glinted in the candlelight. The fabric yielded to the sharp blade with a rending sound and his strong hands tore the delicate fabric from neckline to hem in one swift movement. She gasped as cool air chilled her skin. He pulled the sheet across her.

"You can manage the rest?" he asked the housekeeper.

"Yes, my lord."

"Don't let her fall asleep. It is very important. Do you understand?"

"Yes, my lord."

Travis didn't move. He stared down at her, his expression uncertain and his eyes full of anxiety. He hovered over her like some great eagle protecting its young. His hand reached out to touch her. Blood dripped from the tips of his fingers onto the sheet.

"You're injured," she whispered.

He glanced at his bloody hand with a surprised expression and shook his head. "It's nothing. A scratch."

She wanted to reach out, to touch him, to ease the soul-deep pain lurking in the azure depths of his eyes, but she felt too tired, her arm just too heavy.

"My lord?" Mrs. Pearce raised her brows.

"Yes, of course." He strode away, but turned in the doorway. "No sleeping. I'm relying on you, Mrs. Pearce. Do not leave her alone for a moment."

Victoria's eyelids slid closed. Mrs. Pearce's gentle hands eased her into her nightgown, her cool touch nothing like the warm, strong fingers of the dark, enigmatic earl.

Travis ran downstairs. Thank God. She was conscious and apparently not suffering from anything except a severe knock on the head.

Benton waited for him in his study with brandy and bandages.

"Did I ever tell you what a marvel you are, Benton?"

A small smile crossed the implacable face. "Yes, my lord."

"Hmm."

He sipped his brandy while Benton cleaned and bound the jagged gash in his arm. No need to ruin an expensive rug waiting for the doctor to arrive. God. Where in hell was the doctor? Victoria looked all right, but what if she had unseen injuries? His throat tightened. He resisted the urge to rush back upstairs and check on her. He'd made a vow. He'd keep it.

The vision of Victoria lying on the sheet in nothing but her shift, her black hair spread on the pillow, forced its way into his mind. The fine lawn chemise beneath her stays had left little to the imagination. Small breasts tipped with delicate pink, shapely curves, a dark, inviting triangle at the apex of her thighs. He'd wanted to lie down beside her. Cover her shapely form with his body, hard and wanting. The mental picture sent hot blood racing through his veins to pool, in his groin. Fiery pleasure throbbed in his loins.

Damn. Did he have no control at all when it came to Victoria Yelverton?

He winced as Benton pulled the bandage tight. He welcomed the distracting pain, the sharp reminder of his promise. Lust didn't freeze his soul. He could handle need, even revel in it. The overwhelming desire to protect her had him rigid with fear.

Tenderness. Miranda had taught him to recognize the foolish male reaction to female wiles as a weakness. A primal response designed to trap a man into betraying everything he believed in. No woman would ever hold him enthralled again.

"That should do it, my lord, until the doctor arrives." Benton poured out wine.

Brandy. It would dull the pain in his arm, but would it ease the ache in his chest? He closed his eyes. He didn't have a heart. He'd frozen it out of existence.

He drained his glass and poured another. "Thank you. Let me know the instant Doctor Marsh arrives. He's to go straight up to Miss Yelverton and then to Miss Allenby. In the meantime, I have a note for Wilson to deliver."

"Yes, my lord. I'm sorry I was not able to get the young cleric's name. He just said he was glad to be of assistance and left with the stage."

Good Lord. A Samaritan who wanted nothing for his good deed. Remarkable. "Thank you, Benton."

By the time Wilson arrived, Simon had finished his letter. "Do you know the Marquess of Lethbridge by sight?"

"Yes, my lord."

"I want you to find him and give him this. I don't care if you have to go to every hell and brothel in London; you are not to come back until you have delivered it to him. Do you understand?"

"Yes, my lord."

He frowned at Wilson's doubtful expression. "Well?"

"My lord, do you think the attack could have anything to do with the cove I saw outside in the street this afternoon?"

Simon's heartbeat kicked up a notch. "What?"

"I saw this ugly customer earlier today loitering in the street. Didn't seem to have any business to be there. I had the feeling he paid particular attention to this house. I wondered—"

"Did you tell anyone about this?"

"I wasn't sure, my lord. There's lots of strangers hanging about these days. I thought if he was there again tomorrow I would say something to Mr. Benton."

It made sense. One afternoon might just be a coincidence; a second appearance would warrant comment. He nodded. "I'll talk to you about it when you come back. For now, I need you to locate the marquess. Start at his lodgings, then go on to White's. If he's not there, ask the porter if he can find anyone who knows where he went. If not, try Brookes's, then Madame Berthier's. After that, it's anyone's guess."

"Yes, my lord." The eager young man swelled with self-importance as he took the note and left.

Simon took another pull at the brandy. He ought to go and see how Maria fared. He desperately wanted to check on Victoria, but he would not betray his word. He would stay away from her.

Where the hell was the doctor? The sooner he looked at Victoria, the better Simon would feel.

"God, Simon. I'm so damnably sorry," Lethbridge said. "Genevieve got me so angry, I couldn't think straight."

At well past two in the morning, Simon glared at Lethbridge hesitating in the doorway to the library, clearly unsure of his welcome. His bloodshot eyes and slurred speech told their own story. He'd spent the last hours of the night drinking in his own private hell.

"Tally ho!" a cheerful voice said. A tall redhead nudged Lethbridge forward and stepped around him into the library. Lord Rutherford, Lady Julia's brother.

"What the hell are you doing here, Rutherford?" Simon growled.

"I overheard your man looking for Lethbridge at Brookes's and helped him track him down at the Devil's Kitchen. Sounded like there might be a good mill."

Despite his irritation, Simon smiled. Rutherford loved a fight. He gestured them towards a chair and offered them brandy.

Lethbridge shook his head. "I don't suppose you could locate some coffee?"

Simon nodded, handed a goblet to Rutherford, then stuck his head into the hallway. "Wilson, can you make us coffee?"

Wilson grinned. "Certainly, my lord."

"How are Miss Yelverton and Miss Allenby?" Lethbridge

asked when Simon resumed his seat.

"They were lucky. My cousin has cuts and bruises. Miss Yelverton received a severe blow to the head. The doctor thinks she'll be fine." Simon clung to Marsh's opinion that the lack of further swelling indicated no internal bleeding, although only time would tell. Mrs. Pearce had instructions to wake Victoria every hour and Simon had listened to make sure.

"What exactly happened tonight after I left you?" Lethbridge asked.

Simon, pausing only while Wilson delivered the coffee, succinctly ran through the events leading up to the accident with the stage.

Lethbridge sipped his coffee with a thoughtful expression. "So your driver got off the box and disappeared when the carriage stopped?"

"Apparently."

"And he showed up later and is now sitting outside in the hall?"

"Yes. He arrived just before you did."

"And two men on horseback followed the carriage?"

Simon nodded.

"And two more on foot?"

"I think there were three."

"Then they were expecting you in that spot at that time."

"One of them spoke with a Hampshire accent."

"Interesting."

The throbbing in his arm intensified and Simon eased his shoulder back, seeking relief. "Very."

"I think we should have your coachman in."

Drink-raddled as he was, Lethbridge exuded a businesslike air. He never failed to impress Simon with his phenomenal intellect. He had been one of England's best spies during the war against Bonaparte with his innate strategic abilities and extraordinary facility with languages. If anyone could get to the bottom of this, Lethbridge would. Provided he stayed sober.

Simon invited the coachman in. Bald and overweight, he sat perched on a hard ladder-back chair miserably regarding the three, stern gentlemen facing him.

"So, Griggs," Lethbridge said with an easy smile. "Give us your version of the events of this evening."

Griggs clenched his large, weather-beaten fists on his knees. He looked over at Simon. "I'm sorry, my lord. If you wants to turn me off, I wouldn't blame you."

"Let us hear what happened first," Lethbridge said.

Simon leaned forward. His first instinct was to grab the man by the throat and choke the truth out of him. And he would, if Griggs gave him the slightest provocation. Victoria's face, bloodless and full of pain, flashed into his mind. His chest tightened. She might have been killed. Someone had to pay for this night's work.

"After Lord Travis got out with the ladies, I parked like I always does and went to talk to a couple of the other whips. We always has a chin-wag on theater nights." He glanced at Simon, flushed, then visibly swallowed.

"Go on," Lethbridge said.

"Well, my lord, someone passed a bottle of blue ruin and I had a couple of swigs and the next thing I knows I'm laid out along the wall, no coat, all the carriages gone and my head's like Mother O'Reilly's knocking shop on a Saturday night."

He looked embarrassed at the bemused looks on the faces of his audience. "Banging," he explained.

Rutherford's crack of laughter cut through the tension. "Banging," he repeated. "That's rich."

Lethbridge raised his hand, his expression serious. "So,

Griggs, did you know everyone drinking from the bottle?"

Griggs frowned. The ham fist on his knee clenched and unclenched. He shook his head. "There was Lord Dorset's man, and his two footmen, and Sir Willowby's tiger and a man I didn't know."

"Whose flask was it?"

"I dunno. We always has a drop. Keeps the cold out, like."

"What did this unknown driver look like?"

"Kind of ordinary."

"Tall? Fat? Thin?"

"Ordinary. Like a driver."

The man's stupidity was unacceptable. A red haze coated his vision and Simon rose from his seat.

Sweat beaded on Griggs's forehead, but his soft brown eyes remained steady on Lethbridge's face.

Lethbridge shook his head and Simon reined in his anger.

"Who stood beside him?" Lethbridge asked.

"At first, his lordship's man, then he was next to me."

"Was he taller than you?"

Griggs frowned again, lips pursed. "Taller."

"Young or old?" rapped out Lethbridge.

"Young, and big with it." Griggs beamed as he saw Lethbridge nod.

"Was he in livery?"

"Green and black."

God. This was like pulling teeth. Simon resisted the urge to yell at him to think. This steady elicitation of information tortured him, but Lethbridge knew his business, and any intimidation on Simon's part would have Griggs's mind frozen and useless.

"Whose livery is it?"

Griggs shook his head. "It were kind of odd like."

"Odd?"

"Uniforms are usually a solid color and then trim, you know like braid and buttons. This were odd. Patches."

"Is there anything else about this man you can recall?" Lethbridge asked.

Griggs screwed up his face in the effort of remembering. "He had a scar on his face. On his forehead. I remember noticing it, because it went right through his eyebrow. Lucky he didn't lose his eye, I thought at the time."

"Well done, Griggs," Lethbridge said, smiling encouragingly. "I think that will be all for now."

Griggs swivelled his eyes in Simon's direction. "I suppose I better collect my things, my lord?"

Like most of his servants, Griggs had been a member of the Travis household for many years. Griggs wasn't supposed to drink on duty and his orders were not to leave the carriage unattended, but he was not responsible for the actions of the attackers.

Simon sighed. "No, Griggs. I'll let it go this time. The consequences of what you did could have been disastrous. As it was, Miss Yelverton and Miss Allenby were seriously hurt. I'm relying on you to see nothing like this ever happens again."

Griggs's face reddened as he got to his feet. He pulled out a blue spotted handkerchief, mopped his brow and swiped at his eyes. "Thank you, my lord. I swear on the life of my children, I will never let you down."

The room remained silent as he shuffled out. Simon poured himself another glass of brandy and offered the bottle to Rutherford.

Rutherford filled his glass and paced to the window. "We're no closer now to finding out who did this, than we were when we started."

"I wouldn't say that," Lethbridge said. "We know Simon's coachman wasn't involved."

"He could be lying," Simon offered.

"No. It's too easy to check his story and description with the other coachmen. I think he was drugged."

Rutherford settled back in his chair with a soft whistle. "So what now?"

"Hell," Simon said running a hand through his hair. "I asked Wilson to wait. He said he saw someone hanging around outside earlier today."

"Have at him," hallooed Rutherford.

"Bring him in and let's see what he has to say," Lethbridge agreed.

Within moments, the young footman sat in the chair recently vacated by Griggs, his face rampant with curiosity and excitement. He'd probably enjoyed his foray into the clubs and hells of London tonight.

Lethbridge stared at him intently. "I understand from Lord Travis you observed a suspicious stranger on the street outside today?"

"Yes, my lord."

"Can you describe him?"

"Yes, my lord. About my height, burly. He had a scar over one eye. Balding at the front, hair brown and kind of long at the back. A moustache, but no beard. He wore a black riding coat, kind of old and dirty."

"Egad," Rutherford exclaimed. "The man's a bloody marvel."

"Are you sure?" Lethbridge asked.

"Yes, my lord." Wilson held Lethbridge's stern gaze. "Mr. Benton insists we observe everyone who comes in and out of the house. We have to know who they are the minute they step inside. It's important to address them properly."

Lethbridge smiled and nodded at Simon. "My agents

could use such training." A pained expression crossed Lethbridge's face. He didn't have those men under his command anymore, and Simon knew Lethbridge's forced resignation still cut at his pride.

None of it rang true, Simon thought. Who on earth wanted him dead so badly he would go to so much trouble? No one came to his mind. Whoever it was, he was too cowardly to confront him to his face and had injured Victoria and Maria into the bargain. They might have been killed. Crimson rage surged behind his eyes. He forced a control he didn't feel into his voice. "Have you seen this man before, Wilson?"

Wilson shook his head. "No, my lord. But I'd recognize him in a flash if I saw him again."

Lethbridge got up and strode to the fireplace. He stared down into the embers as if seeking answers in their glowing depths. "Very well," he said after a moment or two. "You can go to bed now. But Wilson . . ."

"Yes, my lord?"

"If you do ever see this man again, you must come and tell either the earl or myself. Do not approach him, just come and tell one of us. Do you understand?"

"Yes, my lord."

"Well, what do you think?" Simon asked Lethbridge, after Wilson closed the door behind him.

"I think, my friend, you have one rather clever and deadly enemy. All we have to go on is this description of Wilson's, confirmed by your coachman."

"What do we do?" Rutherford asked.

Simon grimaced. Rutherford looked for all the world like a man faced with some exciting challenge. While his intellect might not be of the sharpest, he was a good man to have around in a fight. Full of bottom, his talent in the boxing ring came close to matching Simon's.

One arm along the mantel, Lethbridge picked up a fire iron and poked at the dying embers. They blazed and hissed and the reflection of red flames danced on his serious features. "Now, I talk to one or two of my lower-class friends. Perhaps one of them knows who our scar-faced man is. If we can find him, we can find out who sent him."

Exasperated, Simon let out a sharp sigh. He wanted to get his hands on whoever did this now. Tonight. To hell with waiting for someone else to find him.

He stifled his impatience. Lethbridge had a great many contacts in all walks of life. Some of them had worked with him in Europe, some here in London on counterespionage during the war. He knew what he was doing.

Simon nodded reluctantly. "Agreed. But don't do anything without talking to me first." He wanted to know exactly what was going on before anyone took any action. He could not allow his past to be exposed.

Chapter Ten

A gentle snore from across the drawing room drew Victoria's gaze. Maria's turbaned head nodded to the rhythm of her even breathing, while her abandoned embroidery hoop lay in her lap. A purple bruise embellished her cheek and a bandage adorned her forehead. Afternoon sunlight, slanting through the narrow window, warmed the room.

Maria didn't stir at a knock on the drawing room door or at Benton's arrival with the tea tray. Victoria shook her head when Benton cast her a questioning look. "Leave her to sleep," she whispered.

In silence, Benton set his burden on the oval mahogany table. He pointed to a pink note resting on the silver tray.

"Came by hand, miss," he murmured.

Unfolding the paper, Victoria scanned the neatly penned lines.

I am invited to visit his lordship's estate in Hampshire. His carriage will be waiting outside my house at the end of our evening at Vauxhall tomorrow.
Dear Miss Yelverton, you were kind enough to offer me your friendship. If you have any influence on Lord T____ I beg you to use it on my behalf. I cannot gainsay my mother in this.
Your obedient servant and friend, Miss Cassandra Eckford.

An awful sinking sensation in Victoria's stomach left her

feeling sick. Travis's charming friendliness at the theater and his solicitude, both last night and this morning, meant nothing. He'd almost fooled her into believing he wasn't as black as he was painted. One thing she knew for certain, Travis had made no plans for a marriage with Miss Eckford.

She smiled bitterly. How could he be so open, so witty, so . . . seductively attractive one minute and so depraved the next? Attractive? She could never be attracted to a libertine. She was no silly gudgeon like Cassandra Eckford and she had far more to offer than serving as a rake's plaything. She threw the note down. Travis and Miss Eckford were none of her business.

In which case, why did she have such a hollow feeling in her heart?

"Will there be a reply, miss? The servant is still waiting," Benton queried.

What to do? Poor Mr. Runcorn and his sad eyes floated into her mind. Cassandra's chance for true happiness would be ruined if Victoria sat back and let Travis have his way. He would spoil two lives for his own pleasure. Perhaps she should talk to him about it. The thought chilled her to the bone.

Victoria nodded. "I'll answer it in the library. Ask the servant to wait."

She poured a cup of tea, carried it with her to the library and set it down on the rosewood escritoire beside the window. A drawer held writing materials, and after sharpening the quill, she set to work on two letters.

"Miss?" Benton said from the doorway some several minutes later.

Victoria sprinkled the paper with sand. "I've almost finished, Benton."

"It's not that, miss. It's Lady Julia Garforth. She insists on seeing you, and his lordship said no callers today.”

Benton was a treasure and the only member of the household who did not stand in utter trepidation of the earl. The only other member, she corrected herself.

In his apparent anxiety about her health, Travis had left strict instructions for her care. To her annoyance, he had sent a note to Julia cancelling their planned outing. She touched a hand to the painful lump on her temple and had to admit he was probably right.

“It’s all right, Benton. I’ll come right away. A visit with Lady Julia will do me a world of good. Here is the reply to go back with the messenger.” She tucked her other letter, the one to Mr. Runcorn, in her reticule.

The sight of her redheaded friend standing in the paneled hall, riding crop in hand, drove all thoughts of Travis from her mind. “Julia.” Victoria reached out her hands. “How good of you to call.”

“Oh, Victoria. I had to come.” Julia pulled her into a hug. “I received Travis’s note this morning and then Philip told me about Michael. I was so shocked. You must have thought me the most heartless creature imaginable, but I had no idea when we met yesterday. Truly.”

The sympathy in Julia’s voice brought a lump to Victoria’s throat. “It’s all right. I did write, but my letter must have missed you.”

“I had to come and tell you how deeply sorry I am. If there is anything I can do, you must not fail to tell me. How I wish I had been here.”

“Me, too,” Victoria said, remembering how alone she had felt. “It was very hard at the time, but I have grown somewhat accustomed . . .” A sudden rush of emotion stung the back of her eyes.

Julia embraced her. “You poor dear.”

The tenderness in Julia's expression eased Victoria's sorrow. She managed a watery smile. "Oh Julia, it's so good to see you. I do need your help. Can you stay a while?"

"I think so. My horse will be fine with Travis's groom for a few minutes."

Victoria glanced around. Where could they talk alone? Maria would be sure to wake up if they went into the drawing room; Travis might interrupt them in the library. "Come up to my room."

Julia's green eyes flashed curiosity. She nodded and followed Victoria up to her second-floor bedroom. She glanced around and raised a brow. "How very . . . pink."

Victoria smiled. Julia hated pink. She perched on the bed and Julia bounced down next to her.

"This is just like school," Julia said with a grin.

The recollection made Victoria chuckle. "Lord, how we used to look forward to those nightly bedroom feasts after the teachers retired."

Julia laughed. "My word, yes. Remember the cake my mother sent with fruit soaked in brandy?"

"We got into so much trouble that night."

Julia jumped up and struck a pose, her arms akimbo. "If that there cook has put arsenic in the soup and bouillon in the rat trap again, I'll have her guts for garters, so I will." Even after all this time, Julia mimicked their old school matron to perfection.

Victoria laughed and shook her head. "Poor Matron. She thought we'd been poisoned, we were so sick after eating it all in one go."

Julia's expression turned serious. She leaned against one of the bedposts. "But Victoria, what happened to poor Michael, and how did you ever end up in Travis's house?"

A cold shower of reality wiped out the happy memories.

"Oh, Ju. Michael lost all his money to Travis."

"I heard Ogden ruined him."

Victoria stiffened. Julia had never liked Ogden. "The viscount was Michael's friend."

Curiosity filled Julia's lively face. "I'm sorry. I've only heard the gossip. What did happen?"

"Michael called Travis out."

Julia's voice dropped to a shocked whisper. "Travis killed him? Philip said it was an accident."

As a rule, she and Julia never kept secrets from each other. This secret was just too awful. Victoria stared mutely at her friend.

"Victoria Yelverton, don't you dare poker up on me with that prissy look on your face."

Torn between her friendship to Julia and her loyalty to Michael, Victoria debated how much she dared say. "It's the most terrible thing. You must swear never to tell a soul."

"I swear."

"He lost everything at cards, called Travis out, and when he failed to kill him, he . . ." She couldn't say it. She still couldn't put into words what Michael had done. She bunched the counterpane in her hand, staring, unseeing, remembering Michael's last moments and willing herself not to cry.

"Victoria." Julia's voice expressed pity and concern. "Don't tell me he took his own life?"

Victoria nodded. She couldn't utter a word for the choking lump in her throat.

Julia sat beside her and placed her arms around Victoria's shoulders. "How simply horrid for you."

The warm comfort of her friend's arm reminded her of their youth and school, when the worst thing in their lives was a scolding from a teacher about lost stockings. Life had changed drastically. She drew a steadying breath. "He lost everything and Travis offered me a place to stay. I suppose he felt guilty about what happened." She raised her head and gazed into troubled emerald eyes. "None of that matters now. I need your help."

"All you need to do is ask."

"I want to find a position as a governess."

Julia's arched brows drew together and she gave Victoria a sharp glance. "I don't understand."

Victoria got up and paced across the room. She stared blindly at the silver brushes on the rosewood dressing table. Surely Julia would understand why she could not continue to live on Travis's charity. Worse yet was to have him parade her on the marriage mart when she had no intention of marrying anyone. She swung around.

"Travis insists I marry by the end of the Season. You know that's not for me. I want to be independent and make my own decisions."

"The life of a governess doesn't strike me as anything terribly pleasant. You'd have a lot more freedom as a wife."

Julia's expression of disbelief caught Victoria on the raw. She grimaced. They'd had this conversation before. "Not when one is considered to be the chattel of one's husband." She prodded the air with her finger to emphasize her points. "Required to obey his wishes and forced to follow his decisions, no matter how bad. No. I am quite capable of deciding how to live my life."

"You know I'd do anything for you," Julia said, the light from the window glinting in her auburn hair. "I just can't agree with you."

Victoria glowered at her.

"All right," Julia said with a shrug. "If it's what you really want, you know I'll help you."

Victoria prowled around the four-poster bed. "It is what I want." She hesitated. "I do have one more favor to ask."

Julia looked askance. "My word, Miss Yelverton. In all these years you've never asked me for anything and now you want two things in one day?"

Victoria batted at Julia's shoulder on her way past. "Be nice."

"All right. What else?"

Victoria handed the note to Runcorn. "Please mail this for me?"

"Mr. Albert Runcorn," Julia read. She turned up her nose. "Runcorn? You're exchanging the Earl of Travis for a Mr. Runcorn?"

Her heart tripped and faltered and she stopped mid-stride, staring at her friend. What could she mean? Travis disliked her just as much as she despised him. He avoided her most of the time and couldn't wait to be rid of her.

Until last night. Last night he had been quite different, not cold at all, and endearing with his gentle teasing. No matter how she tried to deny his allure, his ready wit and charming smile drew her in. And when she'd regained consciousness in his arms, she could have sworn he didn't want to leave her. The memory of his concerned expression, the shattering pain in his eyes, squeezed at her chest.

She resumed her slow pacing. Imbecile. Tomorrow he'd planned to leave for Hampshire with Cassandra Eckford. "Rubbish."

Julia leaned back against the pillows, her eyes following Victoria's progress around the room, and gave her a saucy smile. "He likes you. He never drives ladies in his curricle. It's unheard of."

An honor indeed, and one that accounted for all the sly stares in Hyde Park. Julia mistook the circumstances. All

157

Travis cared about was finding Victoria a husband. Travis had another woman on his mind, an extraordinarily beautiful one. A hollow ache filled her heart.

She tossed her head. "Nonsense. He barely speaks to me and when he does it's to order me around. He is the most domineering, aggravating man I have ever met."

Julia laughed and caught her arm as she stormed by. "Sit down. You're making me dizzy. I'll deliver the note. Does that satisfy you?"

"Yes." Victoria plonked onto the bed.

"Too bad," Julia said with a naughty twinkle. "Just think, if you married Travis, we would be neighbors in Hampshire."

Marry Travis? When Miss Eckford occupied his mind? The lurch in her chest aggravated her more than her whirling thoughts. She laughed and hoped it did not sound as false to her friend as it did in her own ears. "Julia, be serious for once."

Julia shrugged. "Never. Did I tell you about my most recent conquest?"

"You mean Lethbridge?"

Julia's smile disappeared. "Lethbridge?"

At last, a chance for Victoria to get her own back. She grinned. "I saw the way he looked at you yesterday."

"Not very likely," said Julia with a shake of her head.

"How can you be so sure?"

"Everyone knows he's besotted with Genevieve Longbourne."

"Really? She's engaged to a duke."

Julia nodded and pressed her lips together. "Ever since she got betrothed, Lethbridge has been drinking himself into an early grave. According to Philip, Travis has pulled him out of more scrapes than enough just lately. He's such an idiot."

"Who? Travis?"

"No, of course not. Nothing wrong with Travis, if you can

158

get past his cynical exterior. No, Lethbridge. Anyone could have told him about Genevieve. They call her the winter queen. Nothing to do with her blond beauty, it's the melted snow in her veins."

Julia slid off the bed, sauntered to the window and stared out. "Lethbridge came to London on a brief furlough the year we both came out and joined her court. All the eligible bachelors were doing the same thing. She was *de rigeur*. He had eyes for no one else, and I suppose he went back to war clinging to her memory. He never moved on. At least, that's what Philip says."

"Poor man," Victoria said. "He was certainly in his cups last night at the theater. He left early. Travis said he wasn't well. Genevieve Longbourne and the Duke were in the box opposite."

"That would do it." Julia stared at the floor, then looked up, laughter brimming in her eyes. "But, Victoria, you *must* hear about my conquest."

Leaning back against the pillows, Victoria smiled in anticipation. Julia had a flair for the dramatic. "I'm listening."

Julia perched beside her. "On the way back from my sister's lying-in, Philip insisted we stay nearby the Quorn so he could hunt. I didn't mind. I was glad to get away from everyone cooing over the newest addition to the family. Ghastly, red-faced, screaming brat. He looks just like one of those monkeys they displayed at the Tower of London last year." She shuddered.

Victoria smothered a laugh at Julia's theatrics, knowing she didn't mean it.

"Anyway, after a day of bruising riding, we were invited to one of the local houses for supper. Another member of the hunting party, an old retired sailor, decided he liked the cut of my jib."

Julia imitated the deep voice of her bluff, Yorkshire seaman. "Well, Lady Julia, it's cram on full sails for me. I'll fire a shot across your bow and you'll be in irons before you can reach port."

Victoria giggled. "No one talks like that."

"He does, let me assure you. And he's as wide in the beam as a Newcastle coal ship."

Dropping back into her part, Julia strode with a rolling seaman's gait around the room, her thumbs in her imaginary waistcoat pockets. "Shiver my timbers, matey, splice the main brace."

Victoria burst out laughing.

Julia leaned one elbow on the mantel, crossed her ankles and poked an imaginary pipe at Victoria. "I've a nice little birth in Southampton where a sturdy vessel like you could dry dock and furl your sails."

Victoria collapsed in mirth, laughing as she had not laughed for months, sadness lifting from her shoulders.

Along the corridor, Simon paused in his instructions to his valet at the sound of girlish laughter wafting down the hallway.

"Sounds like the young miss is having a right good old time," his valet said.

Simon nodded.

"Do her good after all her troubles."

Did the servants know everything that went on in the house? Simon supposed it was only to be expected. He frowned. "She's meant to be resting."

"It's probably that little maid of hers. Elsie. Right pert little thing she's turned out to be now she's a proper ladies' maid. Will you be wanting your evening clothes packed, my lord?"

Simon looked with distaste at the black satin breeches and

white silk stockings held up by his valet. He wouldn't need them in Hampshire. Mentally he groaned. If the past meant anything, he'd be dragged all around the continent to keep the foolish chit happy. In that case, he'd be expected to put in an appearance at the British Embassy in every country they passed through. "Yes. Pack the evening clothes. They can follow with the rest of the trunks. I won't need them with me tomorrow."

Giggles echoed down the hallway from Victoria's room.

His lips twitched at the happy sound. It sounded as though someone was tickling her. She was supposed to stay quiet today. He ought to stop the nonsense before she came to harm.

He hesitated. She might not be dressed. Still, he ought to make sure she was all right. He strode down the hallway to her door.

About to knock, the sound of a deeper voice stopped him cold. Who the hell did she have in there? He glared at the door. God damn. If she'd let Ogden into his house and into her room, he'd throttle her. After he killed Ogden.

Victoria's laugh rang out.

Emptiness filled his chest. She would never laugh like that with him.

She'd told him more than once how much she despised him and his dissipated lifestyle, yet she trusted Ogden. Let her have him then, if he was what she wanted. He turned away, sickened.

A man's voice, not Ogden, said in rough tones with a north-country accent, "I'll give you my undying devotion if you'll jump aboard this hearty barque of mine. We'll sail on high seas and wild waters."

"I'll row your boat, you mighty man of the sea," Victoria said between giggles.

161

Rage filled his veins. He raised his fist. The urge to strike at something, anything, gripped him. How dare she? And in his house. He sneered. She was just like all the rest of them, just like Miranda.

The damned little bitch. At the first opportunity, she'd jumped into bed with a servant while he suffered the torment of the damned keeping his hands off her. Row his boat, would she? He'd drown the bastard in his own blood.

He thrust the door open and stiffened his hands into killing blades. "Get the hell out," he yelled.

His eyes veered straight to the bed. Victoria's startled face, flushed and full of laughter gazed at him. She clutched a pillow up to her chest and he caught a glimpse of slender legs in white silk stockings.

Her laughter died, replaced by shock. She sat up and adjusted her skirts.

Simon's gaze took in the rumpled sheets. No one. Perhaps the bastard had heard him coming and now lurked under the bed. "What the hell is going on?"

"Good afternoon, Travis."

Lady Julia stood beside the white marble fireplace with her chest thrown out and a wicked grin on her face.

His mouth dropped open. He thrust a hand through his hair. Hell. Ju Garforth. The little mimic from his childhood days. He should have guessed. He retrenched rapidly. "Lady Julia, what the deuce are you doing? Miss Yelverton is supposed to be resting."

He looked sternly at Victoria. She sat demurely on the edge of the bed, a puzzled expression on her face. Christ. What had he said when he opened the door?

"Nice to see you, too," Julia said.

God. He'd made the most frightful fool of himself. What must Victoria be thinking? "I beg your pardon." He bowed elegantly and smiled. "How are you, Lady Julia?"

"Don't try those ploys on me, Travis," Julia replied. "I still remember the day you and Philip locked me in the hen house playing knights in armor and then promptly forgot to rescue the maiden in distress."

Relieved that his fear of finding Victoria with some greasy servant had proved to be groundless, he laughed as he remembered only too well. Life had been fun then, and the future seemed bright. "Were you ever mad as fire when the scullery maid let you out. My head still rings from the boxing you gave my ears when you caught up to us. It wasn't our fault the gamekeeper offered to take us shooting before we got halfway back to you."

"Hmm. I was taller than you then, but I can still box your ears."

Travis grinned. "Only if I let you."

"You knew each other growing up?" Victoria asked, glancing from one to the other.

Julia smiled. "We have neighboring estates in Hampshire, remember. Philip and Travis were the best of friends until . . ." She frowned, staring at him.

Simon forced himself to stay relaxed, at ease. She didn't know anything. No one knew. There'd been some gossip, some wild speculation locally, but no one knew the truth. His father had paid a king's ransom to keep it inside the family. He retained his smile. "Until I went to school," he supplied. "We didn't see each other again for years. But you are still the same madcap, Lady Ju."

She laughed. "And you are just as wild and reckless as ever, if what I hear is true."

He bowed and smiled, refusing to be drawn into a discussion of his lifestyle. Victoria remained sitting stiffly on the bed. "I'm sorry. I seem to have interrupted you," he said.

"You told me to leave, my lord," Victoria said, all cold formality.

Attack worked better than defense in any situation. "Nonsense. You must have misunderstood. I meant Lady Julia. You are supposed to be resting, not rampaging around here with this hellion."

Victoria tossed her head.

God, he loved the way she did that when she was angry. Clearly, his lie hadn't fooled her. He smiled at her. His most charming smile. The one he kept for his special ladies. "Well, since you are looking so much better, I suppose there's no harm done."

Her gaze slid away. His stomach dropped to his feet. She wasn't prepared to forgive him. Ah, what the hell. It didn't matter anyway.

"I really must be off," Lady Julia said. "Can't keep my horse waiting any longer."

He'd spoiled their fun. What an idiot. He should have stayed away, just as he'd promised. Well, he'd solved the problem. He was going out of Town for the rest of the Season. "Don't depart on my account. I'm just leaving myself."

"It is really time I went," Julia said. She leaned over and brushed her cheek against Victoria's. Simon envied her the whispering touch.

"We'll see you at Vauxhall tomorrow," Julia said to Simon on her way out of the door.

"Not me. Lethbridge is taking Miss Yelverton and my cousin, if they are well enough. I'm going to Hampshire in the morning and won't be back in time."

Victoria's brow puckered. "You're not coming with us to Vauxhall?"

"Did you want me to go with you?" he asked, suddenly hopeful.

She stiffened. "Of course not. It's of no consequence to me what you do."

Blunt and to the point. A sudden flick of anger lashed him. What an idiot for hoping she might want his company. He forced his expression to remain distant. "Then why ask?"

Julia's cheerful tones filled the frigid silence. "Well, I will certainly see you there. Victoria, you have never seen such fireworks as they have at Vauxhall."

"I'm looking forward to it." Victoria's voice sounded flat. Simon remembered how excited she had been about going to the theater. Now she seemed troubled. Perhaps not too surprising after the horrific experiences of last night.

Lady Julia held out her hand. "Good-bye, Lord Travis."

"Lady Julia." He looked intently into her face before he kissed her hand. He recognized her mischievous expression of old. Lady Julia bore watching.

He glanced at Victoria. The light in her face when he first entered had completely disappeared, driven away by his presence. An overwhelming desire to kiss away her frown tormented his soul. He wanted to tickle her and hear her giggle, feel her respond to his caresses. He took in the disordered bed behind her, the most tempting sight he'd seen for weeks, apart from her, almost naked, on that same bed last night.

Desire thickened his blood and surged in his loins. Bloody hell. He'd better leave, before he tried to tumble her.

He nodded. "Miss Yelverton."

Ignoring his pulsing need, he strode back to his room. He had sworn to never again let his desire for a woman control him. He never went back on his word.

He cursed. He hadn't been with a woman since the morning Victoria had arrived in his house. The warm armful he had planned for his delectation for the next few weeks would make him forget all about her.

God, he hoped so. He was starving.

Chapter Eleven

Victoria shivered and pulled her blue merino cloak closer around her. Chilly. But what else would she expect for late April at two o'clock in the morning. If Cassandra Eckford didn't arrive home in the next five minutes, Victoria would march right back to her hired post-chaise and return to her nice warm bed in Travis Place.

No moon brightened the blackness, but the stars and a lamp further down the street cast enough light for her to watch the front door of the Eckford's house. She edged deeper into the shadows of the hedge.

What on earth did people find to do at Vauxhall until this hour of the morning? If she hadn't pleaded a headache and if Maria hadn't still been feeling stiff and sore from the accident, she would know for herself. Try as she might, she'd been unable to think of a way to both go to Vauxhall and help Miss Eckford out of her difficulty. So here she stood, like a garden ornament, stiff and lonely. Waiting.

The part of playing the Good Samaritan no longer seemed like a good idea. Travis would be furious, and if Cassandra had not sounded so pathetic in her note, Victoria would not have considered it for a moment. Travis didn't need to take an unwilling woman. One only had to see the way women ate him with the eyes to know that.

A nagging doubt assailed her conscience. Cassandra had told him she would go with him. His humiliation when she did not arrive would be Victoria's doing.

She shifted her cold feet. Perhaps Miss Eckford decided to join Travis after all? He would be happy. A hollow emptiness spread through her body.

She shivered. Five more minutes and she would leave.

The sound of trotting horses on the cobblestones rang out in the quiet air. Victoria held her breath, not sure if she wanted it to be the Eckfords' coach or not. A carriage pulled up and soft laughter broke the silence. Footsteps tapped up the path and the carriage rolled away. The door slammed.

More minutes passed.

Soft footfalls behind her made Victoria turn around. She closed her eyes and opened them again. No mistake. Cassandra wore a hooded cloak made of some silver fabric that, even in the dim light, sparkled like hoarfrost in a winter sun. She could not have been more conspicuous if she had tried. Victoria reached out and pulled her into the shadows.

"Ouch." Cassandra rubbed her arm.

"Shh. I thought you would never come," Victoria whispered. "Where are your bags?"

"Travis said not to bring anything. He said he had everything I needed."

Victoria rolled her eyes. "But you're not going to Travis, are you?"

"Oh. Shall I go back and pack?"

Victoria bit back her impatient retort. "No, it's too late. Whatever made you wear that?" She pointed at the shimmering wisp that covered Cassandra's gown and hair.

"Travis sent it for me to wear at Vauxhall tonight. He said his coachman would be watching for a lady in silver. So I had to wear it. I mean, you have to wear it. Isn't he romantic?"

Travis was nothing but trouble as far as Victoria was concerned. At the very least, he could have chosen a girl with more sense.

Cassandra began to undo the ties. "It is so pretty. I'm almost sorry to give it up."

Bitterness filled Victoria. "You don't have to, you know."

Cassandra sniffed. "I don't know what to do." Her voice rose to a wail and Victoria glanced around fearfully. "Mama will be so disappointed. She thinks Travis will have to marry me. But I don't want to marry him, I want to marry Albert."

"Hush. All right. If you are sure, then we must hurry." If Victoria was going to do this, she had to do it now. Her heart picked up speed and thundered in her ears. Terror flooded her, cramping her limbs and stomach.

Her hands shaking, Victoria slipped out of her cloak and handed it to Cassandra. In return, she took the silver domino and fastened it around her, tying the strings at her neck and pulling up the hood.

"Travis will be furious," said Cassandra.

Did the silly widgeon have to scare her any more than she was scared already? "I'll deal with Travis. Don't worry about me."

"Oh I wasn't. I wondered if he would come after me. It would be very dashing to have a peer of the realm chasing after me in the dead of night."

Good Lord, the girl was impossible. She had read too many penny romances. "Listen to me. You have to make up your mind. Travis or Albert. If you want the earl to follow you, you might just as well go to him now. Besides," she said thinking it over, "he won't find out until morning that I am you. I mean, that you are not there. By then, you should be safe and sound with your grandmother in Sussex. Everything is arranged."

Cassandra sighed. "I suppose so."

Enough was enough. Assisting someone who desired help was one thing. This ambivalence was quite another, especially when Victoria faced the prospect of explaining what she had done to Travis. He would no doubt consider himself the injured party. "You suppose so? That's it, I'm going home."

"No, no. I mean, I want Albert. It's just I get so confused sometimes. Travis is just so handsome and so noble, but he scares me. I don't think Mama knows just how fierce he can be when things don't go his way. One day at a ball, when another gentleman tried to cut in during a waltz, and he—"

"Never mind all that," Victoria whispered. "Are you or are you not going to Sussex? Yes or no."

The silence seemed endless.

"Yes," Cassandra replied valiantly.

"Then let's go."

Victoria took her by the hand and led her to the waiting post-chaise. The post-boy closed the door and Cassandra let the window down. She stuck her head and arm out. "Miss Yelverton, I forgot to give you this." A silver mask dangled from her hand. "You better wear it. Travis's coachman will be sure to recognize you."

Not such a silly widgeon after all. Victoria took the mask and tied it on. "Good luck, Miss Eckford."

Cassandra bestowed a brilliant smile on her. "Thank you so much, Miss Yelverton. I really am ever so grateful."

Her heart pounding, and scarcely able to draw a breath, Victoria hurried back to the corner of the square where Travis's black carriage, emblazoned with its distinctive silver crest, awaited. At least she'd helped one decent woman escape Travis's evil toils.

"Please wait in here, miss, while I send word to the stables. His lordship is expecting you."

Not quite. Victoria shivered.

Oppressive dark-paneled walls, overstuffed tapestry chairs and an unfriendly-looking brown sofa crowded the St John's Hall drawing room.

Beyond the bow window's lattice panes, a curving shady avenue beckoned. If she left now, Travis would never know of her involvement in Cassandra's failure to show. Coward. When Travis knew the truth, he must understand. No man with as much pride as he had would want a woman against her will.

Standing in the center of the room, Victoria wrapped the silver domino more tightly around her. Fearing recognition, she'd kept the cloak and mask on for the entire journey, even when the coachman had brought her refreshments during the change of horses at first light.

She fought her rising panic. What if she had misread the situation and Travis loved Cassandra? How hurt he would be. And what would he say when he learned of her betrayal?

Firm hands grasped her shoulders.

She jumped, her heart racing unbearably fast. His soft chuckle tickled her ear. Somehow he'd entered and crossed the oak-planked floor without a sound.

"Here you are at last, sweet," he murmured. Long, tanned fingers caressed a path to the fastenings at the front of the domino and his hard body skimmed her back. Pinpricks ran down her spine. "I see you like my gift. I have something much more valuable for you upstairs."

She clenched her jaw to stop her teeth from chattering and turned inside his embrace. She stared up at him boldly. "My lord, I am sorry, but . . ." She slid the hood back from her head. "Miss Eckford has declined your invitation."

His expression of seductive warmth froze. "Has she, by

God?" His narrowed eyes hardened to splintered glass. "And what the deuce are you doing here, Miss Yelverton?"

He reached out and tugged at her mask. The strings held. He cursed, jerking it over her head. Hairpins rattled onto the floor and her hair tumbled to her shoulders.

He smiled, a dangerously rakish smile.

Dread filled her. Not of him, but of herself. A frisson of awareness of his radiant heat, his scent, horses and sandal-wood, and his knowing smile robbed her of breath. She stepped back.

He followed, overshadowing her with his massive form and strength, his jewel-hard eyes probing into her very soul. "Well? I'm waiting for your answer."

Defiant, she kept her gaze steady on his and brushed her hair back from her shoulders. "I came to inform you of Miss Eckford's decision to decline your invitation."

"And?"

His soft tone turned her blood to ice. Instead of fleeing, as every instinct of self-preservation warned her she should, she forced herself to speak with practical common sense. "I wanted to explain. You see—"

"Explain what?" His scornful gaze raked her from head to toe. "You're just like all the rest of them, aren't you? You conspired with her to take her place, Miss Butter-wouldn't-melt-in-your-mouth." His lip curled in contempt. "What a pleasurable surprise. Be warned. I won't marry you, any more than I was prepared to marry her. Does that arrangement suit you?"

She gasped, horrified by his assumption.

Menace emanated from him in chilly waves. His broad shoulders and chest blocked her view of her only path to escape. She dodged around him. In two swift strides, he cut her off and relentlessly backed her against the wall beside the door. With a wickedly seductive smile, he picked up one tress of her tumbled hair and rubbed it between thumb and forefinger. "Like silk," he murmured.

Feet frozen in place, Victoria trembled. Prepared to face his anger, she never imagined he would expect her to fill Cassandra's role. She placed the flats of her hands on his chest, pressing him away. "I did not come here to take Miss Eckford's place, as you put it. I simply came to tell you it's wrong to force her when she loves someone else."

"Force her?" His face darkened. "You think I needed to force her?"

She winced at the suppressed fury in his voice. Now she'd offended his honor. Decidedly unhelpful. He hadn't forced Cassandra; her mother had. He hadn't known.

She twisted in his grasp, felt his thigh against her hip. "My lord," she protested. "Please—"

"Please," he interrupted. His teeth gleamed white as his sensuous smile returned. "I do like the sound of that."

Moving closer, he trapped her hands between them. The heat from his body warmed her skin through her light gown. Her heart beat wildly. She shoved at his wall of chest. "Stand back."

He caught her hands in one of his. Large and strong, hot, his fingers curled around hers. His brilliant gaze fixed on her face, he brought them to his mouth and brushed his lips, warm and dry, across her knuckles. "Or what?" he murmured, his breath moist on her skin.

She wrenched her hands free. "You are no gentleman."

"How very perspicacious of you." His chuckle, velvet soft, sent a shiver snaking down her back.

He stroked her hair, following its length to her shoulder, sliding along the curl that rested on her bosom. One warm finger slipped inside the neck of her gown and trailed over the rise of her breasts, leaving tingling skin in its wake.

"No," she whispered.

He pressed a swift, moist kiss on the sensitive path left by his hand. His glance rose and scorched her face. "Dear God. Do you know how much I have wanted to touch you all these weeks?"

The words fired her blood. Searing heat raced through her veins. Her core fluttered with a deep longing. She wanted him to touch her, to feel his hands on her body, his lips on her mouth.

His mobile mouth curved in a wicked smile. "Of course you do. Women always know when they are wanted. God, but I've wanted you."

She stiffened.

"What is it, poppet?"

The casual endearment pierced her breast. This was not love or respect. It was lust, animal urges she should not know about. One woman was as good as another to him. The thought chilled her blood.

She pushed at his shoulders with all her might. "Stop it. You have to let me go. I only came because I thought it was unfair not to tell you."

His chest rose and fell, brushing her sensitive breasts with each deep breath. His heart hammered against her chest. He frowned. "You little tease. In that case, you could have sent a note."

A note? Her mind scrambled with the thought. Why in heaven's name hadn't she thought of a letter? "I'm telling you the truth. Miss Eckford loves someone else and I offered to help her. I just didn't like to think of you waiting and not knowing she wasn't coming."

A slow, sensuous smile dawned on his lips. "So you do care, just a little."

"I . . ." She couldn't pull her gaze away from his mouth, mere inches from hers. "I didn't want your feelings to be hurt." It sounded lame.

"They are hurt." His smile twisted wryly. "I'm wounded to the quick. Stay, little sweetheart. Heal my pain."

A master of manipulation, he toyed with her emotions. She shook her head, clinging to a slender shred of sanity. This dissolute devil had seduced more women in his life than she had met in hers. She meant nothing to him. She shook her head. "I have to leave now. I have delivered the message."

As if he had not heard her, he pulled her close, nuzzling her neck, his face buried in her hair, inhaling deeply.

He raised his head, desire phosphorescent in his gaze, and captured her chin in his hand. She watched in helpless fascination as his mouth descended. His lips met hers in a blazing kiss. His tongue traced a hot, wet path, exerting pressure on the seam of her mouth. The urge to yield, to open to him, swept her as his thunderous heartbeat resonated against her breasts. She pressed her lips firmly together.

His cupped her head and tilted it until their mouths harmonized, two halves of a perfect whole. With his other hand he stroked her cheek, traced a path down her neck. Tingles sparked to her core.

She jerked her head back and heard his knuckles thud against the wall. His grasp remained firm, his lips affixed to hers. He teased her lips with his tongue, flicking at the corners. She dizzied with her need to taste him.

She held herself rigid, her only defence against a flooding desire to discover all his mouth promised. The pressure softened and his lips moved tantalizingly against hers. His teeth nibbled at her lower lip. She gasped at the sweet streak of torment, which started in her breasts and tore to the pit of her stomach. His tongue slid between her parted lips and swept her open mouth. Struggling to draw breath, her senses swam with heady giddiness, her limbs melted with a strange invasive languor. She clung to his coat.

"Stay, Victoria," he murmured softly against her cheek. "Stay and let me love you."

Raw yearning roughened his voice and caught at her heart.

"I must not," she said, her voice a ragged whisper. "It's wrong."

"How can it be wrong? You feel it too. The needing and the wanting. I see it in your face." His voice, low and urgent, pulsed with tension.

He lowered his mouth to hers again, demanding her surrender. She closed her eyes, powerless to prevent his expert pleasuring of her enthralled body. Fearing she might fall, her hands slipped around his neck, his silky hair caressed her fingers, her sips of air filled with his scent, sandalwood, man, horses, leather.

He eased the domino off her shoulders and it whispered to the floor, a shining puddle at her feet.

"You are so beautiful."

The husky words, whispered against her mouth, vibrated in her core. She leaned into him. His strong, warm hands moved in caressing circles over her shoulders, stroked her back, cupped her bottom. He pulled her tight against his steel-hard body.

Fire-licked and brilliant sapphire, his gaze devoured her. The angles of his face stood out stark and hard in the window's light, his full mouth moist from hers. She wanted to run her hands along his jaw, touch the lips that melted her bones, feel his warm skin. She must not do this. A mewl of longing forced its way from her throat.

"Ah yes, my darling. Don't deny what you feel." His soft

whisper shivered to her core. "You'll want for nothing, I promise. And when it's over, I'll give you enough money to set up a home of your own. You'll never have to depend on anyone again. I swear it."

Cruel torturer. Her dream to be free, to make her own decisions, dangled before her, his to give.

He kissed her neck, nibbled her ear. Pleasure thrummed through her body.

"Say yes, Victoria. I promise, you won't regret it," he murmured.

She would, because he would leave her in the end.

She closed her eyes and let her head fall back, giving him access to her throat, the top of her breasts above her gown. He scattered scorching little kisses across skin that tingled all the way to the centre of her being. She wanted him.

If she did this, nothing would ever be the same. He was handsome, virile, all male, impossible to resist. She wished she wanted to resist him. It would be so much easier if she did. Like a thief in the night, like Romeo on Juliet's balcony, he had stolen into her heart and she was no match for his practised seduction. She had known it for days. When he had looked at her with hungry, soul-deep longing as she lay injured on her bed, she knew her feelings for him went far beyond attraction.

Her calm, ordered life, a millpond, deep and still, had become a raging torrent of emotions. Since meeting Travis, it was out of control, as if rushing unchecked down a mountain slope, carving out a new course only to cast itself over a jagged cliff. A leap into space, with nothing but trust in him to save her from the rocks and boulders shrouded in boiling mists below.

But in the end he'd leave her.

He groaned softly in her ear. "For God's sake, Victoria.

Tell me you will stay. I want you more than I've ever wanted anyone else."

She thrilled to his words. He did not love her, but he needed her. At least for now. And later she would have her precious freedom and her memories.

"I will stay, my lord." The words forced themselves from her lips; tears scalded the backs of her eyes as she succumbed to her defeat at his hands, his lips, his heat, and his torture of her senses.

"Simon," he said.

She opened her eyes. His smile of triumph danced in her watery gaze. "What?"

"Simon. My name is Simon. Let me hear it on your lips."

Still struggling to comprehend the enormity of what she had done, she repeated, "Simon."

He captured the sound in his mouth. His searing kiss spoke of possession. His fingers raked through her hair, he ran his hands over her back, pressing her against his hard body.

Panic filled her. For one brief moment, she fought him for control, and lost. Her body, whether she willed it or nay, moulded to him and revelled in his unyielding strength against her softness. She could not stop now.

He swept her up and carried her out of the door.

Simon drowned in the dark purple depths of her eyes. Her black curls framed her flushed face. The sound of his name, a whisper, had squeezed his chest. A pain so unutterably sweet, it left him breathless.

He ached for her. He wasn't sure he could wait until he got her upstairs. She lay in his arms like a trusting child. He would not destroy her trust. He'd love her well, shower her with jewels, make her happy for as long as she would allow it. He'd let her go whenever she wanted to leave. He swore it. As long as he could have this.

Sweet Christ, he did not deserve her, but he could not stop wild triumph from filling his soul. It swelled his heart to bursting. She was his. For now.

The front door crashed open.

Three steps up the curved staircase, Simon turned with a curse on his lips. Who dared to burst in on him?

Unbelievable. Ogden stood framed in the doorway, sunlight streaming across the marble floor.

"God damn you, Ogden. Get out of my house."

"You had to do it, didn't you? You bastard. You took Miranda from me, and now Victoria."

A black void of horror opened at Simon's feet. He glanced at Victoria, her face drained of color. Had she been Ogden's already? She'd made a point of meeting and talking with him often enough. Christ. He should have known. She had given in far too easily. Ogden had trapped him and nicely.

He tasted acrid bitterness. Idiot. Again he'd been completely fooled. Had he learned nothing about women like Victoria—like Miranda.

He lowered Victoria to her feet. Her body slid down the length of him, jasmine floated up.

Ogden's sneering gaze raked Simon.

"How could you, Victoria?" Ogden said. "I warned you about him. He's a licentious cur. He's the man who caused your brother's death, remember?" Regret filled his expression. "I would have married you one day. You didn't need to go to him."

Red haze filled Simon's vision. Ogden had already bedded the only woman he had ever really wanted since Miranda. He would kill him. Simon leaped down the stairs. Ogden managed two stumbling steps back before Simon's fist crashed into his jaw.

Ogden lay dazed on the floor, his fingers probing his chin.

Simon shook his hand to ease the numbing pain. "Get up, you coward."

Victoria brushed passed him, kneeling at his feet, touching Ogden's shoulder. She glared up. "Stop it. What are you doing?"

Simon turned his back on her. He could not bear to see her hands on Ogden. He began to rebuild the wall of ice around his heart. He had let her get too close. He would not let her do this to him.

"Get out, Ogden," he threw over his shoulder, "before I kill you."

He heard Ogden get to his feet. "Victoria, come with me."

Simon swore. "Oh, no. She's not going anywhere with you. She's going back to London."

"Don't listen to him," Ogden pleaded.

"Simon, please." She sounded angry. "Won't one of you explain what is going on here? Who is Miranda?"

Simon turned to face her. His heart slammed a warning.

"Will you explain it, or shall I?" asked Ogden, his bow ironic and his eyes full of fury.

Simon kept his face expressionless, his voice calm. "You know what will happen if you say anything more."

"Victoria is family now. As good as," Ogden said. "Either yours or mine, from the look of it."

Simon flicked an eyebrow and leaned against the carved baluster, his arms crossed over his chest. He saw the wildness in Ogden's eyes. He would not stay silent. Now she'd hear it all, as Ogden knew it. He steeled himself to bear it. "If you say another word, I'll kill you."

He heard Victoria gasp. He smiled wryly as she placed herself between him and Ogden. So she protected her lover.

"I'm not anyone's family, not yours or his," she said,

glaring from one to the other.

Her temper flushed her cheeks—that and his kisses. Why the hell did the sight cause his heart to leap? He briefly closed his eyes against her allure. He forced himself to speak coldly. "This has nothing to do with you."

"Not so," Ogden said. "You should know the sort of man with whom you are entangled."

"I am not *entangled* with anyone. But I would appreciate an explanation."

Simon felt her gaze fix on his face, sensed her growing bewilderment. He hardened his heart. It didn't matter. "You're digging your own grave, Ogden."

"I have never heard such fustian in my life. Stop it, the pair of you," Victoria said.

Ogden took a step towards her. "Miranda is my sister. Miranda Du Plessy, before she became a St John. Travis keeps her locked up in Yorkshire, isolated and a prisoner, so no one will know what he did to her."

Victoria gasped. She turned to Simon, her eyes dark and full of question. "You are married?"

Fleetingly, he wondered what she thought, what she imagined. It wouldn't be half as bad as the truth. He shrugged. Wanting Victoria Yelverton for his own had been pure madness.

Ogden's expression twisted with malice and loathing. "Miranda, my sister, was his mother, and he debauched her and cuckolded his own father."

Silence echoed in the grand hall.

Victoria shook her head as if to clear her hearing. "You seduced your mother?"

Simon's gut cringed at her look of horror. "Stepmother, actually," he said, and brushed a piece of lint from his sleeve.

Chapter Twelve

The hot knife buried in Simon's heart twisted at Victoria's expression of revulsion—a heart he'd buried deep beneath a wall of ice he thought impenetrable. He retained his faintly bored expression. Ogden must not know she had the power to wound him.

Ogden babbled on as if years of silence had dammed a torrent, which now burst its banks. "Tell her, Travis, how your father sent you away. How he couldn't bear the sight of you after what you did to Miranda."

Hated the sight of him came closer to the truth. The memory of that day was carved into his soul. His father in the library in this house, his broad back implacably turned on a miserable, contrite Simon, his shoulders shaking with suppressed agony and Miranda watching, her eyes full of malicious triumph at Simon's fall from grace. His father had loved his young bride and Simon had destroyed all his hopes for the future, his cherished love and his pride.

Simon never set eyes on him again.

He kept his voice matter-of-fact. "I went away to school, just like you, Ogden."

"But not everyone went to the school you attended, did they, Travis?" Ogden taunted. "Did they teach you well?"

Simon never allowed thoughts of Blackhurst Academy to enter his mind. He raised an eyebrow. "What has that got to do with anything?"

Wild-eyed, his tongue flickering over dry lips, Ogden turned to Victoria. "His father sent him away to a school in the north to learn discipline and self-control. Miranda told me all about it." He swung around to Simon, his white-edged mouth twisted. "She told me how you wrote, begging to be allowed to come home. But they never let you, did they? And when your father died, you had Miranda locked away out of revenge."

Simon shook his head. "Your sister is a sick woman. And you know it."

"Liar. You keep her there, guarded and alone, when she should be here enjoying life, free to live and love again. All she wants is to come home to her family."

What did Ogden expect him to say in own his defense? Was he to reveal his stepmother's madness? A danger to herself and those around her, she had to stay where she was. Simon had broken his father's heart, but he wasn't going to bury a good man's reputation by revealing the truth about the woman he had loved in his old age and the son he hated.

"Simon?" Victoria's soft voice broke into his thoughts, her expression pleading with him to deny it.

He shrugged. "She is well cared for. She has the best doctors and the best care. Her illness requires her to remain where she is."

Ogden balled his fists and took a step forward. "Only because you pay them to say so."

Confusion reigned in Victoria's expression. Her eyes, large in her pale face, turned in Simon's direction, begging him to explain the charges Ogden leveled at him. Let her believe what she liked. He would never release Miranda.

He dropped his gaze and picked at a strand of long, black hair that clung to the lapel of his coat. He let it drift to the floor, watching its progress. It lay on the white marble tile, a fine black question mark.

Ogden took another step and Simon straightened. A physical threat he could deal with. Take pleasure in.

"There's more, isn't there, Travis?" Ogden's eyes blazed with triumph, just like Miranda's had that awful day.

Simon stiffened. Damn him to hell. Yes. There was more and worse. The real reason Miranda had turned his father against Simon until the day he died. But Ogden wouldn't dare reveal it. And Simon would not oblige him. "I think it's time you left, Ogden. Unless you want to find yourself without a feather to fly with. I promise you, if you say one more word I will invoke the necessary clause in my father's will. Your family will be penniless, and they will all know who to blame."

Ogden glared, but pressed his lips together. He needed Simon's money too much to risk losing it for revenge.

Victoria stood unmoving, staring from one to the other. The enormity of Ogden's accusations seemed to have left her stunned and speechless. Simon prayed she would remain so.

He pulled the bell. "You really should not have come here alone, Miss Yelverton. It's not good *ton*. You will oblige me by returning immediately to London and Miss Allenby."

She put out a hand as if to protest, then it fell to her side.

Surely she didn't want to stay after all she had heard? Or did she think he'd let her go with Ogden? Not a chance. He'd kill Ogden first.

The three of them stood in icy silence until the butler answered the summons.

"Bring the carriage around immediately," Simon said. "Assign one of the maids to attend Miss Yelverton. Viscount Ogden is leaving now."

The butler, his face bland and his gaze distant, turned to do his master's bidding.

Ogden cursed. "You really are a cold-hearted devil. You don't care about the innocent woman you keep locked up to protect you from your crimes."

A short and bitter laugh escaped Simon's lips. "Miranda is hardly innocent. A rather willing participant, I would say."

The sound of Victoria's gasp of horror cleaved a hole in his chest. After his earlier behavior with her, how could she not believe Ogden? It was better this way. His lack of control today proved he could not trust himself with Victoria, even if she was Ogden's pawn. Now she would stay away from him.

Unable to bear the condemnation in her eyes, Simon gestured to the door. "Ogden, perhaps you would oblige me by leaving my house. I suggest you crawl back to your cesspit."

Ogden raked him with a pale, scathing glance. "One of these days, Satan, you will receive your just deserts."

Simon allowed himself a small cynical smile. "If that day ever comes, Ogden, I'm quite certain you will be the first to know." Except he'd received his just deserts over and over, and, if today were anything to go by, he would continue to do so for the rest of his life.

Uttering an oath, Ogden flung the front door open and strode to his waiting curricle.

Simon raised an eyebrow. "His manners really don't improve."

"The carriage is at the front door, my lord," the butler announced.

Simon nodded. "And the maid?"

"Waiting inside it, my lord."

"Good. Shall we?" Simon held his arm out to Victoria. "Allow me to escort you to your carriage, Miss Yelverton."

For one sickening moment, Simon thought she might refuse to touch him, then she inclined her head and laid her small hand on his sleeve.

She was stiff-backed and silent. Her fingers trembled against his arm as she allowed him to assist her out into the waiting coach. She hesitated, one foot on the step. Despair he could ill afford washed over him at her questioning glance.

"Simon—"

"Good day, Miss Yelverton." He bowed.

A leaden weight pressed down on his chest at her pained expression. He forced himself to breathe.

She lowered her head and climbed inside, the faint click of the closing door a stern reminder. She was forbidden fruit.

Eleven. The soft knock came right on time. Simon steeled himself to preserve his outward calm.

Having followed Victoria back to Town specifically for this purpose, there was no sense in putting it off. He steeled his spine.

He strolled to the door and opened it. "Come in, Miss Yelverton."

Her manner subdued, Victoria avoided looking at him as she sat. Unlike her. Simon retired behind his desk and took in her pale face and the dark circles shadowing her eyes. If she weren't careful she would suffer a decline in health. More blame to lay at his door.

"Thank you for agreeing to see me this morning. I wish to inform you of the plans for your future," he said.

She looked startled, then hopeful. "Have you heard from my aunt?"

Her aunt. He'd forgotten the damn aunt. He glanced down at the pile of letters on his desk. "Yes, actually, I have."

"So I am to go to her, then?"

Not bloody likely. "No."

"Why not?"

"Your aunt, it seems, is unable to be of assistance to you at this time."

She frowned. "What did she say?" She reached out a hand. "May I see the letter?"

Simon stiffened at her lack of trust. Bitter as the thought tasted, he couldn't blame her. Yesterday he'd been a selfish cur, putting his own desires before her welfare, but no more. He wouldn't let her see the letter. Her aunt was a vindictive, moralizing old witch. "The letter is addressed to me."

"She is my aunt. I think I ought to know exactly what she said."

"If you must." Simon picked up the envelope and pulled out a single sheet of paper. It was short and to the point. He read out loud. " 'Dear Lord Travis, Thank you for your missive of last week. I regret to inform you . . .' " Simon skipped the next few lines. They were far too insulting to Victoria, her father and her brother. " '. . . that no woman who has spent a night under the roof of such an amoral, licentious libertine,' " Simon looked up. "She means me, I believe."

Vivid red spots of color appeared on Victoria's cheeks. She straightened in her chair.

He continued, " '. . . is welcome in my home.' Then there is some more regarding the nature of my moral turpitude. She goes on, 'Even if I were disposed to open my door to my niece, I do not have the financial wherewithal to undertake such an unwanted expense.' And more in the same vein." He threw the letter on the desk. "I won't bore you with it."

Mortification rampant on her lovely face, she dropped her gaze to her hands in her lap. "I apologize, my lord, for my aunt's rudeness."

"Indeed, Miss Yelverton, you need feel no embarrassment on my account. I can assure you I have been called worse and my feelings are not at all hurt."

The blush deepened. Now what had he said? Then he recalled his words of yesterday, almost the same words, under very different circumstances. He sighed. This wasn't going to be easy.

She raised her eyes and met his gaze square on. "I really cannot stay here any longer."

After what she now knew, it came as no surprise. At least Ogden's interruption had prevented a worse disaster. Eventually she would have learned the truth, and Simon had discovered he couldn't stand the thought of it.

Damn it all. It didn't matter what she thought of him; he had a duty to perform. He swept her arguments aside with a dismissive gesture. "I don't agree. We will continue as planned. You will make every effort to find a suitor and marry well before the end of the Season."

Like a pebble dropped in a grotto pool at dusk, her dark eyes reflected ripples of emotion at his harsh words. "And if I don't?" she asked.

Cursed to spend his life hurting those he cared for, he distanced himself, retreated behind his safe wall of ice. Blessed numbness held him in its thrall.

He placed his elbows on his desk and steepled his fingers in front of his face. "You will. A dowry of two thousand pounds a year is more than enough for the most fastidious of men. They will flock to your door, Miss Yelverton."

"I don't have a dowry. And I don't want your money. What will people think?"

"They will think I am your kind benefactor, providing you with a means to make your way in life. What else should they think?" It didn't matter if people thought she was his mistress. Money solved anything.

His stomach clenched at the flush that stained her cheeks with shame. His shame. But her formidable pride, the stiffening of her graceful shoulders, the arrogant tilt of her head, pressed home the dagger she had thrust into his heart in Hampshire. "I won't accept it."

Stubborn to a fault. He held his gaze steady and quirked an insolent brow. "You will. And in return you will do something to oblige me."

"There is nothing I would do to oblige you."

"I think there is. You will promise not to repeat anything you heard yesterday."

Shock crossed her face. "You think you have to buy my silence, the same way you buy Viscount Ogden's?"

Her fury lashed him. He curved his mouth in a self-mocking smile. "Nevertheless, you will accept the funds. Maria will make sure your changed financial circumstances are known. On your death, the funds will go to any children from your marriage."

Children. Yearning ripped his guts apart. What beautiful children she would have. Dark-haired, spirited, maybe with blue eyes. But not his.

"What if I don't marry?"

Knowing her, he'd expected the question. "Then the money will be yours to do with as you wish. There will be more than enough to set up your own establishment. My lawyer will be your trustee. You will never need to see me again."

His bleak future stretched before him. It was the right thing to do. Best for her. His needs did not count.

She hesitated, then rose slowly to her feet. "I thank you for your generous offer, but I cannot accept."

He'd wondered what he would do if she said no. It was a great deal of money. A small fortune. He just hadn't believed she'd refuse it. No woman he had ever met would refuse such a sum.

He leaned back in his chair. "The money is there, whether you want it or no, provided you say nothing, and provided you do not marry Ogden." She would get nothing if she went anywhere near the bastard.

She tossed her head. So he'd made her angry. Better than making her cry.

"I don't want it and you will not tell me who I will or will not marry."

"Ogden will not marry you without the money."

"What do I have to say to make you understand I don't want anything from you? Not your money, nothing at all."

She meant she did not want him. He denied the pain around his heart and strove to remain unmoved. "It's settled. I arranged it with my lawyer this morning."

She opened her mouth to argue.

He wanted this over. Now. If she didn't leave soon, he'd forget all his principles and try to seduce her into running away with him. Persuade her to go somewhere where Ogden and the rest of the Du Plessys wouldn't find them. Somewhere he could make love to her all day long and never see another damned person as long as he lived.

Why torment himself? If he asked, she would say no. His honor demanded he ask, even though he knew he could seduce her into coming with him. Her passionate nature would surrender to him, just as it had yesterday. She deserved so much more. She deserved a good man, a man who did not awake each and every day loathing himself.

"Miss Yelverton, I will not discuss this any further. I am leaving Town again this afternoon and you will be gone from this house by the time I return at the end of the summer. Married or not. Maria has my instructions. She will accept any reasonable proposal on my behalf."

He rose to his feet. "If you will take my advice, you will

marry the Marquess of Lethbridge. He is a fine man with many good qualities." Ian would protect her.

Hurt flashed in her eyes, followed so swiftly by anger, he convinced himself he hadn't seen it. Her top teeth worried her bottom lip for a moment. "You want me to marry your friend?"

No. He wanted her safe and cared for. "You could do a lot worse."

Her lip curled. "Worse than a drunkard? The only man worse would be you."

It hurt like hell to hear her say it. His blood turned to ice. She despised him and she didn't even know the worst of it. He flicked a brow with practiced insouciance. "It was a suggestion, nothing more."

"A suggestion I do not intend to follow."

"As you wish." He bowed, signaling their discussion was at an end.

He watched her stalk towards the door, her slight frame diminutive against the heavy oak panels. A grieving sense of loss flooded his heart.

She stopped at the door and turned to face him. She gazed at him for one long moment. Her voice, when she finally spoke, was low and husky. "Was it true? What the viscount said?"

Bloody hell. "Was what true?"

"You said Miranda was your stepmother, but you did not admit to Ogden's charge."

Shrewd Miss Yelverton. But his guilt, or lack of it, didn't matter. He couldn't care what she thought. More important, his father's memory must not be sullied by Ogden and his lying bitch of a sister. "What did you expect, Miss Yelverton? That I would beg forgiveness? Plead my case?"

He'd done that all those years ago. Knelt at Miranda's

feet, tears running down his child's face, clutching at her skirts, begging her to intercede with his father. She had given him a small cold smile and stepped over him. His father had believed her accusations. Miranda was Simon's first and only taste of love, and she would be his last.

Self-revulsion tasted like bile in his mouth. He would never beg for affection or help from a woman again. He did not need love. A transient emotion, its withdrawal hurt far too much.

She regarded him steadily. "I expected you to tell the truth."

"It really is not your business, Miss Yelverton."

She flinched. Her wounded expression flayed his taut nerves. He had a brief, wild compulsion to deny his guilt, explain it was not his fault.

He buried it. He'd just be lying to himself and to her. He'd earned his father's eternal hatred with good cause. And now he paid the price. Eternal silence.

Sneering at his own weak will, he notched one sure arrow in his bow. He flashed her a mocking smile. "By the way, Miss Yelverton, you will be pleased to learn I have found an exceedingly willing and very lovely replacement for Miss Eckford. We leave for Italy this afternoon."

Shock widened her beautiful eyes. She wrenched open the door and fled. He heard her footsteps as she ran up the stairs and the echo of her chamber door slamming. It was done.

He walked over to the console and stared down at the green-jacketed, porcelain elf perched on the fallen log. It would always remind him of her. The way she'd run her fingertips over it, a brief yet lingering caress. He'd made her angry on that occasion too. She'd almost thrown it at him. He smiled wryly and picked it up, weighing it in his hand.

Cold china. He tossed it in the fireplace. The sound of

splintering porcelain matched his shattered soul.

Victoria threw herself facedown on her bed and slammed her fist into the bolster, wishing it were Travis's sneering face beneath her fists, wishing she could punish him for the sardonic smile of amusement at the shock his words had produced. He'd made her feel sordid, when only hours ago she had felt so wonderfully alive in his arms. She swallowed hard. She would not let him make her cry.

She turned over onto her back and stared up at the rose-pink canopy. What had she expected from this interview? For some reason, she had anticipated Travis would deny Ogden's damning accusations, despite his refusal to do so yesterday. Instead, he'd callously announced he'd found a new paramour. Ogden's interruption had been timely indeed. How foolish to place her trust in such a cynical, cold-eyed devil. Hadn't she learned anything about men?

For all his icy calm, Travis had been unable to disguise the bleakness in his eyes as he all but admitted his culpability. She'd seen it at St John's Hall and again now, when she had offered him the chance to deny his guilt. Awareness stabbed her with a blade honed to keenness. He wanted her to believe the worst of him.

She slid off the bed and paced across to the window. Something in Ogden's words, and in Travis's replies, did not ring true. Intuitively, she felt as if Travis used Ogden's damning exposition as an excuse to avoid a far more awful truth. He hid something beneath his cold exterior. Whatever it was, he did not intend to share it with her. What could be worse than what she had heard?

Steam from her breath fogged the window and she wiped the mist away. What did he have to gain by making a false admission? Stupid idiot, besotted fool. He wanted to marry her off to Lethbridge. She'd spoiled his plans with Cassandra and in the heat of the moment he'd offered to take her instead. In the cold light of day, now his anger at her deceit had subsided, he wanted to be rid of her. What better way to accomplish it than to hand her over to his friend like a used coat? He cared nothing for her.

He could keep his money and his friend and she wished him joy with his new woman. Now Victoria would go somewhere he'd never find her.

The view of the square blurred. No mist obscured the glass this time and she dashed her hand across her eyes. She leaned her forehead against the pane, cool against her skin. Fool. He wouldn't even bother to look.

Chapter Thirteen

"Today?" Julia stared at Victoria in disbelief.

Victoria sipped her tea. "Yes."

"How can you possibly expect me to come up with something suitable in only two days?"

Expect was too strong a word. Victoria slumped against the blue-striped sofa in the Lady Rutherford's drawing room. She had to leave London today, or tomorrow at the latest, or face the very real prospect of a marriage proposal from some fortune hunter or other. Word of her generous dowry would flash through the ranks of the *ton*. She gazed at Julia's shocked face. "I didn't. I just hoped."

Apple-green silk skirts rustling softly, Julia got up from behind the tea tray and came around to sit beside her. "Why not wait until tomorrow. I'm sure I can find something better by then."

"Better?"

"Dash it, Victoria. I did hear of one situation. But it's not at all what I would wish for you. This woman has a history of losing servants very quickly. She's a veritable tartar."

Victoria grasped Julia's hand. "I have to take it, Julia. Travis and Maria are trying to wed me to Lethbridge. I can't live with a man who drinks every time he has a problem. It's what my father did and what Michael did and I won't go through it with a husband."

A strained expression passed across Julia's face. "Lethbridge?"

"Yes. They both mentioned him today as a likely prospect."

Julia dropped her gaze to their joined hands. "I see."

Victoria's heart sank. If Julia agreed with Travis, she'd lose her only ally. "I'm afraid if I stay, they'll wear me down. I've already spent too long enjoying a life of luxury. It's getting harder all the time to face the prospect of earning a living."

Regret mirrored in her expression, Julia stared at her. "You are sure it's what you want?"

"You know it is."

With a jerky movement, her hair a fiery halo against the light from the window, Julia rose to her feet. "Wait here. I'll get the address."

Victoria got up and paced the elegant room. She appreciated Julia's concern, but saw no other choice. Any delay and she would once more be swept up by Travis's machinations.

She'd seen him from her bedroom window first thing this morning. His stern features satanic in the sharp early sunlight, his strength underscored by his control of the skittish stallion, he'd glanced up at the house. For a brief instant their gazes clashed, a distant meeting of two lost souls, and then she wasn't sure he'd seen her at all. He'd galloped away, rending the connection. Forever.

At breakfast, Benton had told her of the earl's plan to ride Diablo to St John's Hall and from there to continue on to the continent. He wasn't expected back for months.

Their lack of a farewell was for the best. They had said everything necessary yesterday and by the time he learned of her departure, her life would be settled on a new path. She sighed. Whether she married Lethbridge or simply disappeared, it made no difference to him. For some reason she wished it did.

Swiping away a foolish tear, she pasted a bright smile on her lips. The future awaited, a future she'd chosen.

Moments later, her face wooden, Julia returned with a slip of paper in her hand. "Here's the address."

"Thank you." Victoria hugged Julia's unyielding form. "Please don't worry about me, Ju. I'll do just fine."

Julia's bitter laugh struck a sour chord. "I'm sure you will." Then, as if she regretted her brusqueness, she hesitated. "Do you need money?"

"No. I have a little. Enough to get me to . . ." Victoria glanced at the paper in her hand, "Selwick in Shropshire. Well, that's certainly far enough away. Oh, Ju, I will miss you. I can't thank you enough."

Julia made a face, then threw her arms around Victoria. "Take care of yourself. Write to me when you can."

Unable to speak around her threatening tears, Victoria nodded. She doubted she would ever see her friend again. They would move in very different circles from now on.

She picked up her reticule, collected her hat and coat from the stolid Rutherford butler and made her way out to the waiting carriage. All she had to do now was pack a small bag and slip out of Travis Place unnoticed.

"He's doing better every day, my lord," the St John's Hall stable master said from his perch on the top rail of the paddock fence.

Simon nodded in satisfaction. Diablo's colt, his coat black like his sire's, had improved by leaps and bounds these past few days. Holding the leading string taut and firm, Simon revolved with the yearling circling the paddock.

A fine colt, with an even gait and long legs, he had

Diablo's strength and the fine lines of his mother's Arabian blood. Simon had named him Devil's Spawn and he had the makings of a champion.

Simon wiped the sweat running into his eyes on his shirtsleeve. After a cloudy start, the day had turned out sunny and hot, and he'd been putting the young horse through his paces for more than an hour. Nothing like physical labor to clear the mind and tire the body. The exercise didn't thaw the frozen lump in his chest.

"Someone's coming, my lord," the stable master said.

Strange. Simon glanced up. Everyone thought he was in Italy.

"It's the Marquess of Lethbridge, my lord."

Lethbridge? Unease stirred in his gut. Simon brought the colt to a stand. "Very well. That's enough for today." He threw the rein to the other man, pulled a handkerchief from his pocket and wiped his face and hands.

He vaulted the paddock fence as Lethbridge drew his horse alongside. Simon ran a hand down the chestnut's sweating, foam-flecked neck. "Still riding this carthorse, I see. What brings you here? I thought you agreed to keep an eye on Miss Yelverton."

Lethbridge nodded a greeting and dismounted, hitching the reins to the fence. "Thor is nothing like a carthorse. I need a big animal. Your lightweight racehorse would collapse under me in half an hour."

Ill kempt, Lethbridge's red-rimmed eyes had a haunted quality, and a rough stubble of fair beard shadowed his cheeks and chin. As usual, he appeared to need a drink to steady his nerves.

Panic slithered in Simon's gut at Lethbridge's avoidance of his question and his sharp stare at the stable master leading the colt out of the paddock. He grabbed Lethbridge's shoulder.

"What's wrong? Has something happened to Miss Yelverton?"

"Bloody hell. How did you know?"

How? Every nerve stretched tight. The fact that nothing about Victoria escaped his attention was no one's concern but his own. He glared at Lethbridge. "For God's sake, tell me what is wrong."

"She's gone."

The word roused his ire to a lashing, venomous rage. "Gone? Gone where?"

"I'm afraid I don't know."

Unreasoning anger darkened his mind. Confident he'd left her protected in London, Simon had come here seeking a shred of peace. Lethbridge had let him down again. "Damn you to hell. Drunk again, Lethbridge?"

Lethbridge grimaced. "Christ, Simon. Cut me some line. She disappeared, and so did one of my men. I need to ask you some questions."

Excuses didn't wash. Lethbridge had let her slip through his fingers and now he wanted to ask questions? He curled his lip. "Don't waste my time. I have to return to London to sort out your mess."

Lethbridge slumped against the rail. "Simon, I've ridden for hours to get here, the least you could do is offer me some refreshment and hear what I have to say."

Lethbridge must have been on the road since first light. Simon nodded grimly. He'd listen to the full story from the sot before he left. "Come up to the house. My man will take care of your horse."

Leading the way, he passed through the barn and crossed the gravel courtyard to the side door. A scullery maid staggered out with a bucket of water and called greeting to a stable boy polishing a pile of tack. The smell of cooking announced the preparation of the evening meal. Simon liked the business side of the house, its disorderly activity a stark contrast to its noble front. It reminded Simon of the human condition, a bland outer facade hiding the inner turmoil of the guts and the heart of the dwelling.

Sick at heart and anxious to leave for London, Simon moved ahead swiftly. He ushered Lethbridge into the small room at the back of the house he used instead of his father's study. He never set foot in the rooms his father had used.

Lethbridge lowered his bulk into the one padded armchair in the room, a moth-eaten remnant from Simon's grandfather's days, and Simon perched on the corner of his battle-scarred schoolroom desk, a relic of abuse by countless generations of young St Johns.

"Brandy?" Simon asked.

Lethbridge stared at the bottle in Simon's hand. Need licked at his expression. "No."

"Something else?"

"Tea." Lethbridge sounded as if he had swallowed grit.

If Lethbridge battled his demon, Simon wasn't about to comment. "Tea it is." He rang the bell and the footman appeared within moments to take his request.

"Now. Out with it," Simon said.

"I haven't seen Miss Yelverton since the night we went to the theater. You already know she cried off from Vauxhall. I was busy looking for your scar-faced attacker, so I was glad she didn't want my escort after you left."

"And?"

"And I left a friend of mine watching the house. I also told your sharp-witted footman, Wilson, my man was there, so he wouldn't get suspicious. I spent my time visiting every tavern in the City looking for our villain."

"No wonder you're too sick for a brandy," Simon said,

unable to contain his contempt.

Lethbridge winced. "I swear, I haven't touched a drop since the night your carriage was held up." He leaned forward, his arms resting on his knees, his golden head bowed. "You could all have been killed and I would never have forgiven myself. I'm off it for good."

He'd had it with Lethbridge's self-absorption. Simon got to his feet. "Until next time."

"Jesus, Simon. You're a hard bastard. You need my help."

Leashing his desire to hurt someone—anyone—Simon exhaled, burying his anger deep, nurturing it for when it would serve his purpose. He'd give Lethbridge one last chance. Only one. Right now, Victoria could be in terrible danger. Bile rose up to choke him. "Very well. I'm listening."

Lethbridge blew out a breath. "I learned the name of the fellow we are looking for. Quigley. But when I got back to my lodgings last night, a note awaited me from your cousin. Miss Yelverton left yesterday afternoon without a word. My man and Wilson are also missing."

Simon swore savagely. Had someone taken Victoria to get back at him? He slammed his fist on the desk. "Christ. I should never have left." He glared at Lethbridge. "I thought you could at least handle a simple task like guarding a woman."

"Damn it, Simon. We assumed they wanted you, not Victoria."

Once more, Simon reined in his anger. "You're right. I thought I'd flush them out by coming here alone."

"I guessed as much. I have a man here watching you, too."

Simon ran a hand through his hair. "Damn you, Lethbridge. You never told me. Your men probably frightened them off, or they are in league with whoever is doing this."

Lethbridge narrowed his eyes. "Not likely. My men are loyal. They might not be under my command anymore, but I would trust them with my life and the life of any friend of mine."

At the footman's knock, Simon got up and let him in, waiting in silence until he placed a silver tray with a pot of tea and two cups on the sideboard. Simon handed him the brandy decanter. "Put this in the library, please." He might as well remove temptation from Lethbridge's sight.

Lethbridge got up and poured the tea.

Simon slouched against the desk. "Devil take it. What do we do now?"

"Did Miss Yelverton have a reason to leave Travis Place?"

Simon bristled and then caught Lethbridge's shrewd gaze. Several good reasons for Victoria wishing to leave occurred to Simon. "She never wanted to be there in the first place."

"If she left of her own free will, there may be nothing to worry about. My man followed her here four nights ago and came to see me when she arrived back in Town. He's probably following her and will report back when she reaches her destination. Here, take your tea."

The bone-china cup and saucer seemed doll-house-size in Lethbridge's large hand. Simon took it mechanically. "It's possible, I suppose."

Lethbridge gave Simon a penetrating stare. "Strange she didn't leave a note."

It wasn't the first time she'd disappeared without saying anything. Ogden. Simon would kill him. And her. He clenched his jaw. Better she was with Ogden than dead or hurt, he supposed. He took a deep breath. "Perhaps she forgot."

Lethbridge sipped at his tea. "Any idea where she might have gone?"

The possibility she might be with Ogden twisted his gut. He didn't want to believe it. "One thing is certain, she didn't go to Harrowgate."

"Harrowgate?" Wheels turned behind Lethbridge's questioning gaze.

"She has an aunt there. She definitely wouldn't go there."

"Exceedingly helpful, that. One place we can cross off the list."

Simon stared at the cup and saucer in his hand and took a mouthful. Disgusting pap. He put the cup down on the desk. "I don't have a clue where she would have gone. Perhaps Maria might know?"

"The day before she disappeared, she visited the Rutherford's townhouse," Lethbridge said.

"Lady Julia." Simon rubbed his rough chin. A surge of hope stopped his breath as he recalled the wicked gleam in Julia's eye when she sauntered out of Victoria's bedroom. "Now that is interesting. Those two are as thick as thieves. I'll bet a pony Lady Julia is involved somehow." Simon leaped to his feet and strode to the door.

"Where are you going?"

"To London, of course, to speak to Lady Julia Garforth."

"I'd like to speak to the man I left here first, if you don't mind."

"How long will it take? The sooner I have a word with Lady Julia, the sooner I believe we will know Miss Yelverton's whereabouts."

"Not long." Lethbridge gave him a sly grin. "Ring the bell for the footman who just brought the tea. He's probably waiting for us to call him in."

The young man appeared the instant Simon dragged on the bell rope. Of average height and build, brownish hair and brown eyes, he blended into his surroundings. He paused in the doorway.

"It's all right, James, his lordship knows," Lethbridge said. "Have you learned anything while you've been here?"

Baffled, Simon shook his head. How could he not have realized Lethbridge had planted a man in his house? Because he'd been too busy trying not to think.

"I saw your man," James said. "He came into the Bell and Cat two nights ago. Scar over his right eye, burly, balding with long brown hair. He's the Marquis of Northdown's gamekeeper."

Ogden. Simon's worst nightmare come true. He cursed.

"Aye," James agreed. "Seems Quigley is away quite a bit. Apparently he often accompanies Viscount Ogden. The viscount has taken up residence at the Du Plessy house."

If Ogden had remained here, then he couldn't be responsible for Victoria's disappearance. "Ogden arrived the same day Victoria did," Simon said. "Seems like they have nothing to do with it."

"There were at least five of them at the holdup," Lethbridge pointed out. "Anything else, James?"

"Not really, sir. Quigley had a couple of pints with me and left the inn around midnight. Seemed very interested in the doings of the earl here and who else was at the Hall. That kind of thing. I followed him when he left. He went back to a small cottage on the Du Plessy land. Then I came back here. He didn't show up at the Bell last night."

Simon exchanged a glance with Lethbridge. Quigley remained a suspect.

"Thank you, James," Lethbridge said. "You can head back to London now. The earl is also going back to Town."

"Right, Major." The young man cut short a salute and grinned sheepishly.

"Not major anymore, James. If you don't mind."

"Yes, my lord. Sorry."

"You can continue to keep any eye on his lordship here, until further notice."

"Not necessary," Simon protested. "What are you going to do?"

"Follow up with Quigley."

"Then take James with you. I am only going to pay a call on Lady Ju."

Lethbridge nodded. "Very well. But wait for me in Town. We'll decide what to do when I get there. You might want to enlist Rutherford."

Simon watched Lethbridge set his cup and saucer on the tray. Despite his seedy appearance, the man had a new purposefulness. He seemed more like the man Simon had grown to respect when he first met him. The man he had been, before he ran aground on Genevieve Longbourne's rocky shore.

He followed Lethbridge out of the room. Right now, Simon needed to talk to Lady Julia Garforth. He hoped she could allay his sense of foreboding.

The imposing cream door slammed in Victoria's face. The lady of the house had taken one scathing look at her husband's leer as Victoria stood on the doorstep and announced the position of governess was filled.

Victoria glanced at the paper in her hand and back at the grimly silent front door. Now what was she to do? Disappointed, she turned her back on the gray stone house and began the trudge back to the nearest village. It lay six miles along the road she had traveled with the carter from Wrexford, full of high hopes, first thing this morning. With most of her money gone, used to pay for her four-day journey, and now no work, her circumstances had changed drastically.

Beautiful Shropshire stretched before her, green in the valleys, smoky gray and purple on the surrounding rocky hills, and peaceful in the afternoon sun. The road ahead undulated into the distance. And when she got to the village, what then? Her stomach rumbled an answer. Food. She would buy some bread and then seek employment. Someone must need her services.

She hefted her valise into her other hand, squared her shoulders and lengthened her stride. She did not want to be out on the road after dark.

More than an hour later a small, irritating pebble found its way into her shoe. The road was rough and rutted enough without this added torture. Victoria climbed up the bank at the verge and, not wanting to be observed with her skirts up as she removed her shoe, put down her valise and climbed over the low stone wall. She unfastened the buckle, removed her dusty, badly scuffed shoe and shook out the offending stone. Blast. It had shredded the foot of her stocking, and she only had one other pair.

She rubbed her aching foot. Finding it soothing, she removed her other shoe and wiggled her toes. A short rest would do her good. She leaned back against the wall and closed her eyes against the bright sun. She had traveled by common stage buoyed up by the prospect of starting a new life; now weariness at her failure invaded her bones.

The drumming of rapid hoofbeats from the direction of the village startled her. She rubbed her eyes. Heavens. She'd fallen asleep and now the sun dipped toward the horizon. She couldn't have slept half the afternoon away. She definitely did not want anyone on the road to see her looking like a gypsy.

She shrank back against the wall, her pulse racing. Oh, no.

Her valise lay on the other side. She clenched her hands. *Don't let him see it.*

The horse passed without a pause and the moment it faded out of earshot, she clambered over the wall and started to refasten her shoes.

Oh Lord. A carriage trundled along from the same direction. One shoe still in her hand, she jumped to her feet. She glanced around, trying to decide whether she should disappear behind the wall or stay put. The road, which had been deserted for most of the day, had suddenly become as bustling as Piccadilly. She smiled at her own foolishness. Two travelers—three, if she counted herself—did not make a road busy.

She bent to replace her other shoe as the carriage rumbled over the brow of the hill. She stood up to watch it pass. It was a gentleman's curricle from its appearance, sky blue, with chestnut horses, but the driver looked rough. He wore a battered hat pulled low over his face and the collar of his shabby coat pulled up around his ears. Odd to be so heavily garbed on such a warm day. He drew up the carriage a short way down the road.

"Miss?"

She ignored the shout, bending once more to fasten her buckle.

"Excuse me, miss?"

Her nape prickled with a strange premonition. She was alone with only bare hills and sheep in every direction.

"Is this the way to Shrewsbury?" he called out.

She stood up. "I'm sorry, I don't know. I'm a stranger here." She groaned. How could she admit to being stranger? Trying not to trip over her loose shoe, she picked up her valise and hurried in the opposite direction.

Behind her, she heard sounds of the carriage turning

around. The driver cursed at his horses. She didn't dare look back. Why, oh, why had she not climbed over the wall?

He drew alongside.

Victoria kept walking, a sort of step-drag-shuffle, as she tried retain her dignity and her shoe.

"Can I give you a lift, miss?"

She kept her gaze fixed straight ahead.

He flicked his whip and pulled ahead of her.

A grateful sigh rushed from her body at his departure. Her relief was short-lived. He stopped the carriage just ahead and jumped down. Victoria's heart began to pound uncomfortably. She glanced left and right. She would never be able to climb the wall before he caught up to her. She halted and watched him warily, backing away as he got closer.

"Stay your distance, sirrah."

He peered at her. "Now then, miss. I only want to give you a ride. Can't leave you out here walking all by yourself."

He wasn't a local. His accent hailed from the west, nothing like the northern voices she had heard these last two days.

"I don't need a lift. I'm expecting someone."

His straggly moustache waggled as his lips split in a grin and revealed yellow-stained teeth. "Are you now? Then I better hurry up." He lunged for her.

Victoria started to run back the way she had come. Her shoe went flying. Sharp rocks dug into her stockinged foot. He grabbed her arm and stuck a foot between hers. She crashed face first to the ground, her breath jolted out of her.

Sitting up, she pressed her stinging palms against her ribs. Tears blurred her eyes at the pain in her hands and knees. A shadow blocked the sun and she stared up at her attacker.

He grunted. "Up you come, missy. It's not me you got to be ascared of."

Still too shaken to run, Victoria shuddered when he hauled her up by her shoulders and started to dust her off. "The master won't be happy if I damages you."

She pushed his hands away. "Who is your master?"

" 'Nuff said. Now why doesn't you get in that there boneshaker, nice like, and everything will be just fine."

Prickles of fear trickled down her back. "No." She swung her valise at his head.

He dodged and grinned. The disgusting smell of his breath, beer, onions and cigars, turned her stomach. She backed away. Before she realized his intent, he grabbed her around the waist and threw her over his shoulder, one hand pressed firmly against her spine, his other arm grasped around her knees. "Let me go!" she screamed.

Seemingly oblivious to her flailing hands on his back and her feet kicking his chest, he toted her to the waiting coach.

Chapter Fourteen

The miles flashed by. Simon knew they were almost there and he let Diablo have his head. His ire had risen with every mile. After a highly unpleasant interview with Lady Julia, who had denied all knowledge of where Victoria had gone, Philip had threatened to speak to their mother. Julia had finally admitted giving Victoria the address of a potential employer.

She wants nothing to do with you, Travis. Why don't you just leave her alone? The words echoed in his mind and stuck in his gullet. Fine. Victoria didn't have to have anything to do with him. But he would not allow her to turn herself into a drudge for some petty member of the gentry in the wilds of nowhere.

Nor was she entitled to leave his house without a word to anyone. Maria had been beside herself with worry about the headstrong, idiotic wench.

When he found her he was going to . . . What? Eaten by black fear and the resentment it caused, he mulled it over. If he had to, he would drag her out of her employer's house by her long, black hair. He would tell them she was his runaway sister. Or wife. Even better. Then he'd put her over his knee and slap her shapely bottom until she couldn't sit down. He would teach her to defy him and to frighten everyone with her disappearance. She would think twice about ever trying anything so nonsensical again. None of his thoughts made him feel any easier in his mind.

Something grabbed his attention.

Simon slowed Diablo to a walk and stroked his neck. The Grange in Selwick lay just ahead, but something niggled at his mind. He glanced over his shoulder at the snaking road behind him.

He'd seen something. A dark shadow. A lumpy black shape on the verge, when all he'd seen for miles were dry stone walls and green grass.

He shook his head. It was nothing. A rock, a bundle of rags. Nothing. Then why this compelling urge to go back and look? He stared up the road toward the Grange. Victoria was there, slaving away for some wretch of a woman. Sent there by Julia Garforth. Damn her.

He'd had a few hard words with that young lady. Only after Simon pointed out all of the evils of Victoria's situation, alone and friendless in some stranger's home, had she crumbled and told him the whole story.

He clenched his jaw. He never ignored his instincts. They made him unerringly successful at cards and everything else. He wheeled Diablo around.

"It will only take a moment or two to check it out," he murmured, the animal's heavy breathing loud in the quiet air. They'd walk back. Diablo could use the rest.

Then he heard it, faintly, back the way he had ridden. A female screaming.

"Sorry, old fellow." He urged the horse forward with his knees. "Seems like we may be needed in a hurry."

Simon couldn't quite believe his eyes as he came over the rise. A woman, her bottom high and her gray gown pulled up to expose slender, white-stockinged legs, kicking at the chest of the man who had swung around to face him.

Victoria. He didn't need to see her face to recognize her. Ogden's hireling, the scar-faced Quigley, had his hands all

211

over her. A red haze filled his vision. He flung himself off Diablo, fists ready.

Quigley dumped Victoria and she cried out as she landed on the bank on her back.

No one hurt his woman and got away with it. He'd kill the bastard.

He stopped short as Quigley drew a pistol from his pocket. Hell. Simon watched the other man warily. He'd left his own weapon in his saddle holster. His fear for Victoria had overcome years of training. He'd lost control of reason.

"Hold it right there, your lordship," Quigley shouted. Simon had heard his voice before. At the carriage accident.

Balancing lightly on his feet, Simon took a deep breath and concentrated on Quigley, isolating everything from his consciousness except the man in front of him. All he needed was a moment, and the weapons of his mind and body.

"Simon." Fear rang in Victoria's voice.

"Stay back, Victoria," he said without removing his gaze from his opponent.

Quigley jerked the pistol. "Back off, unless you wants to die."

Brave in a dark back alley, Quigley seemed ill at ease, despite the gun in his hand. Simon kept his voice easy. "Leave the girl and I'll say no more about this, Quigley."

Quigley flinched at the sound of his name. "Get in the carriage, wench. Or his lordship here gets a bullet in his pretty face."

The sound of Victoria's sharply in-drawn breath told Simon she believed Quigley's threat. "Stay where you are, Miss Yelverton." Simon took a slow step forward. Quigley backed up, licking his lips.

Simon narrowed his eyes. "You won't get away with this. Killing is a capital offence. My friends know I'm here, know about you. You'll be caught."

Quigley grinned. "I got my own titled gentleman to take care of me. He'll make sure I don't swing. If I swing, so do he."

Ogden.

Simon flicked a quick glance at Victoria sprawled on the grass verge. Good. He wanted a clear field.

Crossing his arms over his chest, Simon ran a haughty stare over Quigley. "What gentleman in his right mind would employ a cur like you?"

Quigley cursed. "The Viscount Ogden don't see it like that."

"No!" Victoria's cry of denial enraged Simon. She refused to believe anything ill about the viscount. Loyal to the bitter end.

He prepared to launch himself at Quigley.

A projectile, her reticule, flew at Quigley's head and he ducked, turning his gun to the new source of danger. Damn it all, what did Victoria think she was doing? Desperate to reach Quigley before he fired, Simon lunged and caught him in the midriff with his shoulder. They fell and rolled together on the dusty road.

The gun exploded and deafened him. Searing pain scorched his shoulder.

A scream pierced his ringing eardrums. Victoria.

Simon staggered to his feet, shaking his head to clear the gray fog creeping around the edge of his vision. Quigley lay stunned on the ground. Victoria, on her feet in the grass, looked horrified.

Quigley groaned and pushed himself into a sitting position. The sight galvanized Simon to action. He hit Quigley on the jaw with every ounce of strength he had left. Quigley collapsed in a heap.

Simon had to get Victoria out of here before the bastard

came to his senses. He ran to Victoria and grabbed her hand. "Come on, get in the carriage."

The nervous horses pranced away at their approach, then stopped. Simon tried again, snatching at the reins. They reared up in the traces. Damn. He'd never control them with one arm, and the thought of the carriage tipping over sent cold fear sliding down his back.

They'd have to double up on Diablo. He whistled and the stallion trotted up.

Bending, he held his good hand ready to boost Victoria into the saddle.

"No."

He stared at her. The blood had drained from her face, and her eyes were fear-filled as she backed away. Curse it. He'd forgotten: she didn't ride. "You'll be fine," he said.

"I can't. Go without me. Save yourself."

"Victoria," he urged. "Trust me. You have to do this."

He saw her terror. His heart sank. She had no reason to trust him. He stood upright. He'd have to knock her out and somehow get her on the horse. Dizziness roared in his ears, almost driving him to his knees. He balled his right hand into a fist.

Her eyes widened as if she read his intent. He grabbed at her shoulder. "One way or another you're getting on Diablo."

"All right," she said and reached for Diablo's reins.

"Brave girl."

Diablo shifted. She gasped and clutched at the leather saddle.

"Steady, boy," Simon said, stroking Diablo's flank, knowing the horse sensed her fear.

He cupped his hands. Her small, bare foot rested on his palm. Where the hell were her shoes? He braced his legs and lifted.

Pain burned red hot in his shoulder. He reeled and clutched at the stirrup, fighting the mindless dark.

"Simon. Please. Hurry." Victoria's panicked voice pierced the rushing gloom. Simon glanced over his shoulder. Quigley was on his feet, yanking another pistol from his pocket.

The anticipation of a bullet tearing into the center of his back caused Simon's muscles to twitch. He put one foot in the stirrup and hauled on the saddle with his right hand.

Too weak. He couldn't do it.

Victoria grabbed at his coat collar and heaved.

He was up.

His vision blurred. "Take the reins," he said, putting his arms around her waist. "Set him at the wall and let him go."

He heard her cry of anguish from far away, felt her urge Diablo forward, and then they flew.

Wings. The damned horse had wings.

The bone-jarring jolt as they landed threw him sideways. He fought his way upright. A shot cracked behind them. Victoria flinched. He didn't think she was hit, and he hadn't felt anything. He wasn't feeling much at all.

Victoria's rapid heartbeats echoed through her fine-boned back, and Diablo's hooves thudded dully on the heather-covered turf. Simon locked his fingers together in front of Victoria's ribs and trusted God and Diablo. He rubbed his cheek against her slender shoulders. He was right where he wanted to be, snuggled up against Victoria Yelverton.

"Simon."

Gentle fingers shaking his shoulder, touching his cheek, his forehead. Nice.

"Simon."

"Hmm?"

"Simon, wake up."

Victoria. He opened his eyes. Victoria's face loomed over him. Her hair, hanging around her shoulders, tickled his bare chest above the sheet.

"Hello, poppet," he said.

Victoria Yelverton. In his bed. Just where he wanted her. He put his hand around her neck and drew her close. Her warm breath whispered across his mouth. He pressed his lips against hers, soft, yielding and parting for him. He inserted his tongue in the sweet, hot cavity.

It didn't feel quite feel like his own tongue. Well, that was fine too. Perhaps it belonged to her now.

She pushed him away and his arm dropped to his side, heavy and uncooperative.

"Stop it," she said. "Wake up."

He was awake. Awake, rock hard and wanting. Surely she could see that beneath the sheet. How nice of Victoria to come to his bed. Now, if she would just lie down alongside him everything would be perfect.

Not his bed. He frowned. His bed had blue hangings with the Travis coat of arms. Not hers either. Hers was definitely pink. This was sort of brown. Ugly. No matter. Any bed would do.

He reached for her again and dull pain throbbed in his shoulder. Nails? His last mistress liked to claw his back to bloody ribbons. He hadn't thought of Victoria as that sort. He glanced down. He stared at the bandage and back at Victoria. All of her came into focus. Her face, her hair and a god-awful gray wool gown.

He shifted his head. A mean-looking chamber with barely room for Victoria to stand upright beneath the sloping ceiling met his gaze. Daylight from the latticed window revealed whitewashed walls and peeling paint.

"Where the hell am I?"

She looked relieved. "I don't know."

"What?"

"That awful man attacked us and then we rode across country. I was so frightened, but I just did what you said and let Diablo find the way. I am not exactly sure where here is, I'm afraid. We are in Wales. The people are very nice. They fetched the doctor and he fixed you up and gave you some laudanum."

"Diablo?" Simon tried to sit up. The room swung around his head. He closed his eyes to ward off the nausea. She pressed him back against the pillow. He felt as weak as a baby. "Bloody hell. The bastard shot me."

"Diablo's fine. He's quite wonderful, actually. He found the way all by himself and chose this place."

Simon couldn't follow it. But it wasn't important. He had to get her to safety, then he could think. "We have to get back to London."

She shook her head. Black curls swayed tantalizingly, begging his hands to sink into their depths, cradle her head, pull her close until her lips touched his. He liked her kisses. When was that? Days ago? Weeks? Years? It felt like years. He starved for her kisses.

"You can't be moved."

What was she talking about? He peered at her with a frown.

"The doctor said if you lose any more blood, you could die. The bullet went right through your shoulder. He's worried you might contract a fever." She shook her head at him. "You lost a lot of blood, you know."

Women always fussed about such stuff. "It's just a scratch." He tried again to sit up. The bed ropes protested as he barely moved an inch. He sank back, exhausted.

"You see?" she said. "Simon, I had to use your money to

pay the shot and the doctor."

"Good idea," he said smiling at her.

She looked conscience stricken.

"What?" he asked.

She hung her head. "They only have one room. I told them I was your wife."

Wife. It had a nice sound to it. She looked horrified. He was the last person to whom she would want to be married. Oh well. He chuckled, then winced as the movement jarred his shoulder.

She indicated his bandage. "Does it hurt a lot? The doctor said the laudanum would take care of the pain."

Laudanum. No wonder his limbs and brain felt like sheep's wool. Too bad it hadn't put out the fire in his loins. Hell. There was nothing he could do about that in his present condition.

"It's not too bad. Just when I move."

"Don't move, then."

"No, my lady."

"My lady?"

"If we are married you, my dear, are my lady. The Countess of Travis."

She made a wry face. "I gave our name as Yelverton. I had said it before I realized we needed to be married. So you are Mr. Yelverton."

How like her to strip him of his title. "I see, wife."

A confused blush pinkened her cheeks. She settled in the small armchair by the window and he fixed his happy gaze on her lovely face. He would enjoy every moment of being married to Victoria Yelverton. His eyes drifted closed.

"Eat your broth, Simon," Victoria ordered.

"Eat it?" His flushed face looked like a truculent little

boy's. "How can I eat this pap? Bring me something I can take a bite out of."

"The doctor said broth is the best thing for you right now. It's for your own good."

He glared at her. "Damn the doctor." Then, as if sensing her worry, he sighed. "Fine." He struggled to sit up. "I can't do anything with it lying down."

What a stubborn, proud man he was. He never asked for help. She restrained him with a hand on his good shoulder. "No. You're to lie still. I will feed it to you."

A wickedly amused smile curved his lips and his blue eyes lit with a predatory gleam.

"All right, sit here." He indicated the edge of the bed with a nod.

Her stomach fluttered and a blush flashed to her cheeks. She couldn't prevent it when he looked at her in just that way, and he'd been doing it ever since he awoke.

"Soup," she said.

He made a face. She sat sideways on the edge of the bed.

At the touch of the spoon to his lips, he opened his mouth. "You must be hungry," she said.

She dabbed at his mouth with a napkin before scooping up another mouthful. "Open."

He cursed, but did as she asked.

This time she dabbed at him, he caught her wrist.

"Stop it. You make me feel like a helpless child."

A gem-hard glitter fractured his gaze. His pride made it impossible for him to recognize he needed her help, and he refused to admit he had a fever. "You must eat. The doctor will be coming later. He won't let you get up if you don't get strong."

He moved his head impatiently, his black, tousled hair stark against the white pillow. "Let him try to stop me. We have to leave here. Ogden is probably looking for us."

She shook her head. "You don't know that."

His grip tightened. "Always defending him, aren't you? What is he to you?"

This obsessive hatred of Ogden was quite tiresome. "Nothing. He's just a friend. You don't know for sure he's trying to find us."

He let go of her, a sneer on his lips. "Oh, I know, Victoria. Believe me. What I don't know is your role in all this."

He always thought the worst of her when it came to Ogden. She would not be drawn into this. "I have no *role*, as you put it."

His lip curled. How she hated his cynical expression. "He's going to great lengths to get you back."

She glared at him. "How can he get me back, when I never went to him in the first place?"

"Do you think I believe that? I've seen the way he looks at you. I know you met with him secretly. How can you stomach the cur?"

"He was Michael's friend, and mine, and nothing more."

"Friend?" He spat the word at her as if he tasted poison in it. "He held your hand in the park. Why not just admit he's your lover. You met him the afternoon you disappeared. I'm not a fool. You lied about where you were."

"I was not lying to protect myself or Ogden. I went to meet Cassandra Eckford. She wanted me to help her escape from you."

His expression eased a little, but doubt lingered in the depth of his piercing blue eyes. "Then why did he send his man for you?"

She raised a brow. "Perhaps, like you, he thought he was rescuing me from a fate worse than death."

His laugh was short and bitter.

She glared at him. "I will not be part of your fight with Viscount Ogden."

He shrugged and shuttered his thoughts. As usual, he did not believe her when it came to the viscount. "Come on," he said. "Let's get this over with." He opened his mouth. She spooned in the rest of the soup.

A heavy tread sounded on the stairs. Victoria placed the empty bowl and the tray on the night table and moved to the other side of the bed, leaving room for the doctor.

"And how is my patient today?" Doctor Rees, a grayhaired, jolly Welshman, deposited his black bag on the bed.

"He seems a little feverish, Doctor," Victoria replied.

"Aye, no doubt. You'll have to keep him quiet for a day or two."

"I'm still here," Simon said in arctic tones. "I might be injured, but I've not lost my faculties. And to answer your question, I'm fine."

Impressed by the doctor's calm manner when he'd cleaned and bandaged Simon's wound, Victoria trusted him to know what was best. Under the influence of the laudanum the doctor had ordered, Simon had been cooperative. Today, he had refused the drug and been exceedingly irritable, no doubt as a consequence of the pain.

"Let's see, shall we?" Doctor Rees said, picking up Simon's wrist and feeling his pulse. He pursed his lips. "Thready."

Simon glowered at him. "Thready? What's that supposed to mean?"

How rude he was to nice Doctor Rees. "Simon, shh," Victoria said.

"Don't shh me," he muttered.

"Is he always such a difficult patient, Mrs. Yelverton?" Doctor Rees placed a hand on Simon's forehead. "Husbands are supposed to listen to their wives when they are sick, sirrah."

Sure her guilt showed on her face, Victoria was glad the doctor didn't glance in her direction. Simon caught her blush, though. He waggled his eyebrows and sent her a cocky grin, the cheeky rogue.

"She's a shrew," Simon grumbled. "Won't let me up. Won't give me any decent food."

"Simon," Victoria admonished.

"Hmmp," Doctor Rees said and raked through his bag. He pulled out bandages, wadding and medications. "He must remain in bed. I do not want my good work ruined for the lack of a few days' rest. I am relying on you, Mrs. Yelverton."

Victoria bit her lip. If Simon decided not to obey her, she didn't think she could make him comply. His expression turned flinty behind the doctor's back.

"I'll get up when I damned well please," Simon said.

"Not if you want to live to next week." Doctor Rees gave Victoria a stern look over his shoulder, then began to cut away the old dressings with a pair of scissors.

Victoria shuddered. The doctor's quiet tones frightened her more than any yelling would have done.

"You must make him rest," Doctor Rees said.

When did anyone make Simon St John do anything he didn't want to do? "Yes, doctor," she said.

"He needs to sleep. It is the best cure of all. I'll leave you with laudanum for the pain and cleansing powders for the wound, in case you need to change the bandage before I come again. If he still has a fever then, I'll bleed him."

"Talk to *me*, you goddamn sawbones," Simon said through gritted teeth.

"You'll do as you're told, young man, or I'll send for the

magistrate to investigate this supposed accidental shooting, no matter what your good wife here says."

Simon cursed and subsided into glowering resentment as the doctor's professional hands worked on the raw and ugly mess the bullet had made.

Victoria repressed her nausea at the sight of black, crusted blood around the angry-looking wound. She watched the doctor work, determined to follow his instructions while sincerely hoping it wouldn't be necessary to put what she learned into practice.

The wound cleaned and powdered, Simon supported himself on his elbow while Doctor Rees wrapped the bandages over his shoulder and around his chest. Victoria could only imagine his pain, since no indication showed on his face. In fact, his deep and steady breathing made him appear almost at rest. He lay back with his eyes closed when the doctor finished.

"That's it for now, Mrs. Yelverton. I'll call again tomorrow. Keep him quiet and still and cool, and the fever should be gone by morning. Then he'll start to feel more the thing. Send for me if you are at all worried."

Expressing her gratitude for his kindness, Victoria saw the doctor down the stairs and out to his trap. She returned after a quick bite to eat downstairs to find Simon asleep.

The tiny bedroom barely accommodated the nightstand and an armchair beside the window. She had spent one night in the chair watching Simon, and it looked as if she would spend another one.

Simon's eyes were closed and his breathing regular, if a little shallow. With a view to taking advantage of the afternoon sunlight, she settled into the chair. She had borrowed a needle from Mrs. Davis and, lifting the hem of her gown over her knee, she set to work to repair the only item of clothing she now possessed.

"Why did you take so long?" His voice was a soft whine. His blue eyes peeped from beneath long, black lashes.

She gasped and dropped her gown to cover her petticoat. "I thought you were asleep. I stopped for some luncheon downstairs."

"I'll wager it wasn't soup."

She cast him a saucy smile. "No, it wasn't. It was cold roast chicken, actually."

"Witch." He shifted restlessly, like a spoiled child. "I'm hot."

"I'm not surprised, after the way you argued with the doctor. You really should try to be more appreciative." She got up and mixed his medicine. "Drink this and you'll feel better by the morning."

He screwed his face up.

She sighed. "Please, Simon, don't make this so difficult."

"Fine. Give it to me."

She sat beside him and tilted his head, careful not to disturb his shoulder. His eyes held her gaze as he swallowed it in one gulp.

"There," she said. "That wasn't so bad, was it?"

"You didn't have to drink it."

She started to get up.

"Don't go."

"I'm not going anywhere. Just to sit by the window."

He ran his index finger over her hand and slid it beneath the cuff of her long sleeve. Her skin tingled in its trail and a slow spread of warmth drifted up her arm. She drew in a sharp breath to ease the tension, to deny the danger he represented to her body. He was ill and this meant nothing.

"Stay," he said.

She kept her expression bland and sighed. "All right.

Anything to keep you happy."

He smiled lazily. "Promises."

She resisted the urge to kiss his cheek and instead took his large, overly hot hand in hers and patted it.

"Nice," he whispered. His eyelids closed.

He looked like a boy. Young, vulnerable, and so very different from his normal hard, arrogant self. Her heart filled with a rush of tenderness. He had saved her from the disgusting Quigley and almost been killed himself. He was so impossibly handsome, it was no wonder her heart raced each time he smiled at her. When it pleased him to cast his lures, she had no more defense against his practiced seduction than Cassandra Eckford. And what about his new mistress waiting in Italy?

She gazed at him, running her fingers over the tanned skin of his hand until her back stiffened and her eyelids grew heavy in the fading light. She got up and lit the candle. He would sleep for a while longer. She piled the jug, glasses and soup dish on a tray and took it downstairs.

Mrs. Davis beamed at her appearance in the doorway of the spotless kitchen and announced she had laid dinner out in the snug parlor.

Dinner already? The afternoon had disappeared without her being aware of it.

The table in the parlor was set for one. One plate, one glass, one cup on the tea tray. This would be her life once Simon went back to London. Life for one.

Alone, but hopefully not lonely. Julia would write and Victoria would make new friends, once she found employment. There must be work in Shrewsbury and, if not there, then perhaps farther south in Bristol. She would not go back to London. Simon would be too close.

In the meantime, he was here with her.

There would only be one man like Simon St. John in her life. Brave and sometimes honorable, wicked as sin, he wore his forbidding exterior like a suit of armor, and nothing made a chink in it. Except Miranda, apparently. It seemed that since he couldn't have his stepmother, no one else would either. He protected his own. Her heart twisted.

She pushed her plate away.

Mrs. Davis, plump and red-faced from the kitchen stove, arrived to clear away the dishes. "All finished, ma'am?" she asked, her Welsh accent musical. "Now then, Mrs. Yelverton, you've hardly touched my nice game pie. You need your strength to take care of your poor man up there."

He would never be her man.

"I'm sorry. I'm not as hungry as I thought. I must be tired."

"Ah then, you'll be wanting to retire. I'll fetch you a tray to take up for Mr. Yelverton." Mrs. Davis bustled away with an armload of dishes.

A log hissed and rolled part way out of the grate. Victoria got up and poked it back with a fire iron. The flames danced and flickered as she gazed unseeing into the glowing embers.

Travis seemed to want to be more than her friend. Her lover. How strangely decadent it sounded. The kind of sordid thing ladies whispered about behind their fans.

And what she did want? She had no family to care if she was ruined, and she wasn't looking to make a good marriage. If truth be told, she was already ruined after spending two nights alone with a bachelor. Why not let him have his wicked way and enjoy what all the ladies in London panted for.

His mistress? She didn't want to be dependant on anyone. Nor could she abandon him, after he had risked his life to rescue her. And what if Quigley did come looking for them? She pushed the terrifying thought aside. No one would find them here, hidden away in the depths of the Welsh foothills while they played husband and wife.

Heat rushed from her head to her toes. Enough of this nonsense. As soon as Travis recovered, he would return to London and she would go her own way, no matter what he said to the contrary.

Mrs. Davis returned with a jug of water and a bowl for washing on a tray, and Victoria carried it upstairs. Hoping not to wake Simon, she eased open the bedroom door.

Her stomach flipped over. Travis lay spread-eagled, the covers at his hips. His broad shoulders, one marred by the heavy bandage, took up most of the width of the bed. But it wasn't his upper body that took her breath away, she'd been witnessing the sculpted curves of his bronzed arms and chest for the past two days.

Eyes averted, she set the tray on the bedside table. She'd seen drawings in books, and statues in galleries, taken hurried glances at risqué artwork, and clearly Simon was one very beautiful male.

And he had almost been hers. If Ogden had not disturbed them, she would still be at Travis's house in Hampshire.

A tiny, secret smile curved her lips. She had succumbed to him like soft clay in the hands of a master potter. Her will had fled and left her needing him. Unfortunately, he didn't need her.

She risked a peek. He'd kicked the sheet so far down the bed it revealed the flat, hard plane of his stomach and an intriguing navel surrounded by dark hair, which followed a straight line towards . . . Victoria swallowed. Thank God for the sheet. All virile male. Slim hips. Long, muscled legs stretched wide apart. Pulled tight around him, the linen betrayed a significant bulge at the juncture of his long thighs.

He kicked out and she snatched at the sheet before it

ended up at the foot of the bed. Yanking it up to his neck, she drew in a ragged breath and then tucked it in.

His head rolled toward her.

"Victoria?"

She gulped. He had developed an unnerving way of watching her from beneath his lashes. She hoped he hadn't seen her staring. "I'm right here," she replied. Thank goodness his eyes were closed.

"Victoria."

The fractious child again. She sighed. "Yes, my lord."

His hand shot out and grabbed her arm. Shocked by the burning heat she felt through her wool gown, she tried to pull away.

"You'll not escape me this time," he said, his voice hoarse. He swallowed painfully, and his breath rasped in his throat. His brow furrowed, but his eyes remained closed.

"I'm not going anywhere, Simon. Please release me."

"Swear it. Promise me."

"I promise."

Her words seemed to reach him. His grip relaxed.

She should not have left him alone. Racked by guilt, she put a hand on his forehead. An inner fire burned him up. She mixed another draught of medicine.

"Simon, drink this."

He turned his face away. She tried to lift his head and guide the glass to his mouth at the same time. His neck, a column of corded muscle and sinew, resisted her.

Again she pressed the glass against his lips. "Drink."

He pressed his lips together, a naughty boy defying his nurse.

"Simon St John," she said, at her wits' end, "if you don't drink this, I swear I will walk out of here for good."

He opened his mouth and Victoria tipped in the bitter

draught. With a sudden premonition he was about to spit it out, she dropped the glass and clamped his jaw shut. He swallowed.

"Damn," he cursed, following up with a string of oaths she'd never heard before and hoped never to hear again. She clapped her hands to her ears and backed away. Men. How typical.

He stirred. His face, glistening with sweat in the flickering candlelight, held an expression of such agony it frightened her. Perhaps she'd mixed the draught wrong. Deep lines of pain showed around his mouth.

"No," he cried out in a hoarse whisper, misery etched on his stern features. In the throes of his dream, he reached out, groping, seeking.

She caught his clawed fingers in hers. He clutched and held fast, crushing her hand in a painful grip. He stilled.

Victoria took a deep breath and her heart slowly returned to its normal steady rhythm. She wiped his face with a towel. His skin burned to the touch. She had to cool him. Fevers were dangerous.

She cupped his chin in her hand while she bathed his face. He twisted his head and pressed his hot, dry lips against her palm. Fire raced from her hand to the pit of her stomach. She leaped back, scorched and trembling.

She closed her eyes. How did he do this to her? Out of his senses and with no idea who she was, he set her body quivering with one small kiss. She'd lost her wits.

She forced her mind to rational thought. His dissolute past made him a master of seduction. It wouldn't matter who nursed him. Her, Cassandra Eckford, Miranda, Mrs. Davis downstairs, it was all one to him. She meant no more to him than any of them.

He battled with the sheet and heaved it to one side as if it weighed a hundredweight. In the candle's soft glow, he lay like a burnished statue, glorious in his nakedness.

Strong, lean and dangerous. She had already discovered the beauty of his torso, now his lower half was laid out before her wickedly curious gaze. His hips were even narrower than his waist. His long legs were covered in dark, curling hair, a finer version of the curls surrounding . . . She blinked and put her hands to her hot cheeks. His manhood lay against one thigh, surrounded by a thatch of black curls. Nothing she had seen in books had prepared her for the real thing.

He lifted his hips. His stomach muscles were ridged in hard curves. Her appreciative glance drifted up to his face.

Blue sapphires glinted, his lips curved in a sultry smile. "All for you, sweetling," he said, his voice thick and strange.

Catching up the sheet, Victoria threw it over his lower anatomy, which, even as she covered him, changed, grew larger, lifting away from his body.

Her gaze flew to his face.

Unconscious again, he had no idea she had stared at him like a first-time visitor to the Elgin Marbles. Dear God. She hoped not, or she would never be able to face him again. She waited for her heart to cease its clamoring.

He lay immobile, his expression set like granite. She touched a hand to his forehead. Raging hot. She dipped the towel in the water jug and ran it over his brow.

He sighed. She dipped and wiped again and his tight expression relaxed a little. The lines around his mouth softened. She continued stroking the damp cloth down his cheeks, across his jaw, his neck, his shoulders, his body, careful to keep the sheet where her gaze dare not rest. His breathing deepened and his sleep seemed more natural. She relaxed.

Once more, she straightened the sheet over him. Dark

stubble shadowed his cheeks; long black lashes fringed his closed eyes. He slept, handsome, dark and the devil's temptation. Satan.

Just as she had the previous evening, she stripped off her gown, washed as best she could and wrapped the quilt around her, prepared for another long night in her chair.

Pitch black. Neck aching and joints stiff, she must be cold, from the sound of her chattering teeth. Victoria clamped her jaw shut. Not her. Across the room.

Simon. She shook her head to clear the veil of sleep.

She let the quilt drop and leaped to her feet. What ailed him now?

Shaking hands were of no use for lighting candles. Thank heavens for the faint glow of the dying fire in the grate and the pale diagonals of moonlight creeping through the lattice.

Finally a spark. The candle flickered, then steadied. She picked it up and held it above the bed. He squinted against the light, shuddering, his lips bloodless and his teeth clicking.

"G-God," he managed. "I'm f-freezing."

She laid her hand on his forehead. Slick with sweat and still hot to touch, his hair stuck to it in damp black curls, and yet he shivered. She pulled the sheet higher, then grabbed the thick quilt from her chair and threw it over him. His glittering eyes followed her every movement.

"Any better?" she asked.

He nodded, but his shaking, shivering body said otherwise. Stoic. The word came unbidden to her mind. He never asked for anything. Except that she stay.

"I'll go and ask for another blanket."

He grabbed her hand. "You're not going anywhere."

She stared at him. Awareness had gone from his eyes, replaced by glazed pain and fury. She worked at his fingers, trying to break their grip. "Travis, let me go."

He didn't seem to hear her. If anything, the pressure on her wrist increased. How could he be so strong in his weakened state? She raised her voice. "Let me go."

"No. Not this time. By God, I'll not let go this time. I mustn't let go."

The tallow, when she held it higher, revealed a face set in bitter lines, his brows drawn down in a deep frown. Gooseflesh raced up her arms as she stood, practically naked, shackled to a man imprisoned in his dreams and shivering like a kicked cur.

She set the candle down. No sense in setting light to him. She couldn't break his hold, nor could she stand for who-knew-how-long, waiting for him to come to his senses. She eased back the quilt and lay beneath it, on top of the sheet that covered him. She settled herself in the narrow space between the edge of the mattress and the man who guarded its center.

He sighed and snuggled up to her. She stiffened. Her heart raced at the feel of his warm breath on her skin, his fiery body tight against her. She felt hot all over as one of his legs slid over the top of hers, only the thin sheet and her shift for protection.

His shivers decreased and slowly died away. He drew on the warmth he fired in her blood. She pulled at her hand. His fingers clutched convulsively. She gave up and lay still, praying for dawn to arrive.

Chapter Fifteen

A heavy weight pinned Victoria's legs. She opened her eyes. The gray light of dawn cast shadow and light on the chiseled planes of Simon's peaceful face beside her on the pillow. She was free of his hard grasp. She eased away from him. He rolled toward her and she held her hand to his forehead. Cool. She sighed with relief.

"No," he cried out.

Startled, she drew back from him. His eyes remained closed.

His head dark against the linen shifted restlessly. "Miranda." The whimper of a thwarted child escaped his lips. He dreamed of Ogden's sister. His father's wife. No wonder he suffered the torment of the damned.

She tried to ease her legs out.

He groaned. "I didn't mean it. I couldn't have . . . I would never . . . Forgive me." His voice broke and Victoria's stomach clenched at the heartbreaking sound. To hear him beg instead of demand revealed depths too frightening to contemplate.

Tears ran down his hollowed cheeks. Unable to listen to his agony a moment longer, she touched his chest.

"Simon."

He stilled.

"Simon. You're dreaming. Wake up."

God, he hated himself.

Simon opened his eyes.

Victoria. He must be still asleep. Warm, vibrant, her hair floating around her shoulders, a glorious tangled mess, her lips a hairsbreadth from his, she was in his bed. If he was dead, then somehow he'd made it past St Peter into Heaven.

"Hello, angel."

She frowned.

He knew he was grinning like an idiot, but he didn't care. The ghastly bitterness, which always surrounded his awakening, fled at the sight of her beautiful face.

He slipped his hand around her neck and pulled her lips to his. Yes. Soft, warm and full of promise. He felt her yield. Not a lot, not all, but a definite softening.

God. Bliss. She wanted him. He always knew when a woman slipped beyond the boundary into need. He really had reached Heaven. He deepened his kiss, flicked her lips with his tongue and nibbled. So sweet. Like sugar on a cake, like a taste of lollipop on a baby's lips, like . . .

She pulled away and he didn't have the strength to hold her.

"Simon, wake up."

He chuckled at her indignant expression. It didn't match the misty haze of desire in her violet eyes. "I do assure you, I am wide awake."

"Oh," she said and tossed aside the cover. She wasn't exactly in the bed with him, he realized. Not quite.

He caught her arm. "Where are you going?"

"You were cold. I just lay down beside you to keep you warm."

So that was it. But it did not account for the kiss. Not this one or the last one. He recognized the signs, the flush of desire, the shivers, the softening, yielding body. She wanted him as much as he needed her.

Something else stuck in his mind. He recalled her staring

at some point during the night. Staring at him naked. Not the little innocent she made out, Miss Victoria Yelverton. Well, he wasn't entirely surprised after Ogden's declaration. He hated to imagine Victoria bedding a cur like Ogden, but Simon would enjoy showing her there was more to loving than pain.

"I'm cold now," he said, casting her a sly smile of invitation.

"I'll cover you with the quilt and you'll soon warm up."

She wasn't playing. Not yet. "Not good enough."

"Simon, please don't do this."

The pleading tone in her voice served as a dash of cold water. He released her and shrugged.

He eased himself up into a sitting position.

"Are you feeling better?" she asked. "You had a fever in the night."

Better? Of course, the bullet wound. "Yes, thank you." Might as well be polite, even if the one pain she had it in her power to alleviate would go unattended.

Her expression held puzzlement. "Are you sure?"

He tried a careless laugh. Anything to ease the tension thickening his blood and pulsing in his loins. "The merest scratch."

He shifted. The pressure on his throbbing shaft from the heavy quilt only made things worse.

Unable to resist, he eyed her beautiful bosom. The shift hid nothing of her breasts' up-thrusting perfection beneath the filmy fabric, astonishingly alluring in the faint dawn light. He wanted those soft pink tips budding in his mouth. Even as his glance grazed across them, they tightened, hardened to points beneath the sheer muslin.

Pure torment. How like a woman. "Get out, if you are going," he grated. He would not let her see how weak she made him.

"Simon." Her breathy whisper made his stomach clench. "You were having a nightmare. It wasn't me you kissed when you awoke, was it?"

He frowned. "Who else would it be?"

Victoria's face contained hurt. "You called out to Miranda and then you kissed me."

His nightmare. Miranda always got in the way of anything good in his life.

He breathed evenly and called on every ounce of control in his command. He reached up and dragged his fingertip down the line of her jaw, across her lips, down the slender column of her neck until it came to rest in the hollow of her throat.

"Victoria, I knew exactly who I kissed. I haven't been able to think of kissing another woman since the day I saw you run across Hyde Park."

She glowered. "What about Miss Eckford?"

She couldn't be jealous. A spark of hope flickered into life. His reckless heart hummed with cautious joy. He kept his tone carefully neutral. "I didn't think I had a hope in hell with you."

He held his breath. He never knew where he was with her. She was unlike any female he had ever met. She had a mind of her own.

"Oh."

What the bloody hell did she mean? Oh. Oh, good? Oh, bad? Trying not to look at her glorious breasts inches from his chest, he let his finger slide lower, waiting for her to push him away, hoping she would not. Her face, her beautiful, exquisite face, hovered above his. But this time it had to be her choice. If she chose to get out of this bed now, he would never touch her again. Never. He swore it—and he would keep his promise this time.

Her decision.

She lowered her face closer. He was dreaming. A nightmare, because when he woke up, he'd know it hadn't happened. He closed his eyes, not wanting to see her disappear.

Her lips brushed his. A whisper of a kiss. Just the kind of kiss he liked, sweet and temptingly innocent. Her tongue touched his bottom lip.

His balls tightened. White-hot flame licked his groin rock hard. His control abandoned him to his fate. A moan of desire escaped him. She pressed her mouth harder against his, touching his tongue with hers.

He needed her close, her softness pressed against him. He wrapped his arms around her.

Burning pain. A groan ripped from his lips. He slumped back onto the pillows fighting a wave of dizziness.

"I'm sorry. Forgive me. I'll get some laudanum," she babbled, touching his face, his chest.

"I'm fine," he said, hauling air into his lungs, trying not to gasp. "Don't move. Just give me a moment." Nothing would get in the way of this. He would just be more careful. He forced the pain into the recesses of his mind.

"Now, where were we," he murmured and pushed her riotous curls back from her anxious face.

The sweetness of Simon's expression and his blue eyes, softened by the haze of desire, took Victoria's breath away.

His hand slipped down her back, caressing her hip. She ought to stop him now, while he wasn't strong enough to hold her. She should just get up and explain she did not want this.

She did, her body shouted, relishing the heat surging through her veins and the sweet longing trembling in her core. She wanted him.

Unable to resist his blatant sensuality, even knowing he only felt lust, she pressed against him. If it was all he had to give her, it had to be enough.

His glorious, sensuous smile made her heart skip.

"Kiss me, please, sweetheart," he requested.

If only she knew more of kissing. She'd only ever kissed one man, him, and then only twice. If he scorned her lack of skill, she would die of embarrassment. She pressed her lips against his and they parted. Emboldened, she edged her tongue into his mouth. A throat-deep growl of pleasure pierced her core with the sweetest ache she'd ever known. She moved her mouth on his, imitating him. She flicked her tongue across his lips then plunged it deep into his mouth. He sucked on it gently. Pleasure shot between her legs.

She gasped and drew back, panting.

He breathed just as hard.

"Damn me," he said, his voice thick. "Don't stop now. You're killing me."

So, in this she had some power over him. She smiled and leaned closer.

His hand cradled her head. He gently eased her against his mouth.

He moved his lips against hers and she parted them. He caressed her tongue with his. Her eyelids drifted closed. There was no reality except his mouth and the sensations storming her defenses. She ought to fight him off in outraged virtue, but the gate stood open and the horse had gone. She pressed closer. She felt his thigh hard against the top of her legs. She pushed her hips against him and moaned at the heightening pleasure of the hard feel of him between her thighs.

Her body burned, nerves stretched taut to breaking point. His hand slid down and then drifted up again. She felt his palm's rough skin on her thighs, her buttocks. He lifted her shift with his steady caress up her body.

He broke the kiss. "Help me take it off," he whispered.

It? Off?

She glanced down the length of her body. Her chemise rode high above her waist. She glanced back at his face; his eyes gleamed wickedness, daring her.

His hand roamed higher, hot and heavy against her ribs, brushing the underside of her naked breasts. His thumb teased her nipple and the tension in her core tightened.

Trembling, wanting to please him, she sat up and swept the shift over her head.

His smokey gaze caressed her body. His face darkened with need. "Victoria," he breathed. "You are the most beautiful woman I have ever seen in my life."

Fire lit her racing blood. Her wantonness shocked her. She buried her face in his shoulder, ashamed that she could not stop herself. His musky, male scent filled her nostrils as heat warmed her cheeks.

Placing his hand under her chin, he forced it up. "Look at me." Sincerity burned in his eyes. "Believe me. You are glorious, pure poetry, a goddess." He pressed his lips to hers.

She surrendered to the delight of his wooing mouth. His tongue flickered on her lips and she opened to him. He explored her mouth and she tasted his in turn. She lost herself in the bliss of his mind-numbing kisses.

His lips moved from her mouth to her chin, to her throat, to the rise of her breasts. A tension built inside her. Too tight. A flame of desire flared in the pit of her belly and sent her mind reaching heavenwards.

His mouth found her nipple and she gasped, clutching at his hair. Before she could pull him away, his tongue circled and she shivered in torment and delight. He moved to her other nipple and it puckered and hardened under his slick, hot tongue. Her breath came in small gasps. She was going to die of pleasure.

No turning back, she decided. Not now.

Careful to avoid his bandage, she ran her hands over his back and shoulders, up through his hair. She never wanted this to end.

He drew her nipple into his mouth and she spiraled out of control. She could think of nothing but his mouth and the pulsing need between her legs. She arched her hips toward him.

"Will you let me love you, Victoria?"

She knew she should say no. "Yes," she gasped.

"Slip between the sheets, so I can touch you more."

More? There was more? She felt his hand tugging the sheet beneath her and saw his grimace of pain as he tried to pull it out from under her. She scrambled to thrust it down with her feet and saw the way his gaze focused on the tops of her thighs.

He groaned.

"Does it hurt?" she asked, conscious stricken, starting to back off the bed. They should not be doing this. His wound would open.

He grasped her hand and pressed it to his mouth. "God, yes, it hurts. Let me show you."

He gently guided her hand down, across his chest, over his stomach. She looked down and saw him hard, pulsing and rigid, thrusting towards her. He brushed the back of her hand against the engorged, purple tip, silky-soft and hot. She snatched her hand away.

"It hurts?"

"Pleasure pain. You feel it too. I can see you do," he said. He brought his mouth to her lips.

Pleasure, laced with the pain of needing more, rippled in her belly. She yielded to his kisses. Nothing between them, his chest pressed hard and hot against her breasts, the rough hair of his thigh brushed rhythmically against her hip and his hard maleness pressed against her thigh. His palm caressed her breasts. He brought her to a state of endless, mindless longing.

His kiss hardened, deepened, and enslaved her.

Gliding over her ribs, down her stomach, so lightly her skin flickered at their passing, his fingers explored the curls of her womanhood. She ought to be afraid. She wanted him and she wanted this with him.

The sweetest agony Simon had ever endured forced him to lean on his good shoulder to hold her close. He had to move slowly and carefully or he'd be incapacitated by pain.

He'd learned to isolate pain, to ignore it, to cut himself off from all feeling, physical or mental. Blackhurst had taught its lessons well. Years of petty misery interspersed with physical cruelty had honed his skill of stony endurance until nothing could touch him. Nothing until now, when his heart soared with the joy of her yielding and left him defenseless against his body's hurt. He didn't care. Nothing would stop him.

He ran his fingers through the crisp curls protecting her slick, swollen, female flesh. Damp for him.

The heat of her core pulsed against his hand as he delved his tongue into the cavern of her mouth. Traces of her jasmine perfume lingered in her hair and mingled with the essence of her woman's desire.

Her trembles ran the length of her deliciously slender form. She hovered on the brink of her ecstasy, and his.

Her need called him and he slipped one finger between the delicate folds of flesh into hot wetness. Her back arched and she gasped into his mouth, a hot rush of moist air he swallowed greedily. Catching her tongue gently between his teeth, he sucked it into his mouth.

His woman. He pressed his thumb against her pleasure nub and eased his fingers deep inside her, seeking the place that would drive her wild with wanting him.

She writhed beneath his hands and mouth, her hips grinding into his cock. She cried out. Yes. He'd found it. Another finger followed the first and heated, wet flesh stretched to accommodate him. He released her mouth, allowing her to catch her breath. Her gasps and moans drove his own surging want higher and harder than he ever remembered. He had no control.

Drawing back, he tried to set himself apart, to watch himself bring her pleasure and take his own, the way he always did.

Her puzzled frown revealed she sensed his detachment. It ruined the moment. He wanted to be a part of her, have her blend with him until they became one. He gave himself up to her. He had never felt this close to anyone before, and he didn't want to think.

"Open your legs," he said, nudging her thighs with his knee.

Now came the test.

He must not fail her.

He raised himself above her. The bed ropes creaked and groaned as he adjusted his weight to support himself on his good arm, his hand beside her shoulder. He carefully eased himself against her entrance, the path to heaven on earth, to death in life.

He was big and she was small and tight. He ran his other hand over her flat stomach, dipped into her navel, teased her breasts, plucking at her taut nipples, dark with desire, then moved lower, circling the small nub that would bring her close to what she wanted. She cried out for him and he thrust inside her.

She quivered with shock at the brutality of his entry. Her eyes squeezed tight shut.

Dear Lord. A virgin. She'd told the truth about Ogden. Simon hadn't dared believe her. Women always lied. His heart surged with triumph. She was his.

"Victoria."

Victoria kept her eyes shut.

"Look at me, sweet."

Victoria glared into his strain-filled face. How could anything that had started out so wonderful, feel so awful?

His hips pinned her thighs. He lay suspended, motionless, above her, a slight trembling of the arm holding his bandaged chest inches from her body. He remained inside her, stretching her, filling her.

"I'm sorry, Victoria," he said, bending to seduce her mouth.

More lying kisses from his sensual lips. They had promised something other than this.

"Relax, love," he pleaded. "It will be all right in a moment. I promise."

In her heart, she knew to trust his word and released her breath. Once more his mouth descended to hers, his hand caressed her breasts, moving from one to the other, his thumb flicking at the nipple as his tongue licked at her lips. Against her will, her desire surged. A master of the sweet torture of her senses, her body could not resist him, even as her mind berated him.

He moved, pulled away, left her bereft. But not for long. He eased back slowly and the delicious friction drove her mindless. She cried out, but not with pain. Her body vibrated with need. She lifted her hips, wanting more of him.

"Yes," he said, pushing home. "Lift your legs around my waist."

She did and he surged deeper.

"Simon," she cried.

"Hold on, my darling," he whispered.

He began to thrust with steady, ever-increasing urgency.

There was nothing else, just the sensation from their joining filling her mind with a desire and need so distant she reached for the universe and clenched her body around his, holding him tight inside her as she clung to him with her legs and hands.

"Oh, Victoria," he whispered and reached between them, stroking, pressing. "Now, darling. Come to me now."

She felt his tremors, saw pain on his face, his jaw clenched in the grip of sweet agony.

The dam broke. She rushed headlong and breathless into a maelstrom of sensation centered at her core. Heat spread through her limbs in bone-melting bliss.

He groaned and pulled out of her body, fixing his mouth to hers as he heaved and shuddered above her. She felt wet heat on her belly where the hard length of his manhood pressed between them.

He drew his mouth away and grabbed for the towel on the bedside table. He wiped her stomach, then lay down beside her, pulling her close. She glanced at him with a question on her lips.

Simon smiled at the misty wonder in her face. "No babies, Victoria. No children, fatherless, lost and alone." He knew what it was to be alone. His lips touched her temple and her cheek, he nuzzled her ear, stroked her arm. He petted her hair where it lay on her breast. He adored the silky feel of her hair. "So beautiful," he murmured. "You were wonderful. Kiss me, sweetheart."

She turned her face to him and Simon gazed at her full lips, bruised and swollen from his kisses, her skin red from his rough, unshaven cheeks. Christ, but he was a brute and he would not change one moment, not for all the world. She was the sweetest and best lover he had ever had. Would ever have. He kissed her tenderly and pulled the quilt over her wanton nakedness. Her eyes slid closed. She slept.

He would keep her forever, if she'd let him. He didn't deserve her, never would, but now she belonged to him, he'd make sure no harm befell her because of his selfish wanting.

He drifted on a gentle sea of satisfaction. For once, no bitter regrets clouded his sated contentment.

Chapter Sixteen

Simon couldn't tell how long they'd slept. The light streaming through the window indicated a morning far advanced, and pots and pans clashing below reminded him he hadn't eaten anything but soup for two days.

Her head cradled on his shoulder, Victoria's black hair veiled both of them. A faint pulse beat beneath the translucent skin below her ear, and her shoulder rose gently with each peaceful breath. He didn't want to wake her.

God, she was beautiful. And a virgin, despite all his doubts. The thought sent heat surging to his loins. He forced his body under control with practiced ease. She would be far too tender for him to touch again soon, and he didn't want to disturb her in case, in the reality of daylight, she regretted their love-making.

Throbbing pain in his shoulder drove the breath from his lungs. The spreading dark red stain against the white of his bandage indicated he'd disturbed the wound. Another ache to be isolated from his awareness.

Blackhurst Academy had taught him to master hunger, thirst, pain. Pride made him vulnerable to humiliation, but in the end, it forced him to overcome weakness by refusing to acknowledge it.

He rested his gaze on Victoria. Food for his soul and all the sustenance he needed. She had given herself to him with sweet abandon. His heart squeezed painfully with a welling emotion he had never expected to experience again. He would endure anything for such a rare and precious moment. He tightened his arm around her, pretending he could hold on to her forever.

Her eyes fluttered open and he watched in delight as recollection returned. The flush, which traveled up her throat and colored her face, enchanted him.

"Good morning," he said, smiling at her and pulling her to his lips for a satisfying, open-mouthed kiss.

"Good morning," she said with shyly lowered lashes and a smile warm enough to melt a glacier.

He cradled her cheek against his chest again, anxious not to lose connection with her. Not yet.

She lay peacefully against him, her hand resting on his belly. If her hand should wander lower and touch him, he would be hard pressed to hold back. His need already throbbed deep within him.

"Simon?"

"Um-hm."

"Tell me about Miranda."

He froze. Cold anger replaced contentment in a heartbeat. Her name always did that to him. He inhaled deeply. He owed Victoria some sort of explanation after what she'd heard Ogden say. "What did you want to know?"

"The truth. You're hiding something. You loved her didn't you? You called out to her in your dreams."

Dream? It was a nightmare, and it had stayed with him all his life. How much dared he tell her? He had never spoken of Miranda to anyone except Lethbridge, and only then because he got disguised. He never allowed it to happen again. "I loved her until I discovered her true nature."

"What was she like?"

Like? How could anyone truly describe Miranda and not

be accused of lying? Certainly he had been unable to explain it to his father. "She is Ogden's older sister. A year older I think. The same coloring, fair, gray-eyed, blond hair, so long she could sit on it when it was unpinned. I saw it loose many times when she came to live at St John's Hall."

God. How long ago was it? He first saw Miranda Du Plessy at her wedding to his father, the only time his father permitted him to go to London. His father took his duties in Parliament very seriously and relegated Simon to the Hampshire family seat with only servants for company. Sometimes he'd managed to escape from his tutor and racket about with Philip.

"She and your father lived with you?"

Simon shook his head. "Not at first. They were married in London. Miranda loved the *ton* parties and my father was rich, unlike the Du Plessys. He gave her everything she wanted, escorted her to balls, held routs and masques in her honor. They were one of the most celebrated couples in London. I read all about them in the newspapers. But they never came to Hampshire. She wasn't enamored of the country."

"It must have been awful for you when your father spent so much of his time with his new wife."

A wry smile tugged at his lips as he remembered how delighted he'd been when he heard of his father's impending wedding. His heart had thrilled when he learned he would have a mother just like other boys.

Simon remembered his hopeful longing for Miranda to love him as her son, his desire to be part of his parents' life. God, how utterly devastated he'd been when the young Miranda completely ignored him on her wedding day.

He brushed Victoria's hair back from her inquiring face. He bent his head and kissed the small frown between her delicately arched black brows. "My father was one of those men who fell hard. When my mother died in childbirth, he blamed himself, and me."

Victoria nodded wisely. "It was the same for my father. He went to pieces when Mother had the accident. He blamed himself so much, he couldn't bear the pain and so he drank and let everything go to ruin around him."

Simon pondered. That might almost have been preferable to his father's total withdrawal into his work. Some emotion might have been better than none at all. "Things changed for him when he met Miranda. She was twenty-three and he was in his fifties. He seemed younger and happier than I ever re-membered. He was not a warm man, but she definitely thawed him."

He shrugged. "It made little difference to my life. My father never spent any time at St John's Hall, and nothing changed after his marriage. At least not for the first few months."

She wrinkled her nose, her face revealing her mind at work. He anticipated her next question with interest, hoping she wouldn't delve too deep.

"She was twenty-three when she married your father?"

Safe. "Yes."

"And you were what age?"

A fair question. "Twelve."

"I see."

Now what the hell did she mean?

"But Miranda came to stay at St John's Hall later?" she asked.

"Yes."

"And that's when . . ."

For a brief moment, Simon considered taking her in his arms and diverting her with passion. But she wouldn't forget what Ogden had said, and Simon would have to answer her sooner or later. Better to get it over with while she was happy in his arms.

"My father sent her home to St John's Hall when I was about thirteen. To be honest, I think he couldn't keep up the pace." Liar. In retrospect, he believed his father had started to guess about Miranda's illness and wouldn't face it.

"How did she feel about that, if she hated the country so much?"

The bitter crux of the matter. Trust Victoria to see it straightaway. Miranda had been furious. She'd stormed around the house, screaming at the servants, complaining about the weather, writing letters to his father, which demanded he come and fetch her. His father's tactic had been to avoid the issue, sending flowers and jewels. Anything, except sending for Miranda to come to London.

"She wasn't too happy about it," he said.

"And you?"

Simon sighed and stared up at the low, discolored ceiling. After all these years and the events that followed, it was hard to remember how he had felt when Miranda first arrived. He'd been just too young and far too innocent for someone as worldly as Miranda.

"I think she fascinated me. I had never seen a woman like her. She wore gowns that skimmed her magnificent bosom, had a face which would have put Helen of Troy to shame and, when she wanted to be, she was devastatingly charming."

"Like her brother, Ogden," Victoria said in a small voice. She drew a line down his chest with one small finger. It felt delicious. He took a deep breath, stilling his desire.

Probably Ogden would have the same effect on women. Simon curbed a sudden rush of jealousy. Ogden was older now and Miranda, by everyone's account, had been a diamond of the first water in her prime. "Maybe. Anyway, after a few weeks, she realized my father planned to leave her there. Since I was her only source of entertainment and I had more or less avoided her while she was angry, she set out to win me over."

Victoria got up on her elbow and leaned over him. Deep purple eyes with amethyst glints of sharp intelligence searched his face. He kept his expression bland. The hurt belonged in the past. He didn't let it touch him anymore and wouldn't trouble Victoria with his torment. He captured her chin and coaxed her sweet mouth to his lips. Her response inflamed his need, but she broke away and snuggled back into the crook of his arm. Forcing himself to restrain his want, he pushed away the dark strands of hair tickling his face.

"Go on," she demanded.

He ran a hand over her creamy shoulder. "You made me forget where I was."

She ignored his hint. "You said Miranda set out to charm you."

"She did. It wasn't particularly difficult."

How could it have been? To a boy starved for companionship, Miranda could be such fun. "At first we just talked and sometimes, after dinner, we would read aloud to each other. Then we started taking exercise together, walking or riding. She always complained of boredom and I tried to think of things to amuse her. I neglected my studies to keep her entertained. She loved to gamble and on rainy days we played silver-loo."

And always the stakes had been something intimate: a touch, a kiss, a smile, a glance under her skirts at her calf. Simon had become her shadow and a willing slave. It wasn't just her companionship he wanted. Her flirting, teasing ways had him dreaming of her at night, imagining her in his arms, touching her, and his body had become a confused bundle of heated lust. If the old wives' tale had been true, he would have gone blind in a week. He'd obsessed about her and her luscious body.

"She must have had things of her own to do?"

"Like?"

"I don't know. Don't ladies of great houses visit the sick, or their friends, and receive guests?"

"My father didn't allow it. He was very protective of Miranda." He'd probably decided to keep her out of temptation's way in Hampshire with Simon. A dreadful mistake for all of them.

"I see."

The familiar snake of shame slithered in his gut. Simon hesitated. Still, she'd heard most of it already. "One day she kissed me. She'd kissed me before, on the cheek. I'd kissed her hand. I thought she was a goddess. I had her up on a pedestal. I can still remember that kiss. Wet, with her tongue in my mouth, she pushed me up against the wall. She scared the hell out of me." He chuckled wryly, remembering his red-faced embarrassment at the way his cock had hardened so obviously beneath his tight breeches.

Victoria stroked his arm. A gentle, comforting touch.

"I stammered and stuttered and ran away. She wasn't impressed. She called me a stupid little boy the next day. Mortified, I swore I would do better, but she just laughed at me."

"So did you do better?"

"No. Strange as it may seem, she lost interest. She ignored me. She started riding out on her own or with Ogden. The Du Plessys have their house near ours, and Ogden became a regular visitor when he came down from Oxford for the summer. Hidden in the schoolroom, I watched them ride away each day. She never invited me along and I was far too jealous to ask to be allowed to join them."

He'd practically cried when he'd realized Miranda scorned his company. He'd retreated into hurt silence and she had teased him unmercifully, if she deigned to speak to him at all.

"Later that summer, my father came to visit. Miranda threw herself into his arms declaring she had missed him and begged him to take her to London. He couldn't resist her pleading and they left the day after he arrived."

"Did he even talk to you, Simon?"

Dear God. How had she sensed that his father's total oblivion to Simon's adoration had cut him to the quick?

"No. Her weeks of absence from his side seemed to have driven him to new heights of besottedness. I knew how he felt. I missed her too, and we lived in the same house. She had withdrawn all her friendly glances, her secretive smiles, everything I had come to rely on for my happiness. I felt bereft when they left. Just a stupid child, I suppose."

Simon pulled the sheet over Victoria's shoulder, smoothing it flat, the feel of her beneath his fingers blunting the edge of ancient pain. "The next time he sent her to the Hall, she was six months pregnant. She was to await the birth in the country. No more parties. She hated it, and she spent her time visiting her mother at their country house. Ogden had gone back to university. I was back in favor and in heaven. She taught me how to kiss her, just how she liked it. She showed me how to give her pleasure without actually, well, I suppose you'd say, without consummation."

He could see her confusion. Why the hell well-bred young women never learned anything about their sexuality, he never understood. But if they did, there would never be such a thing as a virgin bride among the nobility.

"Our bodies never actually joined together," he explained.

"Oh."

He wasn't sure she understood, but he would teach her about that some other time. "My father arrived for the birth of his son, stayed a week and left again."

"You have a brother?"

Simon steeled himself to answer calmly. "No. He died."

"How sad. Miranda must have been heartbroken. And your poor father must have been upset to lose another person so close to him."

Upset did not describe his father's emotions at baby John's death.

"Yes, he was devastated, especially when Miranda told my father, I seduced her, took her against her will. She blamed my father for leaving her in the country with me." His father had turned to stone while Miranda played out her revenge for the loss of her child.

Indignation filled Victoria's face and she sat straight up, pulling her knees under her chin beneath the quilt. "It wasn't true. She seduced you. You were just a little boy. I remember Michael at that age. He was impossible. He followed the up-stairs maid around like a moon-eyed calf. You were thirteen and she was twenty-three, a woman. Why would she say such a thing? And how could he believe her?"

Simon took her hand and kissed it. Tenderness, an emotion long forgotten, swamped him with such force it clogged his throat. He wanted to squeeze her tight for her understanding, for her defense of the confused and frightened boy he'd been. He longed to tell her everything. He swallowed. She'd despise him if she knew.

"I don't know," he lied, even as the recollection painted vivid images in his mind.

He'd caught Miranda with one of the footmen. Moans

from her room had panicked him. He'd charged in to investigate. He almost threw up. She lay sideways across the bed, with her legs up on the footman's shoulders. Baby John, in his cradle in the corner, screamed while Miranda writhed and the young footman, fully clothed, his wig askew and his face red, thrust into her.

Miranda had opened her eyes and stared right at Simon. She'd poked her tongue out and said, "Run away, little boy." And he did. He ran and hid, shaking and sick. His goddess had smashed to the ground.

The next day, she'd behaved as if nothing had happened. But Simon couldn't. He hated her for betraying his love and threatened to tell his father.

After that, everything had happened too swiftly for him to comprehend. Baby John's death, the accusation, and before he knew it, he was packed off to Yorkshire to school.

"My father sent me away to school and I didn't see Miranda again until after he died. But I don't love her, Victoria. I hate her."

She frowned at him. "It's not good to hate her so much you dream about her."

Simon forced himself not to shudder at the ghost crossing his grave. He didn't dream about Miranda. He didn't care about her. It was the dead child who haunted his dreams, a life cut short because of Simon.

He struggled to remain relaxed. "You're right. It's not at all healthy." There was nothing he could do about it.

"You must have been glad to leave Miranda and go away to school."

Christ. The ridicule he'd suffered year in, year out at Blackhurst for his supposed crimes against nature. He'd buried the aching, bitter memories of cold and hunger and didn't want to resurrect them. The headmaster had been given *carte blanche* over his discipline, no doubt at Miranda's suggestion, and he'd never been able to do anything to please the sadistic bastard.

"No, I didn't particularly like it."

"You had company of your own age, at least."

"I didn't make many friends there," he said in the matter-of-fact tones he'd practiced for years. "There was one boy I got to know quite well, Arthur Prentice. He disliked Blackhurst as much as I did." He'd defended poor Arthur with his fists on more than one occasion.

"It was a special disciplinary school. They taught unruly boys to obey, weak ones strength and bad boys were re-formed. Arthur was counted with the weak, and I was definitely counted with the bad. A veritable son of Satan."

"Your nickname," Victoria said softly.

"Umm. It stuck somehow."

He'd been proud of it. Played on it. He grew taller and stronger than all the other boys through his long hours of physical toil. The gardener, Alexander McIver, a man who'd traveled to the east as a soldier and embraced its mysteries, had taken Simon under his wing. Simon grew to respect and ultimately love the strangely patient old man as much as he could love anyone. Then McIver died and left him alone again. But McIver had taught him the meaning of real control, the ancient art of discipline of body and spirit.

In the end, they'd all feared Simon's fists and his cutting tongue, the teachers and the other boys, while he had been afraid of nothing. He had nothing to fear. He'd already been hurt as much as it was humanly possible.

He hadn't merely trained his body. Mr. McIver hadn't allowed it. Simon went to as many lessons as he could between his enforced labor. Fortunately, he had intelligence and he'd worked hard to keep up with his classmates. Always his shining hope, the beacon in the dark surrounding him, was that, somehow, his dedication would impress his father and make things right.

"Do you still see Arthur?" she asked.

Arthur. Poor sod. "No. He died at Waterloo. His father wanted him to be a soldier. Arthur was just a gentle, scholarly boy who liked to read. He didn't stand a chance in the army, but his father insisted on buying him a commission to prove his son's masculinity."

Simon stroked his fingers through her hair, trying not to remember Arthur's pale face the day he set out for war with the French.

"It was not a very nice school, Victoria. The boys were taught through fear and ridicule."

It had brutalized him.

"And you spent four years at that awful place?"

He shrugged. "I learned a lot."

When his body had been tested to its limits, he had learned to focus his mind, a valuable lesson taught by Mr. McIver. It had served him well. Until now. Until Victoria had disturbed the careful order of his life.

"So then you went home again to your father and Miranda?"

"My father died when I was seventeen, then I went home."

His father discovered Miranda tupping a groom in the stables one afternoon, became apoplectic, and died hours later. Simon hadn't even known of his father's death until weeks later, after the will was settled, when one of his trustees had come to take him away from Blackhurst. He never had the opportunity to prove his worth to his father.

"How sad. And Miranda?"

It hadn't taken Simon and the rest of the family long to discover the full extent of Miranda's madness. The freedom she gained after his father's death seemed to tip her over the edge. She became insatiable as far as men were concerned and wandered the streets at night, sometimes barely clothed, in search of satisfaction. She'd stabbed her maid when she tried to prevent her from going out in only her nightgown. It had been terrifying. Miranda had been a danger to herself and a stain on his father's memory. They had been lucky the maid accepted a handsome settlement rather than dragging the family through the courts.

"Miranda is unwell." Later they'd discovered that Lady Northdown, Miranda's mother, suffered from a similar disorder. Simon hurried on, hoping to forestall more questions. "My mother's brother and an old friend of my father's became my guardians. They arranged for Miranda to be nursed on my Yorkshire estate, where she can rest and be at peace. They sent me off to university." He grinned. "Cambridge was the best time of my life. I met Lethbridge there and ran into Rutherford again."

"I'm glad."

He flicked the tip of her nose. She seemed satisfied and not disgusted or dismayed. He breathed a sigh of relief. She did not need to know the full extent of his crime or his humiliations. It was no one's business but his own. "And now, *Mrs. Yelverton*," he said, throwing her a cheeky grin, "I'd be very much obliged if you wouldn't mind fetching me some breakfast, or perhaps lunch."

"My goodness," she cried, looking at the window. She started to rise and pulled the sheet off him.

"You're bleeding," she said, staring at his chest accusingly. "I better change the bandage. You shouldn't have . . ."

The quilt slid to her waist, revealing small breasts, rose-tipped, translucent mounds in the morning sun. "Oh," she gasped as she saw the direction of his glance and clutched the quilt and pulled it up.

"Spoil sport," he teased. "Really, I'm fine."

She frowned. "I think I'd better call for the doctor."

"And will you tell him how it happened?"

"What? Oh." Her blush almost sent him past the point where he could hold his body in check. He pulled her close and began a slow, heavenly kiss.

"Simon. Stop it. You'll only make it worse."

He blew out a breath. She was right. "Very well. Off you go and fetch the quack. Then, I beg you, get me something to eat, before I starve to death."

"Whatever is the time?" she muttered. She wrapped the quilt around her and shuffled around the bed to find her clothing.

"I really don't know," he replied. And he really didn't care.

Chapter Seventeen

The aroma of roast duck filled the low-beamed private parlor set aside for their use. In the center of a table covered with an embroidered white cloth and surrounded by side dishes of oysters, pudding and asparagus, the duck held pride of place on a cream-colored oval platter. Soft light from the candles on the sideboard and set in sconces on the paneled walls gave the room a cozy feel.

Simon, seated opposite Victoria, his beard freshly shaved and wearing an open-necked shirt borrowed from the publican, laughed ruefully and glanced down at his arm resting across his chest in a sling. "Would you carve? I think I might have a little trouble with only one hand."

"Of course." Victoria hadn't actually ever carved a bird before, but how difficult could it be? She picked up the large knife and fork and attacked the golden-brown bird. The knife skidded off the crispy skin and hit the plate with a ringing sound.

"Damn." Simon lurched across the table and grabbed the knife. "Here, you hold the fork and I'll cut."

He looked so terrified, she giggled.

He grinned. "What are you laughing at?"

"The fear in your face."

"Not funny. You could have cut off your hand."

Victoria stabbed the fork into the roast and he hacked at the duck's brown, juicy flesh. When he finished, she served the chunks of meat and the rest of Mrs. Davis's delicious fare. "Would you like me to cut up your meat?" she offered.

"Thank you, but I think it will be safer if I deal with it my way."

He picked up a morsel of the duck and tore at it with strong, white teeth.

She raised her eyebrows. "How ungentlemanly of you, Mr. Yelverton."

"Better than losing my fingers," he retorted with an upward tilt to his lips. He poured himself another glass of wine.

The noise of the taproom, chinking glasses and lilting Welsh voices, filtered into the quietness of their secluded haven, accompanied by the smell of old ale and pipe smoke.

Today's earlier dreamlike quality lingered like a fragile fragrance waiting for the wind of reality to blow it away. They had laughed at foolish things. He insisted on seeing Diablo and she accompanied him to the barn. She loved the way the fierce stallion responded to his gentle petting. From there, they wandered in the garden for an hour or two, lounging in the warm sun. He lay on the bench, while Victoria, on a stool near his head, read to him. He'd fallen asleep and snored. She could almost imagine this could last. She smiled at him.

Red wine caught the light as he lifted his glass in a toast. "To Mrs. Yelverton," he said. His seductive smile melted her bones.

She raised her glass in return. "To you, Mr. Yelverton."

They drank, his gaze intent on her face.

"Do you think Lethbridge will come tomorrow?" Victoria asked trying not to let disappointment creep into her voice.

Just before dinner, Mr. Davis had brought one of the local tradesmen to talk to Simon. The man had business in Shrewsbury and Simon sent a message with him to the marquess, whom Simon had arranged to meet there with a post-chaise to take Victoria back to London. He and Lethbridge planned to seek out Quigley and then Ogden. Simon refused to listen to any suggestion that Ogden might know nothing about his gamekeeper's activities.

Simon finished his wine in one swallow and refilled it. "I would expect so."

She sighed. She would not go back to London. It would be better if they separated now, before she became totally dependant on him. His moving on later would devastate her far more than saying good-bye now.

"What are you thinking?" he asked, watching her from beneath his lashes.

Ever since he had spoken to the tradesman in the garden, she had sensed his growing tension. A building recklessness had invaded his normally cool expression. His candle-lit eyes glittered ominously as he observed her over his wineglass.

She smiled, desperate to hold onto the lighthearted mood of today, to retain the easy warmth between them. Tomorrow they would go their separate ways. She pushed the thought aside. "Nothing," she lied.

"Tell me."

Somehow she could not prevaricate with him, not even to save herself. "Your toast reminded me that this is our last night as Mr. and Mrs. Yelverton."

He raised one dark eyebrow, a wry smile curving his lips. "You're right. Soon we will be the Earl and Countess of Travis."

For a moment, her heart leaped in joy, then the bottom fell out of her stomach at his cynical expression. She set her knife down carefully. "I beg your pardon?"

His face darkened. "Did you think I would ruin you and abandon you?"

Victoria swallowed. "Is this a proposal of marriage?"

He grimaced. "Something like that," he said, his voice gritty. He sighed. "Yes, dammit."

He had been quite explicit, that day at his country estate, about not wanting to marry. And he certainly hadn't said anything about love. "Why?"

"Why? I just told you why."

Guilt. He'd ruined her and now he thought it his duty to rectify the situation. A rake plagued by an overactive sense of duty. If she wasn't so close to crying because she yearned to say yes, she might have laughed.

He had no reason to feel guilty. She had made her own decision. She shook her head. "I am much obliged to you for yet another generous offer, but just as before, I must decline."

With a short laugh, his gaze dropped to his wineglass. "I'm more than you could possibly stomach, I suppose. I won't take no for an answer, I'm afraid." He twisted the stem of the glass and the ruby liquid glimmered. He tossed it off and set the glass down with a snap. "You must marry me. Honor won't allow anything else."

Victoria rose to her feet and he stood up with her, ducking his head to avoid the low, blackened beam. Devilishly handsome in the flickering light, his expression turned dangerous. The charming, easy man of the last few hours disappeared. Satan St John, stone-faced, eyes like frozen glaciers, flashed her an insolent smile.

Victoria steeled herself against his anger. "I don't care about your honor. You can't force me to marry you."

"Really?" He prowled around the table, lithe and lean. "Are you sure I can't?" he asked, his murmur terrifyingly soft, his gaze fixed, unblinking, on her mouth.

She backed away.

Fast as a whip and stronger than steel, he grasped her arm and pulled her close. He lowered his head and captured her mouth in a slow, torturous kiss. Her senses reeled and shock waves crashed to her core. Instantly, she wanted him.

When at length he raised his head and gazed into her eyes, her body trembled with yearning.

His breath grazed her lips. "Tell me I can't, Victoria."

Every nerve craved his touch. Have this for all time, her body tempted. Say yes, it begged. She knew better. Trap him and he'd tear himself apart. And her.

"Simon," she pleaded, "you don't want to marry me, any more than I want to wed you."

His lips twisted. "Don't I? What *do* you want? If you could have whatever you wanted, what would it be?"

Your love, her heart cried in tune with her body's aching demand. Duty, not love, drove him. What would be acceptable to his honor?

"When my father was alive, before we came to London, I worked on a parish project to raise funds for a school for farm laborers' children. We hoped to provide those who couldn't find work on the land with a better future than slaving in factories in the north. I'd like to teach them."

Simon stepped back a little, his gaze searching her face for answers. "That's it? A school? No broken-hearted squire left in your wake?"

Heat rose in her face. Until this moment, she'd forgotten her crush on the vicar's son and her bitter tears when he bade her farewell.

"I see," Simon said, before she could answer.

"You see nothing," Victoria stormed. "You just make up your own mind about what's best for me. You never think to ask me for my opinion."

"I thought I just did."

"Yes. And then you scorned it. Damn you, Simon St John. I don't want—"

"I can make you want me," he said. His hot gaze raked her body and she gasped at the answering flare deep in her veins.

She'd never seen him so wild. His mood scared her. "You've drunk too much. You'll feel differently in the morning."

Blue eyes narrowed, he placed his hand on the ancient beam above her head. "And how will you feel in the morning, Victoria?"

"I'm not going to change my mind." She couldn't. If she let him do this, she would be just like Cassandra, snaring him into a marriage he didn't want.

The expression in his eyes unreadable, he stared down at her. She raised her chin.

"We'll talk in the morning," he said. "Right now, we're going upstairs."

His piercing glance dared her to fight him. She didn't want to. She wanted this last night together to be a memory she could keep in her heart.

He tensed, as if he expected her to flee. She stood her ground, staring boldly back at him.

"Damn you, Victoria Yelverton," he muttered.

Before she could respond, he swept his arm around her and pressed his lips against hers, hard and harshly demanding. She leaned into him, putting her arms around his neck, running her hands through his hair, across the broad shoulders which, after tonight, she would never feel again. He smelled of soap and fresh air and smoke. He tasted of wine.

He groaned deep in his throat and picked her up, his one good arm around her waist.

"Simon," she exclaimed. "Your shoulder."

"Hold on then," he said. "I'm not letting you go, until we are upstairs and in bed."

Afraid he would reopen his wound, she clung to his neck

and he headed out of the room and up the narrow winding stairs. "You mustn't do this," she said.

"Oh, but I must." The torment in his deep voice shocked her to silence.

He stopped when he reached the landing outside their room. "You'll have to open the door."

He let her slide down his body. Her desire pitched higher. He stood blocking her path to the stairs. As if she would try to escape. She reached up and placed her palm on his hard jaw and felt a muscle jump.

He reached around her and turned the doorknob. He bowed with a flourish of his hand. "Your chamber awaits, my lady."

My lady. She would never be his lady. She would have the memories of these few days and nothing else. The candle flame on the night table blurred. She blinked. She could not bear to let him see her cry on their last night together.

He kicked the door shut with his heel and pulled her close, kissing her with a savagery she could barely comprehend, trying to dominate her with his will.

She resisted.

"Damn you," he said against her mouth, then softened his lips, skillfully teasing and enticing until her body melded with his. With a groan of satisfaction, his hand went to the buttons down the back of her gown. Nimble fingers released the fastenings. The rake, he was an expert at removing ladies' gowns.

He must have felt her stiffen. "Stop it," he growled.

She ran her hands over his chest and encountered the rough fabric of the sling. "We mustn't do this."

He stepped back and roughly pulled the cloth over his head and dropped it on the floor. "I'm fine." He pulled his shirt out of the waistband of his breeches and, one-handed, fumbled with the shirt buttons.

"Let me," she said with a smile.

Surprise on his face, he let her undo them. She eased the loose garment over his head. The candle cast the hard planes of his face into sharp relief; the light glistened on the sculpted contours of his arms and chest. She skimmed her hands over his bare, warm skin.

He sucked in a hiss of breath. Flames leaped deep between her thighs.

He plucked the pins from her hair, raking urgent fingers through it. "I love your hair, glossy like a raven's wing. Don't fly away from me, Victoria."

His words tugged at her aching heart.

Working with one hand, he pushed her gown first over one shoulder, then the other. He worked it down her arms one side at a time until she pulled her hands free.

Sensuous awe glazed his expression as he gazed at her breasts.

"Simon I—"

"Shh," he whispered, pressing his finger to her lips, devouring her with his eyes, starving and hungry for her. Her heart clenched. He never asked anything of her, except that she stay. And she couldn't.

He didn't love her.

She would take what he had to offer tonight and gladly. Her heart picked up speed, her pulse raced. She kept her gaze fixed on his beloved face, observed his darkness turn seductive as he watched his hand roam her breasts through her shift. His palm, hot on one, his fingers brought the nipple of the other to a tight, hard peak. Her knees weakened and she clutched at his shoulders.

He winced.

"I'm sorry." She dropped her hands.

"Don't. It's all right."

"No. We shouldn't. What if it starts to bleed again. The doctor said—"

"Damn the doctor. I won't let you do this to me, Victoria."

The pain in his expression stilled her. Did he think she deliberately tried to injure him? "I just don't want you to be hurt," she whispered.

He laughed, a hard bitter sound. "Now where have I heard that before?"

She ignored his irony. One of them had to have some sense. She leaned forward and kissed his cheek, a warm, motherly kiss. "Remember what happened last time? You can't risk opening your wound again. Not if you want to leave here tomorrow."

He grasped her face in one lean, strong hand, forcing her to look into his eyes. "*We* are leaving here tomorrow, together."

Unable to lie, she shrugged.

"Dammit, Victoria. You will marry me." His mouth captured hers in a kiss that punished even as it rewarded.

Immersing herself in his urgent desire, her own want reaching unsuspected heights of longing, she forgot everything except the need to feel his hard body inside her. She pressed her hips against his thigh, desire streaking to her core.

In one sure movement, he stripped her gown over her hips. She stepped out of it and he pressed her back onto the bed.

"Now," he breathed.

She lay back and watched as he fumbled with the buttons on his breeches. His chest rose and fell, his dark hair falling forward, then he pulled the tight fabric over his hips and down his long, beautifully muscled thighs.

She gasped as his erection stood bold and free and he shot

her a wicked glance. "I'm ready for you," he said. "Are you ready for me?"

Ready? She burned. Her core, tight and demanding, begged her to scream for him to take her, to bury his hard length inside her, to make her his and take her to completion. Only with him did she truly feel complete.

He swept her legs up onto the bed then lay next to her, one leg across hers, his lips finding her mouth, her throat, and through her shift, her nipples.

Shivering and gasping, she reached down for the hem of her chemise. She wanted to feel him next to her skin. All of him, his heat, his hard male strength and form. She wanted nothing between them.

Simon groaned.

Naked, she was perfect. Small, pointed breasts, a flat stomach, black curls at the apex of her thighs hiding the wonderful heat and passion he desired, waking and sleeping. She would marry him. He would make her want him as much as he needed her.

Simon focused on her pleasure. A slow torment of her senses with mouth and tongue and lips that would leave her mindless, unable to resist his will.

He laved those beautiful rose-tipped breasts with his tongue. Her moan of delight sent blood to his shaft. He was so hard he could scarcely think. He drew in a shuddering breath and traced a path of kisses to her belly. He swirled his tongue in her navel. A brute to want her so, he didn't care. She wanted him. Her soft cries, deep in her throat, told him she did.

He placed his hands on each side of her shoulders and moved to cover her with his body.

Agonizing pain ground from his shoulder to the recesses of his mind, leaving him rigid and motionless. Darkness edged his vision. He'd lost control. He groaned.

"Simon."

Fear rampant in her expression, her face floated in front of his and he swore. She made him so weak, even here, where he should dominate. He was cursed.

He gritted his teeth and levered himself up again. She pushed at him and, unable to resist, he collapsed on his side. He squeezed his eyelids shut, reaching for the distance that kept him safe from pain and humiliation.

Warm and moist, her lips brushed his, her tongue traced the seam of his mouth. Scorching heat fired his blood. He opened his eyes and caught her saucy smile.

"My turn," she said.

Damnation. She was unbelievable.

Surrendering to her, he forced himself to lay still. Her mouth followed the line of his jaw, her breath whispered in his ear, sending a thrill of exquisite pleasure to his cock. He moaned.

The torture didn't stop. Relentless in her exploration of his body, her hands fluttered over his arms, her lips traveled to his chest and found his nipple. She licked it. He could not prevent his gasp as it pebbled and sent an arrow of desire to his bollocks.

She nibbled with her teeth at his tit's sensitive nub and his hips rose off the bed, seeking her, wanting her tight around his throbbing shaft.

"Victoria," he groaned.

"Simon," she whispered against his chest. "Tell me what to do next."

"Straddle me, sweet, ride me."

On her hands and knees, she lifted herself over him. The dark curls of her mons rested on his belly, hot and moist against his skin.

"That's it, darling." He reached down and slipped a finger into her soft folds, gently massaging her where her body touched his. Her faced tightened, and her glazed eyes slid closed. He cupped his palm against her hot womanly flesh, swollen ready for him.

"Let me inside you. Lift your hips." He raised her up.

Dazed and uncomprehending, her eyes gazed down at him. He rubbed the tip of his pulsing shaft against her scorching, wet opening.

Sudden comprehension filled her expression and she smiled. She lifted herself up and began a slow slide down his shaft. Languor filled his limbs. His mind spun out of control as pleasure radiated through his body and his soul.

The intense pleasure of him deep inside her made Victoria gasp. His hand, hot on her buttock, encouraged her to rise again. She savored the searing heat traveling from where they joined to the tips of her breasts as she moved along his length. She learned how his body fit into hers to produce unimaginable quivers of pleasure. Each slide of hot flesh against hard arousal produced an unendurable stomach-clenching shiver and teased her need for more.

"Oh, Victoria." The deep longing in his voice jolted in her belly. She squeezed him tight inside her and rocked her hips.

"Yes," he breathed. "God. Yes."

Her spirit soared as she knew her own power to give him delight. There was only him inside her, his body hard and thrusting to her downward stroke, his palm and fingers on her breasts. She leaned forward to his lifted head. He latched onto her nipple and suckled. Heat and tension vibrated in her body and her mind. She pressed down harder, clutching him inside her, tighter. They were one.

Blackness filled her mind. Urgently, she launched herself over the edge and felt him fly with her. They soared as bliss

271

exploded. His ragged cry of joy told her he had reached his own fulfillment.

She collapsed on his chest.

She couldn't move. Warmth invaded every part of her body, her heart thudded in her chest and Simon's knocked loudly against her ear.

He wanted to marry her. She tried to think about what it meant, but her mind quaked with the aftermath of him.

She shivered. Her source of warmth had gone. Simon. He was out of bed and stumbling around, the soft gleam from the window outlining his lithe, muscular shape. Need tugged at her bottomless well of desire. "Come back to bed."

The bed ropes creaked beneath his weight as he sat on the edge. He slanted her a smile over his shoulder. "In a moment. I heard a noise. It's probably nothing," he whispered.

He pulled on his breeches. She groped around, found her shift on the pillow next to her head and slipped it on.

"Stay here," Simon said over his shoulder as he pulled on his boots. "I'm just going to make sure everything is all right downstairs."

The sound of booted feet on the stairs brought him up-right and he swore softly as his head struck the low ceiling.

The door burst open.

Victoria pulled the sheet up under her chin.

"Well, well. And what do we have here?"

Ogden? Terror robbed her of breath. A pistol in his hand gleamed evilly in the light of a candle held by the man peering over his shoulder. She shuddered. Quigley. Simon had been right.

"Bugger off, you stupid bastard," Simon said wearily. "And take that oaf with you."

"Who, Quigley?" Ogden's voice crackled with scarcely

contained excitement. "He's got a score to settle with you."

Ogden ran his gaze over the bed. "Victoria. Good evening. I see you didn't heed my warning." He bowed.

A blush heated her face at his sorrowful tone. Simon moved to block Ogden's view. "You leave her out of this."

Ogden moved inside the room and took the candle from Quigley. "Tie his hands," he said.

Bringing his fists up in front of him, Simon squared off to Quigley. Ogden directed the pistol at Victoria. "Don't give me any trouble, Satan."

"Coward," Simon taunted. "Your grievance is with me, not her."

What was Ogden doing here and why had he brought Quigley? If he had come to rescue her, he had arrived too late. Victoria found her voice. "My lord, I am here of my free will. This is not your concern."

"Is it not?" Ogden asked walking around the far side of the bed toward her.

Simon turned, his gaze fixed on the hand with the pistol.

Quigley punched at him. Simon dodged, but Quigley's fist caught him on the jaw.

The blow resonated through her body. "Stop it!"

Simon staggered and Quigley lifted his fist to strike him again. She couldn't let them kill him. "He's wounded." She threw herself at Quigley striking at him with her fists.

"For God's sake, stay back," Simon said and warded her off with his forearm. She fell to her knees on the bed.

She could not believe this. She desperately wanted to wake up from this nightmare.

Ogden put the candle down and grabbed her arm. She shivered at his cold, reptilian touch. "He's right, Victoria. Stay out of it and you will be fine." He feathered his fingers across her cheek. "I'll take care of you after I've dealt with him." His caressing voice sent waves of nausea crashing through her.

A knowing smile twisted his lips. "Come quietly, Travis, and I promise Victoria will be well looked after."

Anxiety creasing his brow, Simon swung his attention away from Quigley,

"Don't worry about me," she said, more confidently than she felt.

Quigley's fist slammed into Simon's bandaged shoulder and Simon sank to his knees with a groan. The sound tore at her heart.

Victoria slipped from Ogden's grasping hand and leaned over the bed, trying to help Simon to his feet. "Stop it, you brute. You'll kill him."

Ogden ran his hand over her back, then grabbed her around the waist. "You'll forget all about him in my arms, my dear." She lashed out at him as he lifted her back onto the bed.

Simon lurched to his feet. "Take your hands off her, Ogden, or I'll kill you. Cover yourself, Victoria." Murder shone from his blue eyes, his face granite-hard.

Embarrassed, she pulled the quilt around her.

Quigley punched Simon in the stomach. Simon doubled over, coughing and gasping for air.

Against her every urge, Victoria remained still; her interference only made things worse.

Moving behind Simon, Quigley dragged his hands behind his back and tied them with a rope he pulled from his pocket.

Simon bit out a curse as Quigley yanked the rope cruelly tight.

Red blood blossomed on Simon's bandage. If they didn't stop this, he would surely die. She had to do something. "Please, my lord. Don't do this."

"Don't beg, Victoria." Simon's voice rasped a warning.

Ogden gave her his familiar courtly smile and captured her hands in his. "She'll beg all right. She will beg for me and forget you."

How could she have been taken in by his superficial charm. He was a snake. She edged away from him.

Rigid with mind-numbing fear as Ogden fixed his strangely glittering gaze on her face, she froze at the venom in his voice. "All those weeks, while you sat in that hovel in Golden Square, keeping me dangling on a string, I relieved your idiot brother of every last penny, apart from what Satan took on the very last night." Putting an arm around her shoulders and tipping her chin, he forced her to meet his eyes. "Do you think I cared about Michael or his pathetic bit of money? You were always the prize."

How stubbornly blind she had been. Ogden had ruined Michael to get to her. The man she had defended as her brother's friend had driven Michael to desperation. She wanted to weep. She jerked her face away.

"Why did you suggest I take her in, if you wanted her?" Simon asked, his eyes glittering slits.

Ogden's expression became rueful. "If I had thought for a single moment you would act on it, I never would have taunted you."

"I thought as much. You're too stupid to live, Ogden. Far too damned stupid."

Quigley hauled on the rope and Victoria heard a sharp hiss of pain between Simon's clenched teeth. His expression remained unmoved.

"Now then, Satan," Ogden said. "There's a lady present, watch your language." He smiled. "She's a tasty morsel, isn't she? I shall enjoy getting to know her better, much better."

Victoria couldn't repress her shudder.

Simon lunged at Ogden. Quigley jabbed an elbow in the side of his head. Simon would have fallen if Quigley hadn't held him up by his bound arms.

"Leave her alone, you bloody bastard," Simon grated out. Blood ran down his face from a cut over his eye.

Victoria desperately tried to calm her shaking nerves. She had to do something to help Simon. She ran her gaze around the room. There had to be something she could use as a weapon.

"Stay out of this, Victoria," Simon warned.

Ogden leered at her. "Do as he says. Be a good girl and I won't have to punish you. You'll like what I have for you, Victoria. I'm a good lover, you'll see."

Simon cursed. "I'll kill you if you lay a finger on her."

Victoria tasted sour bile in the back of her throat. What a fool she had been to trust this man over Simon. She gazed with longing at the heavy candlestick on the night table just out of her reach. The thought of Quigley hitting Simon again prevented her from risking it.

"Sun's coming up, my lord," Quigley said, peering out of the window.

Ogden straightened. "Indeed," he said. "We must hurry. Get him out of here." He nodded at Simon who glared back at him.

"Victoria, you will remain here until I come back for you," Ogden said with an elegant bow. Following Quigley, who pushed Simon ahead of him, Ogden closed the door behind him. The key turned in the lock.

Victoria listened to the sound of their progress down the stairs and the front door slamming. Then silence.

276

Chapter Eighteen

Dressing swiftly, Victoria considered her options. Surely the Davises must have heard Ogden and his henchman and would come to their aid?

The thick-planked door with iron hinges offered no chance of escape. She crossed to the window and peered out. A rosy glow lit the sky to the east and trees and bushes took shape in the garden below.

She gasped and drew back. Trapped. Two men stood conversing in the deep shadows. More of Ogden's villains.

Peeping around the window frame, she made out one giant of a man, his light hair reflecting the pale dawn as he gestured toward the inn. The slighter man nodded his head. At length, the tall man slapped his underling on the shoulder and strode off through the gate. His henchman entered the inn. Now she had another obstacle to overcome.

Rusted shut, the window latch refused to budge. Victoria knocked the candlestick against it, fearing discovery at any moment. It inched across the wooden window frame until finally she nudged it clear. She flung the window wide and stared at the drop to the ground.

Oh, Lord. She'd break her neck. She dashed to the bed and pulled off the linen. She grinned to herself. Obviously, Viscount Ogden hadn't considered the fact that every female who ever read a romance novel knew to use bed sheets to escape. She fastened the makeshift rope to the bedstead and threw it out of the window. Without looking down, she clambered over the windowsill and slid down the knotted length. She landed amid a rather scratchy privet. She pulled her skirts free and held her breath to see if anyone had heard her. Nothing. Only the sound of awakening birds.

Afraid to risk going to find the Davises in case she ran into the man she'd seen go inside the inn, she followed the tall man into the woods beyond the courtyard. Simon had to be there.

While the sun was on the rise, no light filtered down to the forest floor. The earth-damp smell of leaf mold scented the air as she followed the path, a short cut to the nearby village.

Voices carried on the still air, one man shouting and cursing, another reasoning. Victoria hid behind a holly bush. Peering around the prickly greenery, she saw a clearing ahead of her, and in its center, Ogden paced in front of a still-bound Simon held fast by Quigley.

Using a thicket of brambles for cover, Victoria crept closer. The gloom did not hide the blood running from Simon's injured shoulder or the cuts on his bare chest and face. Three other men with guns stood facing out like guards. Ogden had brought a small army.

Ogden halted in front of Simon. "Admit it, damn you."

"Go to hell."

Ogden struck him on the cheek with the back of his hand. Simon's head snapped back. He spat blood. Victoria muffled her scream with her fist against her mouth.

This had to stop. Victoria started from her hiding place.

A hand grabbed her wrist, another covered her mouth and her captor pulled her back against his large form. He hustled her behind the trunk of a large oak. She stared into the grim face of the Marquess of Lethbridge. Of course. She should have recognized him as the tall man in the garden.

"What the hell are you doing out here, Miss Yelverton?" he asked.

"You have to help Simon."

"All in good time. He won't thank me if anything happens to you. Do not move from here."

Relieved to know help for Simon was at hand, she nodded and leaned back against the rough bark. The marquess strode off into the forest. She peered around the tree.

Simon lay on the ground at Ogden's feet. Tears rose in Victoria's eyes as he dragged himself up onto his knees and then onto his feet. Why didn't he just lie down and stay there?

He swayed, his expression insolent as he stared at his tormentor. "Is that your best shot. My last mistress had a better right hand than you," Simon said.

Victoria winced. Was he deliberately trying to bait Ogden into killing him? If so, he was going about it the right way. Ogden, fists clenched, closed in on Simon. Oh, where was the marquess? If he didn't do something soon, she would have to intervene.

The sun rose over the trees and the clearing burst into vibrant colors. Ogden's hair gleamed gold, his clothes and linen immaculate. Simon, bare-chested, dirty and bloody, would have looked like a beggar beside him, if not for his aura of warrior's pride.

"We has to get going, my lord," Quigley said, glancing around.

A sneer on his face, Ogden pulled out his pistol. "Say your prayers, Satan."

Triumph blazed in the pale eyes staring at Simon. Spittle flecked Ogden's lips. Damn the twisted bastard. But for Victoria, Simon wouldn't care one way or the other. He recalled with horror the rumors about Ogden's sadistic use of women. It had never occurred to Simon to suspect Ogden of being as insane as his sister, but looking at him now, he wasn't sure. For the first time in a great many years, the maggots of fear crawled in his gut. Fear for Victoria.

He held his anger in check and his excruciating pain isolated from his sharply focused mind. "Leave Victoria out of this, Ogden and I'll give you what you want."

Ogden smirked. Simon's blood ran cold at the madness in the leering gaze.

"All right," Ogden said.

Simon needed more assurance. "Swear it. On your honor as a gentleman."

"You'd trust my word?"

His mouth filled with salty blood from the cut inside his cheek. He spat. "I don't have much choice, do I? But yes, I do trust your word."

Ogden straightened.

"Besides," said a calm voice from the trees, "you have a witness."

Lethbridge, a golden god, sauntered into the open space and stood in a patch of sunlight.

Bloody hell. Lethbridge, and hours earlier than expected. Simon repressed his smile. Now this was something like.

"Good day, Ian." Simon grinned and bit back a wince at the sting from his cut upper lip. "Nice of you to drop by."

"My pleasure," Lethbridge replied with a bow.

"Get on with it then," Simon said to Ogden.

The nervous bobbing of Ogden's Adam's apple made Simon smile inwardly. Ogden had been waiting for this day for a very long time and could not resist the challenge.

"Mark this well, Lethbridge," Ogden said. He fisted his hands on his hips, his expression a mask of pure hatred. "You remember the day of the carriage accident at Danson's ford, don't you, Satan?"

Simon nodded. Never a day passed that he didn't remember.

"Speak up, man."

"Yes," Simon said.

"You had hold of the baby, didn't you?"

"I pulled him out of the sinking carriage."

"Just answer yes or no."

"What is this, Ogden, some kind of trial?" Lethbridge asked.

Ogden flicked a glance his way. "Something like that. It's justice after all these years. Yes or no?"

"What are you? The judge, jury and executioner?" Lethbridge questioned.

Ogden smiled, a chilling, mirthless little smile. "Yes."

Simon glanced at his friend. He stood, one fist on his hip, staring at the nails on his other hand, a picture of nonchalance.

"Well? Yes or no?" Ogden pushed his face into Simon's.

"Yes," Simon said.

"And you let him go."

"Yes." Simon forced the word out.

"You purposefully let an innocent child drown."

He hadn't done it on purpose. At least he always told himself he hadn't. "No. He slipped out of his blanket. The current carried him away."

"Liar. You miserable liar," Ogden screamed.

Simon tensed as Ogden's fist bored into his gut. He didn't resist, following the blow by doubling over, cutting off all sensation one limb at a time, preparing, just as Mr. McIver had taught him.

Spit ran down Ogden's chin. He flexed his knuckles as if to ease the sting of his blow. "Tell the truth, Satan. You hated Miranda for giving your father another son. A son he loved better than you. You were jealous of the child."

All the old guilt swept through Simon. He had been jealous of his father's love for the new child. A love he'd never been able to capture for himself.

Ogden sneered, his face loathsome in its confidence. "You were jealous of a baby. Come on. Admit it."

He had been. His father doted on baby John, because he was Miranda's child. His father, who had all but ignored Simon most of his life, adored the newcomer.

"Yes," he muttered. "Yes, damn you. I was jealous of . . ." He couldn't prevent the catch in his voice, no matter how hard he tried to control his emotions. "My father cared for him more than me. But I didn't let him go on purpose."

"You drowned him."

Miranda had cried out in alarm. He'd looked around for a second. When he looked back, all he held was the empty shawl. John's round head with its wisp of blond hair had bobbed above the rushing water and then disappeared. Simon bowed his head. "Yes."

"Murderer. See, Lethbridge, he admitted it. He murdered his own brother, my sister's child."

Lethbridge shook his head. "Not quite. He said he didn't do it on purpose."

Ogden's eyes narrowed and his lips curled in a snarl. "He admitted it. We all heard it, didn't we?"

The other men all nodded.

Ogden turned to Simon, speaking softly. "Tell the truth. You said you'd give me what I wanted."

His pint of blood. Simon had given his word and Victoria's life depended on it.

"Don't admit to something you didn't do, Simon," Lethbridge said.

The air rushed from Simon's chest. Didn't do? Had it

really been an accident? Or had he, like a cuckoo in the nest, let the child drown to keep his father's affection to himself. Miranda said he had and his father believed her. Simon didn't know anymore. It didn't matter. He had to make sure of Victoria's safety.

"I admit it," he said, loud and clear and the devil take his soul. "I killed him."

Someone moved to his right. The atmosphere shifted in anxious waves. Not Lethbridge, he had already taken account of his presence. Simon refocused.

"And now you die," Ogden said.

"You can't just kill him in cold blood," Lethbridge said, his voice calm and quiet. "It would make you a murderer. You will hang, unless you kill me and my men."

Lethbridge. The master of the bluff and always full of surprises. Simon chuckled silently.

Suspicion filled Ogden's face. "If you had men here, they'd be on us by now."

Lethbridge raised an arm. Rutherford, Wilson and James moved silently from behind the trees and stood at the edge of the clearing. They must have caused the disturbance Simon felt. Ogden's men muttered, raised their weapons and moved closer to their master and Simon.

"You will hang, Ogden, I promise you. Unless, of course, you do the honorable thing," Lethbridge said.

Ogden turned his attention to Lethbridge. "What do you mean?"

The sly old fox. Simon laughed. Pain nudged at his chest. Ogden or Quigley must have cracked a rib or two. "He means a duel, you whoreson. Or are you too cowardly?"

Simon watched with sardonic amusement as Ogden looked him over. He knew how bad his condition appeared. He wavered on his feet, one eye was closed and blood was running into the other. This would be easy, for Ogden.

"Fine," Ogden said. "A duel."

"Ogden," Simon said. "If I die, have you thought about what happens to your family? According to my father's will, the golden goose dies with me or disappears if you reveal the truth to anyone else." His father, despite believing his guilt, had done his best to protect his oldest son and the family honor.

Ogden backhanded him. Simon rocked on his heels and let the blow caress the side of his face, moving precisely to reduce force of the impact. He shook his head to clear the blood from his eye.

"I say, bad sport," Rutherford shouted.

"*If* you die," Ogden shrieked. "You mean when. I don't care about your bloody money. It's Miranda I care about."

Christ. Simon's nagging suspicion of something unmentionable between Ogden and his sister churned in his gut. "It's not just you, Ogden. What about the rest of your family?"

Ogden thrust his face into Simon's. "They abandoned her. Let them find out what it's like." He jerked his head at Quigley. "Free his hands."

Ogden paced the twenty paces. Kind of him not to make Simon walk the distance. Ogden's first mistake.

The pistol Lethbridge handed Simon felt familiar. His own dueling pistol. Another of Ogden's mistakes. Simon let it fall to his side. He nodded slightly at Lethbridge's questioning look.

"Good luck," Lethbridge murmured.

Simon gave him a cocky grin. "The devil's own luck."

Like the military man he was, Lethbridge marked ten even paces and stationed himself halfway between the duelists. He held out a white handkerchief.

Simon staggered slightly and then planted his feet apart. He fixed his gaze on Ogden.

A cry of anguish rang in his ears.

Victoria. Pain sliced him with a thousand cuts. She was here.

He swung around and saw her running from the trees. His heart shattered. Not Lethbridge's men, it was Victoria who had disturbed his concentration at his admission of guilt.

She'd heard it all. Knew his mortal sin. His control deserted him. Blood roared in his ears, his body screamed out in agony, his shoulder, his chest, his head, his heart.

Streaming with tears, her face held the same expression of dread as on the day her brother died. Damn her. Why could she not have stayed at the inn? He preferred death to her knowing.

"Get her out of here," he shouted at Lethbridge.

One of Lethbridge's men rushed toward her.

"You'll be killed," she cried out.

Ah, she was anxious for him. The thought gave him comfort, strengthened him. No one had ever cared what happened to him. He would not let Ogden harm her.

"Take her back to the inn at once," Lethbridge shouted.

"Simon, no. Don't do this."

Sorrow ached in her voice. It was Ogden she worried about. Bitterness filled his soul.

He refused to look.

Shutting everything from his mind, he absorbed the feel of the gun in his hand, his weapon an extension of his arm, a living part of his body, like his finger, his palm, he was the weapon in his hand.

He distanced all emotions, pain, grief, love, until nothing but the pistol in his fist and a living thread connected him to his enemy. Each movement, each breath, became a fragment of time, filling the space between them. He saw only Ogden and the fine thread guiding the bullet into Ogden's brain.

A flash of white midway along the thread.

The signal. He lined up with the gossamer web.

His heartbeat picked up speed. He breathed deeply through his nose just as Mr. McIver had taught him all those years ago. Peace flooded his mind.

The white square hit the ground. He aimed along the thread.

The image of Victoria's face, frightened and anguished, flashed before his eyes. The thread wavered and flickered. She hadn't left, and she made him weak. He would not allow it.

He inhaled. The gleaming line steadied. He pulled the trigger.

Explosions roared in quick succession.

Ogden's bullet drifted toward him. Wide.

His own bullet slid quietly along its guideline. A hole appeared in Ogden's forehead.

Victoria was safe. *Thank you, Mr. McIver.* He knelt and offered reverence to his old teacher, the only person who had ever believed in him.

Shots made Victoria jump. They echoed through the silent woods. Birds squawked and fluttered skywards. Freeing her arm from Wilson's fettering grip, she turned. Simon was on his knees. For one heart-shattering instant, she thought he'd been hit. Relief washed through her as he hauled himself to his feet.

Arrogant in his victory, he glared around, his face an expressionless mask. She saw his eyes. Flat, dead, they looked out from the stygian depths of hell, as empty as the death he'd inflicted on Ogden.

This was the real Simon St John. Satan. A dark, vengeful

angel, a murderer of children, he killed on the field of honor as calmly as other men ate dinner. She didn't know him at all.

She froze in his gaze.

He stared at her. Recognition, like ripples on a fathomless, crystal pool, fractured the still surface of his eyes. He clawed out from his dark world and into hers.

He raised his hand as if to reach out to her. She jerked away. He stiffened, a flash of anguish sweeping his face. Then he smiled, a cynical curve of his lips. He sauntered over to Lethbridge bent over Ogden's still body.

"Please, miss, come with me." Wilson tugged on her arm.

She stumbled away, dry sobs racking her chest. How could she have thought she loved such an unfeeling devil?

Bars of afternoon sun fell across the scrubbed faces of ten children of varying ages. They gazed solemnly back at Victoria, immobile in neat rows of desk and chairs.

Victoria smiled. "And that's the end of the story."

The spell broke on a collective sigh.

"Good afternoon, children," she said getting to her feet.

"Good afternoon, Miss Yelverton," they chorused.

Bert Johnson threw his hat in the air. "No more school," he crowed and they were off: an unruly group of farm children, clattering and laughing their way back to their chores in the fields. School was finished until autumn. All gone in an instant, except Neddy, a black-haired, brown-eyed scamp, sporting a green and black bruise around one eye. Ned's father was the village drunk.

The lad couldn't be more than seven, but he'd suffered numerous broken bones and he dragged one leg. Ned never complained about his dad, and Victoria had discussed his situation with the vicar, who thought nothing could be done to protect the child.

"Not leaving yet, Ned?" she asked, halting beside his desk.

"Me da don't get home from the pub yet, miss," he said and wiped his nose on his ragged, dirty sleeve.

"Would you like to stay and have a cup of tea and a biscuit with me?"

"Cor, yes, miss."

She smiled and held out her hand. It was not unusual for Ned to break his fast with her, for he often went hungry. She thought of another boy who had gone hungry, starved for affection and human warmth as well as food. At least she could help this one. The other did not want her help.

"Come along then, young man."

She took his grubby hand in hers and they crossed the schoolyard to her cottage. Roses framed the door, chintz curtains stirred in the light breeze drifting through the open windows and the smell of baking wafted from the kitchen. Elsie loved to cook.

After Ned drank his tea and ate his cake, she waved goodbye to him and he ran up the lane. Back in the house, she sat down in her bright and airy drawing room.

"Here you are, miss," Elsie said. "The London paper and today's mail. Fair exhausted you must be. Good thing it is too for you have a break from them little horrors."

Victoria laughed. Elsie, who had asked to stay with her when she left Travis Place, had become a formidable woman now that she ran Victoria's small house in Crayford.

Had it all happened only three months ago? Twelve weeks since Ogden had died at Simon's hand and two long months since Simon St John had arranged for her to have her wish for independence. What she said she wanted above all else.

She rubbed her arms with her hands.

"You cold, miss? Let me light the fire."

"A fire in July?" Victoria replied, scandalized by the extravagance. "It was just gooseflesh."

"A ghost walking over your grave," said the superstitious Elsie with relish. "Never you mind. Supper'll be along shortly."

Victoria scanned the paper. She smiled at the notice of Mr. and Mrs. Albert Runcorn's wedding with Lady Elizabeth Halsted in attendance. She silently wished the very best for Mr. Albert Runcorn and his new bride.

She hesitated. She always said she would not, then she always did. She turned to the society column.

Travis. He'd been in the paper a lot lately. One of London's most eligible bachelors, he always attracted attention. Occasionally, they coupled his name with one of the Season's debutantes. He only had to stand up to dance with someone more than once and they announced an engagement was in the offing. She usually ignored that kind of gossip. Simon had no real interest in marrying anyone, as she well knew.

Mostly his name was associated with a Lady B____, a very merry widow, by all accounts. Victoria couldn't remember a Lady whose name began with B.

The words drew her eye: *The earl of T____s,* it said, *danced twice with Lady Julia G____h at the Smythe's ball on Saturday night. If this writer might be permitted an opinion, they make a very handsome couple. From the amusement on their faces, they seemed well entertained by each other. Lord T____s left the ball early with Lady B____ and was not seen until Tuesday.*

Victoria blinked at the burning sensation at the back of her throat and behind her eyes. Why should she hurt because of Julia or Lady B, whoever she was? Victoria should be glad for him. His life hadn't changed one iota since she left him in Wales. And why should it?

She had waited for weeks for his return to London after the duel. He never came.

Only Lethbridge had paid her a brief visit.

"Will Simon be charged with murder?" she had asked Lethbridge in Travis's drawing room in Grosvenor Square.

"The witnesses will say Ogden forced the duel and Simon responded in self-defence. The rest will depend on the local magistrate." Lethbridge patted her arm and smiled encouragingly. "He's fine, Victoria."

"He looked so cold, so evil. He scared me. He really is a devil."

Sadness hollowed Lethbridge's expression. He shook his head. "Listen, Victoria, Simon has been through a lot in his life. The business with Miranda and the baby hurt him badly."

"Simon said he killed the child. I heard him."

Lethbridge held her gaze. "The baby drowned, swept away in the river in a carriage accident. Simon was a boy. The two adults present watched Simon dive into a torrent to save the baby. The pair of them blamed Simon, little more than a child himself, for his failure."

Lethbridge ran a hand through his hair. "He tried, Miss Yelverton. The child's loss and their accusations still haunt him."

The horrendous picture he conjured up made more sense than Simon's admission, knowing him as she did.

"Why did he admit to it?"

"To save you. Ogden promised to leave you alone if he admitted to murder."

Victoria felt sick as she remembered how she had recoiled from Simon in the forest. Tears filled her throat. "I didn't know."

Lethbridge nodded. "The trouble is, Miranda lied to save herself, and his father believed her over Simon. She planted the seeds of doubt in Simon's mind. His father disowning him was bad enough, but sending him to Blackhurst almost destroyed him. Did he tell you about it?"

"He said he didn't like it much. He didn't make many friends there."

"It was far worse than anything you could imagine. You must never tell him I told you this. I only learned some of it when he was in his cups. I'm not sure he remembers he told me." Lethbridge stared solemnly at her, waiting for her promise.

She nodded.

He went on in a low voice. "It was a crime sending him there. He was publicly flogged as a regular punishment. They called him unnatural, but never explained what it meant or gave him a chance to answer the charge. The other boys thought he was . . ." he hesitated. "Blast. I don't know if I should say this or not. They thought he lusted after other boys."

Victoria gasped. She knew what he meant, and she knew how reviled Simon would have been.

"The other pupils would have nothing to do with him unless it was to torment him. He worked long days or went without food. He had to give up sleep to complete his lessons."

Victoria shook her head. "I can't believe they could be so cruel to a child."

Lethbridge held her gaze, his hazel eyes demanding she listen and believe. "It's true. He was publicly humiliated every day of his stay there. Once, they made him stand outside all night, naked, in the dead of winter with a sign around his neck declaring him to be the son of the devil. He began to believe what they told him."

He ran a hand through his hair as if he could scarcely understand it himself. "They didn't take his pride, Victoria.

291

What they did was make him deny he has any kind of heart. Miranda and Blackhurst forced him to avoid all forms of human closeness. Apart from me, you are the only person I have ever seen him come close to admitting affection for."

Reeling from what she had heard and scarcely able to comprehend what Simon must have suffered, Victoria whispered, "I had no idea." She recalled his expression of raw suffering when she rejected his proffered hand. "What should I do?"

Lethbridge sighed audibly. "Give him some time. Try not to think of him as Satan. God, I should have made sure you were gone from there. I knew what he was capable of, you see, and it's not pleasant. It's an inner power, a strength he used to get through Blackhurst. It's almost as if he has no soul when he's like that. I knew he would kill Ogden."

Soulless. The word described what she had seen when their eyes had met across the clearing.

She had never seen him again.

He was recovering from his injuries in Hampshire, excused Maria, at first. He had pressing business at his estate, he'd written later. All her letters were returned unopened, all her requests to see him denied. He avoided her, fearing she would keep him to his rash promise of marriage, she finally concluded.

Then his lawyer had come to see her with the deed to this house and school. An ironic smile tugged at her lips; she'd told Simon how to be rid of her on their last night together and he'd taken her up on it.

Less than a month later, she'd moved here. Welcomed by the neighbors as an eccentric woman of means, she took over from the retiring schoolteacher because it pleased her.

The only contact she had with Travis since then was through his lawyer. Everything arranged and ordered just as she wanted. She was her own mistress, making her own decisions. She *was* happy. She just hadn't expected never to see him again.

The words on the page blurred. Dash it all. Surely she wasn't crying still? She blew her nose and continued reading.

Lord T___s, it is rumored, is expected to leave for Italy at the end of the Season.

Probably with bloody Lady B____.

She threw the paper down. It was the last time she'd read the stupid column. She turned her attention to sorting her letters and bills.

She wiped her eyes and smiled at Julia's familiar handwriting. They'd kept up a steady correspondence since she left London. Julia had recently come into a considerable fortune of her own and planned to travel. On several occasions, she had tried to persuade Victoria to go with her. Victoria always said no. She looked forward to Julia's letters, always full of droll tales and humorous descriptions of the doings of the *ton,* but she never mentioned Travis or Lethbridge, even though she must see them frequently, as noted in the newspaper.

Victoria would have liked Julia's impression of the earl's activities, his health, his happiness. Pride prevented her from asking.

This letter invited her to spend two weeks with Julia at her parents' country home in Hampshire. Why not? School was finished for the summer. She was her own mistress.

She went to her desk and pulled out her writing case.

Chapter Nineteen

Simon leaned against one side of a pillar overlooking the dance floor. Lady Corby's ballroom, for some reason unknown to rational man, was decorated like an eastern potentate's harem with blue and pink muslin. The last ball of the Season and the year's crop of debutantes hadn't improved in Victoria's absence.

He ran a bleak, assessing glance over the group of young ladies waiting to be asked to dance. None of them engaged his interest for a moment. No female had since Victoria left. He stifled a yawn as one girl caught his gaze and batted her eyelashes. Simon raised a haughty eyebrow, the chit blushed and turned away.

"Satan." Lethbridge, leaning on the other side of the same pillar, sent him a sly grin. "Leave the poor little things alone if you're not going to ask them to dance. You're frightening them."

"More like they are frightening me," he replied, returning the glance of another saucy miss peering over her fan at him. She held his look boldly. She might do for him. She looked hard enough to marry a man who had nothing to offer but a fortune and a title. What had remained of his battered heart lay buried in Wales, shattered by the expression of horror in Victoria Yelverton's eyes.

Barely a year ago, he would have taken the bold wench up on her ill-disguised interest. He would have seduced her into

294

taking his money. It no longer challenged him. He just wasn't interested.

Not so surprising after he'd known real fulfilment with Victoria. The shallow game of amour held no lustre anymore. These days he was practically a monk. And yet he couldn't stay away. Restless in the country, his stables no longer absorbed him. Bored here in Town, without Lethbridge to push him through the motions of living, he'd be mad by now.

"So, are you going to offer for any of them?"

He had always intended to find a bride one day, someone as heartless as himself, before he met Victoria. Now, he wasn't sure anymore. What did it matter if the St John name died with him? "There are a couple of them who might suit," Simon drawled.

He lifted his quizzing glass and observed Hawkfield, sporting a new *fille de joie,* dance past them.

"But," Lethbridge prodded.

"But," Simon said, unable to contain a weary sigh, "I think I'll wait until next year and see if anything better comes along."

"Hmm," Lethbridge murmured.

Simon followed the direction of his friend's abstracted glance. Genevieve Longbourne swirled by with a flash of diamonds and flurry of cream satin in the arms of the Duke of Rockingham.

"You're a fine one to talk," Simon said. "Stop gazing at her like a moon-calf before the Duke calls you out. Surely, now the wedding day is set, even a stubborn fool like you can see it's hopeless."

"Mind your own business."

Simon raised an eyebrow, but said nothing. Lethbridge's stubborn clinging to Genevieve was not a topic either of them would discuss without heat.

Lady Julia Garforth floated by on Colonel Monteith's arm. He wore full military regalia. The ladies couldn't resist a uniform. He frowned. "I thought Monteith had already left for India. Do you think he's going to offer for Lady Ju?"

Lethbridge stiffened. "Damn the fellow for his impudence."

"Hmm," replied Simon, remembering Monteith's proposal for Victoria's hand all those months ago. He should have convinced her to agree. Then she never would have discovered his past and despised him more than she already did.

Thank God he hadn't foisted a child on her in his careless passion. He'd waited for Maria to report things were safe on that front. He would never have forgiven himself if he'd had to force her to marry him. The thought of Victoria large with his child tore open the gaping hole in his chest. Bloody hell, would the acid of regret never cease to eat away at him?

She ought to marry someone else; then perhaps he'd finally be free of her. He grimaced. A wealthy woman living alone risked danger, especially one as beautiful as Victoria. According to his lawyer, Victoria had attracted a persistent suitor and the problem might soon be solved. He clenched his jaw.

"For Christ's sake, Simon, stop glaring at them. I swear the blond one is going to swoon."

Simon hadn't realized he was glaring. Damn. If he didn't watch out he'd have a steely eyed mother dragging one of them over here to dance.

He resumed his perusal of Lady Ju. "I suppose I could always offer for Julia," he said. "She's sensible and we get along all right. We always have."

"I thought you were a friend of hers."

Simon frowned. "I am."

296

"Pretty poor friendship, marrying her when you love someone else."

Simon stared down his nose at the smirking Lethbridge, resenting his knowledge. "You have nothing to crow about."

"I'm not offering to marry anyone else," Lethbridge pointed out.

"Well you should. And since when do you care so much about Lady Julia, anyway?"

Lethbridge glanced in her direction. He shrugged. "She's a great girl, that's all. Don't ruin her life the way you . . ."

The way I ruined Victoria's, Simon finished in his mind. He regretted the outcome bitterly, but he would not have missed those nights in her arms for anything in the world. The memories of those few short moments were all he had. They'd been the only good part of his life.

He shook his head. "You're right. She's better than any of these other hen-wits, but it would be hard to bed a girl who's more like a sister."

Lethbridge's face turned flinty, a glint of steel reflected in his normally placid eyes. "Damn you, Satan, she wouldn't have you anyway."

The rigid set of Lethbridge's back gave Simon the odd sensation he'd missed part of the conversation. Who cared? He eased away from the pillar. "I'm going to find a game of piquet."

Lethbridge cast one last, long glance at Genevieve. "I'll join you." Lethbridge took his arm and they strolled toward the card room. "Are you going to Pelham's for the hunt this weekend?"

Simon curled his lip. "I wasn't. Pelham's an idiot."

"Come along, why don't you? Do you good to get out of Town for a few days. You don't actually have to talk to Pelham. I never do."

Simon chuckled. "Maybe. I'll let you know."

★ ★ ★ ★ ★

The library door swung open. Victoria, reclining in one of the window seats and cosy behind a heavy curtain, glanced up from her book expecting to see Julia.

"Damn you for a fool, Philip. Why the hell did you allow Pelham to talk you into getting on that mare of his in the first place? I told you she was unpredictable."

Travis's sardonic drawl pierced her ears like nails dragged down a slate. For a moment, she considered fleeing behind the drapes or diving under the desk. Too late.

Heat flushed her face as Travis stopped short at the sight of her. Rutherford, right behind, collided with him, then pushed on past.

"Miss Yelverton," Rutherford said. "Didn't know you were visiting." His right arm in a sling, Lord Rutherford took her hand awkwardly in his left.

Victoria's heart had not yet returned from her throat to her chest. She wasn't sure she could utter a word. "Yes. Lady Julia invited me." Idiot. Of course Julia had invited her. She looked at his arm. "You are hurt?"

"Fell off a horse." Rutherford grinned. "It's just a strain, but it put paid to hunting."

"I'm sorry," she said unable to think of anything else to say. She was exceedingly sorry.

A cool smile curved Travis's lips. He barely touched her fingers as he bowed. "Nice to see you again, Miss Yelverton." He moved to the window and stared out over the formal gardens.

"Miss Yelverton," Lethbridge said with a friendly smile and an elegant bow.

Julia had arranged this. Victoria would murder her. "Excuse me, gentlemen," she said, happy to discover her voice did not shake like her body. "I'm on my way out."

"Don't leave on our account," Travis said without turning around. "Indeed, I believe I am the one who is leaving."

"You can't," Rutherford said. "You just promised m'mother you'd dine. She will be most affronted if you cry off now."

"I'd forgotten a previous engagement at the Hall," Travis snapped.

This was intolerable. Victoria curtseyed. "Well, I may or may not see you later." She left as quickly as she could without actually appearing to run away. She heard Travis's hard laugh as she fled down the hallway.

How could Julia have invited both her and Travis? Victoria could not stay with him under the same roof, or even nearby at his own estate. He ought to be in Italy with the infamous Lady B____.

After a brief search of the downstairs rooms, she found Julia in the herb garden at the east end of the red brick Tudor mansion. She wore a huge straw hat tied with a big green bow under one ear, while she dug in the soil around what appeared to be a large weed.

Julia looked up at her approach. "See this, Victoria, meadowflower. It's the best cure for a headache known to man."

"You and your weeds," Victoria said staring at the leggy plant.

"Herbs, Victoria. Healing plants."

"Never mind them, Travis is here with your brother and Lethbridge," Victoria blurted out.

Julia paled. "Lethbridge, here?"

Victoria stared at her. "Oh, Julia, not you too. Yes, both of them. Were they expected?"

Julia laughed. "Me too? Whatever can you mean? And no, I promise you, I had no idea. Philip wasn't supposed to be back until the end of the month. I had planned to leave before then."

"I have to leave now."

Julia clipped a bunch of ragged leaves, inspected them and dropped them in her basket. "Why?"

"Because I can't face him. He was appalled to find me here. I'm his past, Julia. No one likes their past thrust under their nose."

"Then he will have to leave. Where is your bonnet? You will get freckles out here in the sun."

"I don't get freckles," Victoria replied.

Julia sighed. "If you must leave, go in the morning. We'll send you home in the carriage."

Julia was right. It was too late to depart this afternoon, and besides, it would be very rude to her hostess, Lady Rutherford. Perhaps Travis would play the gentleman and take himself off.

Travis, it seemed, had also changed his mind. Already in the drawing room when Victoria and Julia came down for dinner, his scorching, ironic gaze drifted from her modest gown and traveled up her face to her hair. She colored. What did he expect? She was a schoolteacher. Her severe style of dress suited her new life.

Victoria joined Lethbridge and Julia's mother, a tall, thin lady with faded red curls, while Julia went to speak with Travis and her brother. Strange how Julia avoided Lethbridge's company after her earlier attraction. She never mentioned him now and Victoria did not like to pry.

"Dinner is served, milady," announced the butler.

"Oh dear, yes, yes." Lady Rutherford seemed rather flustered by her sudden house full of guests. "Now, Philip, you take my arm. Julia you go with the marquess and perhaps Travis you wouldn't mind escorting Miss Yelverton."

"My pleasure." Travis bowed. A wicked glint lit his bright blue eyes at her gasp.

He had a nerve, laughing at her. She pulled herself together. It was missish of her to act like a stranger to him. She could do this. She smiled. "Thank you, my lord."

It went without saying, she was seated next to Simon for dinner. She decided to make the best of it. The footmen served a first course of mock turtle soup.

"You are looking well, Miss Yelverton," Travis said in lazy tones.

"Thank you, my lord. As are you." He wasn't. He looked thinner and paler than she recalled. His face seemed more granite-like than ever.

He flicked a sardonic look her way. "You are too kind."

He'd guessed her thoughts. She felt her face go red. She concentrated on her food.

"How are you enjoying Kent?" Simon asked.

He obviously wasn't going to stop tormenting her. "I love it. My school is doing well. I have ten pupils. I think the local people are becoming accustomed to me." She glanced sideways at him. He wasn't eating. He leaned back in his chair, holding his glass of wine and watching her from beneath lowered lashes. Blue ice froze her heart.

He curled his lip. "I hear you have some local squire in your clutches already." Boredom filled his voice.

Victoria almost dropped her fork. She glanced around the table to see if anyone listened to them. No one seemed to be paying them any attention. "You mean Sir David Enterly?"

Twisting the stem of the glass, he watched the liquid swirl. "Do I? I'm sure you're right. Has he made you an offer?"

Heat rose in her face again. Insolent and dark, he seemed more devastatingly handsome than ever, or had she just forgotten? "If it's any of your business, yes, he has."

Travis sipped at his wine, then gave her a mocking smile. "And will you invite me to dance at your wedding?"

What a question. "No, of course not. You see I'm—"

"No need to explain, Miss Yelverton. I'm wounded, but I can't say I'm surprised."

He turned to Lady Rutherford on his left before she could compose a reply.

Victoria struggled to swallow some of the food on her plate. How could he have known about Sir David? Perhaps it was better if Simon thought she was to be married. At least he wouldn't think she hungered for a man who cared nothing about her.

A roast of beef removed the first course, supplemented by a platter of pig's trotters and assorted vegetables. Barely aware of what she ate with Travis's dark presence and his pervasive chilly anger looming large at her side, she kept her gaze fixed on her plate.

"Allow me to help you to some green beans," Travis said. "You need to keep up your strength for your bridegroom."

Victoria jumped at his deep voice close to her ear. "No, thank you," she said, refusing to look at him.

"No?" He gestured at her plate. "You must eat, Miss Yelverton. It wouldn't do for your looks to fade. What would your country swain say?"

She couldn't stand any more of him. She had to leave. "You are intolerable, sir," she whispered. She started to rise from her seat.

"Sit down, Victoria," he said quietly. "Don't make a scene."

Now he blamed her for this? "You are the one making a scene, with your innuendoes," she replied, keeping her voice low. She let him hear her anger. "I would not have come here, had I known of your presence."

She heard his light exhale of breath. "I won't tease you

anymore, Victoria. I promise. I'll be gone in the morning."

He turned back to Lady Rutherford and Victoria smiled shakily at Philip, who, having assuaged his hunger, was now ready to talk to her about his favorite hunter.

Travis studiously avoided speaking to her for the rest of the meal and Victoria declined tea in the drawing room after dinner, citing a headache, which was the truth.

She waived off Julia's proffered remedy of herbal tea and withdrew to her chamber.

In front of her dressing table, she stared into the mirror at her pale reflection. She had been so nervous, felt so threatened, her brain and her manners had gone begging. At the very least, she should have acknowledged his assistance. She ought to have taken the opportunity to thank him for the house and the school, since the lawyer had refused to deliver any messages on her behalf. How unforgivably rude she had been.

She would speak to him in the morning before he left. She got up and looked out the window into the dark. What if she missed him? She would never have another chance. She dare not risk coming to visit Julia again; he lived too close. Seeing him hurt too much.

She had to go back downstairs now and find an opportunity to speak with him alone. She took a deep breath and straightened her shoulders, stepping out into the hallway before she changed her mind.

She walked quickly down the ornate oak staircase into the green and gold painted entrance hall. A footman passed her carrying a large tray of dirty dishes from the dining room. The gentlemen must have finished their port. "Have you seen Lord Travis?" she asked him.

"On the balcony, miss," he said pointing to the dining room.

Victoria passed swiftly through the room, avoiding the servants busily clearing the table and stepped through the French doors onto a balcony that overlooked the formal gardens at the back of the house.

Dark and deserted, there was no one there. She turned to leave.

The aromatic smell of smoke drifted on the air and she saw a glow at the far end as he drew on his cigar.

"Travis," she said softly.

He coughed.

"I'm sorry. I didn't mean to startle you."

"What in hell's name are you doing here?" He sounded far from pleased.

"I came to thank you."

"For what?"

She frowned. The civilized conversation she had imagined had not sounded like this. She pressed on. "For the house and the money and . . ." It sounded awful. Like a paid-off mistress. He thought of her that way. Prickles of embarrassment ran down her back.

"I mean, I'm grateful for your generosity." Worse. She shouldn't have come. "Anyway, thank you." She turned to leave.

"You are very welcome."

He spoke the words so softly, she almost didn't hear them. She stopped.

"Run away, Victoria," he said, louder now. "I can't promise to behave if you stay. I might gobble you up like the big bad wolf."

She faced him. "Simon?"

"Go. Now. Off to your Kentish knight or he will have even more to blame me for."

"Oh, that."

"Yes. That."

"I think you misunderstood. I'm not going to be married."

"What? The bastard."

Victoria smiled at the anger in his voice, guessing his thoughts. "He asked me to marry him, Simon, but I said no."

"You did? Why?" He laughed, a harsh sound in the dark. "I suppose you think it's wrong to offer a man used goods. He won't care if he loves you."

Blunt and angry as ever.

Her own temper rose in response. "Love, Simon? What do you know about love?"

"Nothing." He tossed his cigar into the garden, its tip a brief, red shooting star.

She heard his bitterness and knew her words had slashed at a man who had never known love, and that he deliberately pushed her away. An ache hollowed her chest for him. It always did.

"I can't marry Sir David. My heart belongs to someone else."

He stilled, a motionless figure, staring out into the dark, a black shadow against the jewel-pricked sky. "It does?"

"Yes."

She heard an in-drawn breath in the dark and moved closer to him.

"Anyone I know?"

She thought she heard repressed hope in his voice, even though he sought to hide it.

"You might know him."

He bowed stiffly. "I wish you both happy."

Wrong again. He clearly didn't care. She feared his ridicule if she said more.

A dawning realization pierced her heart. He wanted to frighten her away. Fate had offered her this one chance and if she did not take it, she would regret it forever. She forced herself to go on. "He doesn't admit to loving me, I'm afraid."

He muttered a curse.

"You might know him, he's a rather elusive gentleman," she went on.

"Name begin with S by any chance?"

"Yes," she whispered.

"You don't mean it, Victoria. You can't." His voice caught as he tried to say more. His fist struck the balcony. "Don't do this."

She had to ask him. This was the real reason she wanted to speak to him tonight; she knew it now. Knew it as well as she knew her own heart. "Why did you ask me to marry you, then send me away?"

He stepped closer. She felt the heat of his body inches from hers, smelled his familiar sandalwood cologne. The light spilling from the dining room cast his beloved, sternly chiseled features into sharp angles. His fractured gaze bored into her. "I was wrong to ask you. Ogden proved it to you. You deserve a whole man, not an empty shell with nothing but blood on his soul." He laughed, rough and low, and turned back to the rail. "You'd better leave before the devil takes your soul too."

"I'll leave, Simon, if you'll tell me you don't love me."

He'd never mentioned love. Never told her he loved her. But she knew him better now. He feared to love. No one with a past as dreadful as his would ever fully trust anyone.

Making her own life for herself wasn't such a wonderful thing if she had no one to share it. She needed him so much.

"Damn you, Victoria. Leave." His voice sounded angry and anguished.

"I'm not going anywhere unless you tell me."

He inhaled, deep and steady. His chest rising and falling. Another deep breath. "I don't," he said, his voice calm, full of frost and from a great distance.

Disappointment gouged at her heart. But she would not give up without a fight. She needed him, no matter how little he could give her.

She swallowed the lump lodged in her throat. "You don't what?"

He took another deep breath. "I . . ." His voice ragged, he trailed off into silence, then swallowed. "Damn. I don't . . ."

She moved closer and touched the hand clenched on the railing.

He stiffened.

"Simon, even if it's only a little bit, it's all I want. I've missed you."

"Victoria." Her name seemed to be wrenched from somewhere deep inside him, as if it hurt to bring it forth. He caught her hand, brought it to his lips. "Victoria, my own heart. I do love you. I love you so much I feel as if I'm dead inside because you aren't with me. But I don't deserve you. You heard. You know what I am, what I've done. You saw me as I am. Satan. A devil."

As if they burned, he released her fingers. "Don't torture me more than I do myself."

She reached up and caressed the hard planes of his jaw. Tears wet his cheeks. She wiped them with her palms while her own ran unchecked.

"Simon, you were not responsible for the poor child's death. Ogden forced you to admit your guilt."

He jerked his head away. "He didn't make me say anything I don't believe." His voice contained bitter despair.

Her heart wrenched. She prayed to find the words to ease his agony. "Simon, you tried to save him. You were a boy. His mother should have saved him. The coach driver . . ."

He swallowed. "But I had him. I had him." Simon choked

and dashed his hand across his eyes. "He was there in my hands. Miranda screamed at me. I looked. I thought she was in trouble. I turned back and he'd gone. I held nothing but the blanket. God, Victoria, I dream it every night. He cries and then disappears under the water. I can't reach him. I was a bloody coward. The water was deep and I got scared. I let him drown."

She covered his hand with her own and found it shaking.

All these years he'd taken the blame, punished himself more than anyone should be punished. "It wasn't your fault."

He shook his head in denial. "I can't ever be sure. Not in my heart. I envied him my father's love."

She wanted to shake him, but knew one wrong word and he would splinter into a thousand pieces and she'd lose him forever. "Simon, you tried to save him."

"Dear God, Victoria. Don't make me out to be better than I am, you'll just be disappointed. Don't do this."

"No. Don't *you* do this. I love you, Simon."

He turned and gazed at her. Tension, anger, fear all radiating from his powerful body, a steel spring wound so tight with hard-won control, if it let go it would annihilate everything in its path. "You can't."

"I can, and I do. You have to trust me, Simon, or there's no hope for either of us."

Arms crushed her hard against his well-remembered hard frame. His deep voice rumbled low in his chest. "I love you so much it hurts," he murmured. "Hold on to me. I'll never let you go. I won't let you slip away, I swear."

She wrapped her arms around his lean waist. Too thin. "I'm not going anywhere without you," she promised. She laughed and reached up to stroke his hair back from his forehead. "I need you, Simon."

His mouth found hers with all-consuming tenderness. She

floated on his kiss. Her heart swelled with so much joy, it hurt to breathe. Her body trembled with longing.

"Marry me," he demanded when he finally allowed her to breathe. "Let me love you forever."

"I thought you would never ask again," she said with a quiet laugh as he swept her up in his arms.

"Say yes, Victoria," he said, his tone flat and hard as if he feared her answer.

"Yes. Yes. I love you, Simon. Believe me," she whispered against his neck, inhaling the familiar sandalwood, filling her senses with his wonderful male scent.

Carrying her in his arms, he marched past the astonished servants in the dining room, who tried not to see them as they headed for the stairs.

"Thank you," he breathed, raising his eyes heavenward. "And you, Victoria. I swear you will never regret it. I would give my life for you."

"I know you would, Simon. I think you did."

He lay her gently on his bed and lay down beside her, his hands trembling as he caressed her face with such gentleness, she thought she'd die of yearning.

Later, they lay entwined within the depths of the canopy. Pale light from the window illuminated their sated bodies.

"Simon?"

"Um-hm."

"You said you don't want children."

He pressed his lips against her skin. First one kiss, then another, a heated trail. Flames flared in her belly. "Simon, stop. Answer me."

"Not true," he said. "I just didn't want illegitimate children. It's hard enough when you are born in wedlock."

"Oh."

"I don't trust your 'oh', my lady. What?"

"Well, you see, there is this little boy in the village where I have my school."

"Had."

"I beg your pardon?"

"Had your school. We will have to find a new teacher to replace you. You are going to be too busy keeping me happy and being a countess to teach a school."

"We will discuss that later." She held her breath.

He sighed. "What about the boy?"

"I'd like to take care of him. Perhaps foster him. He's so brave and so hurt. He reminds me of—"

"Fine."

"Truly?"

"If it makes you happy, Victoria, it makes me happy too."

She caught his face between her hands. "I love you, Simon St John."

His smile gleamed in the starlight. "How lucky can I get? What did I do to deserve you?"

"You love me," she said running her hands through his hair and kissing every inch of his face.

He groaned. "Let me love you, my darling Victoria," he whispered softly against her mouth. "Now and forever."

About the Author

Growing up in England and Scotland until her early twenties, Michèle Ann Young developed a keen appreciation of British history and culture and took business with a history minor at college. The Regency era, a time of flamboyant extravagance, elegance, social upheaval and discovery, seems to Michèle to mirror our own age. She finds it fascinating to imagine how her historical characters must deal with the problems and events still besetting us today. This is her first Regency historical in print, but she promises many more to come.

Michèle lives and writes in Richmond Hill, Canada, where she resides with her husband and two beautiful daughters. Each year she goes back to Britain to steep herself in family and history as well as explore new settings for her novels.

To make Michèle Ann Young's acquaintance, please drop in at: http://micheleannyoung.com.